THE HORIZON WAR

by Robert Weinberg

Book 2
THE ASCENSION WARRIOR

a World of
Darkness
Trilogy

Cover Illustration: Jason Felix

White Wolf Publishing
735 Park North Blvd. Suite 128
Clarkston, GA 30021
www.white-wolf.com

Printed in Canada

AUTHOR'S NOTE:

While the locations and history of this world may seem familiar, it is not our reality. The setting for the Horizon War is a harsher, crueler version of our own universe. It is a stark, desolate landscape where nothing is what it seems to be on the surface. It is truly a World of Darkness.

Certain concepts and characters have been inspired by those originally created by Bill Bridges, Steven C. Brown, Phil Brucato, Elizabeth Fischi, Chris Hind, James E. Moore, Nicky Rea, Allen Varney, Mark Rein•Hagen and Stewart Wieck.

"When the hurlyburly's done
When the battle's lost and won."
    —*Macbeth*,
    Act i, Scene i

Prologue

"Wake up, wake up!" his mother shouted, her voice shrill. She sounded a million miles away. "Get moving!"

Groaning, Ernest squeezed his closed eyes tighter shut. It couldn't be morning already. It wasn't fair. He felt worn out, battered, bruised, barely able to move. Pain shrieked like an enraged harpy through his muscles and joints. Just like always. There was no way he could get out of bed and go to school. Not today. Not ever. He just wanted to sleep.

Medication and exercise did little to ease the physical pain. It was intense, everlasting. He had lived with it all his life, and unless some miracle cure was discovered, would die with it. The agony of each day drained him of his strength, his energy, his will. But it was nothing compared to the mental pain he endured in the classroom.

The other children in his class made his life hell, mocking him, taunting him about his twisted bones and stunted body. Called him freak and cripple and worse. Ernest hated them, every one. He couldn't face their hatred any longer. No matter how loud his mother screamed, he would refuse to budge. Better death than another day of torment. Sticks and stones had broken his bones, and names could always harm him.

"Snap out of it, you fuckin' metal head!" screamed the voice he suddenly realized was not his mother's. Groggily, his mind filled with fog, he hunted for a name. Reed, *Sharon Reed*. Instantly, he remembered a tall, slender woman with short clipped hair and gaunt, grim features. He hated her with an unquenchable fury. Ernest seized the image, holding onto it like a life preserver in the sea of blackness. Struggling against waves of pulsating red agony, he clawed upward out of the darkness towards consciousness. "Wake up, wake up, you stupid sonofabitch!"

Something warm, hard and stinging slammed into his head. Then again. A third time. Relays embedded in his flesh snapped into action. Microcircuits hummed with information. A woman's hand, reported the sensor units. The attacker slapped with inhuman power. Enhanced flesh and reinforced bone indicated extremely sophisticated biological engineering. Memory circuits confirmed identity. *Sharon Reed, Progenitor Research Director of the Gray Collective*.

Fire exploded behind his skull. Ernest remembered everything. But he wasn't Ernest. That identity was long gone. It was part of the past. This was the present. He was X344.

Pain blockers, sensing major injuries, went into action, cutting off all feeling from those areas of his body badly damaged. His nose was broken. Major damage had been done to his spinal column. Standing erect was going to be difficult. At best, he was functioning at forty percent capability. Back-up processors sent desperately needed chemicals to critical areas of his arms and legs. Energy, drained from a dozen less-important functions, poured into his major motor controls. He couldn't survive very long using this emergency system, but without it, X344 knew he was dead. Both options had drawbacks.

X344's eyes popped open. He found himself staring directly into the face of Sharon Reed. The woman gasped in a mixture of surprise and relief. Astonishing, considering she hated him nearly as much as he despised her.

"You're dead," he declared, his voice barely a whisper. His smashed nose gave him a raspy tone. "I saw your buddy, *your damned assistant*, Velma, stab you in the back. She killed you."

Reed shook her head. "Injured, not killed. Over the years, I've made some major body modifications. Velma thought she knew all my secrets, but I kept a few to myself. She stabbed me in the wrong heart." The director half-turned. A silver-handled knife was still buried in her back. "It's wedged against a bone. Painful. But not fatal. My second heart went into action instantly. It just took me time to recover."

X344 swiveled his head, looking around the smashed laboratory. The huge chamber was in shambles. The bodies of their companions, Technomancers engaged in the AW project, littered the floor. In the far corner of the room, a huge mass of flesh stirred fitfully. One gigantic tentacle twitched sporadically against the lab floor, sending shock waves rippling through the entire building.

The cyborg stared at Reed, his eyes unwavering, trying to read answers in her face. She was his worst enemy. They belonged to rival Conventions of the Technocracy. Before the disaster, they had actively been trying to kill each other. "This place is finished," he declared. "Why didn't you leave me? In a few hours, my energy would have run out and I would have died. End of story."

"It's not so simple," said Reed. She pointed in the opposite direction, to a spot twenty feet away. "Remember the gateway into the Deep Universe you opened? It's still functioning. Something on the other end wants to examine the contents of the Gray Collective. I'm not sure how, but it's drawing power out of the station. Slowly but surely the entire Realm is being drawn into the depths."

"Hell," said X344. Following the instructions of his leader, Comptroller Klair, he had wrenched apart the Deep Universe tube. Wisely, he had thrown the device across the room upon activation. The move had saved his life. Klair had not been so lucky. The beacon opened a pathway between this Horizon Realm and someplace else. The gateway, a shimmering ten-by-twelve rectangle of absolute blackness, had sucked the Comptroller right through. The last thing X344 could remember was strange, unearthly robots emerging from the portal. They had not looked friendly.

"Perhaps the beacon ends in the netherworld," said Sharon Reed, treating his statement as a question. "I'm not sure where it leads. Nor do I have any desire to find out. The pull isn't strong but it's been increasing at a constant rate over the past hour. If we remain here much longer, we'll both be swept to the other side."

"What happened to the robots?" the cyborg asked, his voice shaking.

"I missed most of the action," said Reed. "Much of the time I was semi-conscious. I have impressions, nothing more. Evidently, a group of Tradition willworkers led by Prisoner 17 broke into the Collective. Somehow they defeated the robots and rescued their fellow wizards from our cell block. By the time I was functional again, they were gone."

The cyborg clenched his fists. His energy supply was running dangerously low. "I knew all along that escaped mage would bring back trouble."

"Forget him," said Sharon Reed, her voice dripping with venom. "He's not a major concern. Worry instead about the AW Construct. *He's gone*."

"Impossible," said X344, knowing deep in his heart that she wasn't lying. "The clone had no mind. He was just a superhuman body, created without intelligence."

"I know what he was *supposed* to be!" she screamed. "I helped *design* the fuckin' thing, remember! But he's not what we set out to create. The damned thing possessed self-awareness. He was *somebody*. Someone who knew exactly what he was doing. That's why Velma knifed me. She was acting on his orders!"

For over a year, nearly fifty expert technicians of the Technocracy had worked on the top-secret AW project. The research was designed to produce the ultimate weapon in the ongoing war against the annoying group of willworkers belonging to the Nine Traditions. Blending the computer technology of Iteration X with the biological engineering skills of the Progenitors, the Technocrats had developed a prototype model for the most advanced clone ever conceived. The being was physically perfect—stronger, smarter, quicker than any human in the world. With a reinforced skeleton, genetically designed internal organs, and nanobyte blood, the AW clone was virtually indestructible. Wounds healed in an instant and no disease could harm it. Nor did it age.

Mentally, it had a brain larger and more powerful than any human's. It possessed total control over its every body function. Electronic enhancements throughout its nerve system gave the clone incredible powers over machinery and computers. One touch was all it needed to take control of any operating system.

The clone was the most dangerous being the Technocracy had ever created. An army of such beings would have easily destroyed the Nine Traditions. It had been designed to end the Ascension War. Thus, the name for the project and the being itself. AW—

The Ascension Warrior. Now the clone was fully functional, self-aware, and missing.

"Whose mind controls the AW unit?" asked X344, as he tested his arms and tank treads. They seemed functional, though he knew he did not have enough energy to stay that way very long. "One of the Tradition fools who broke in here?"

"No," said Sharon Reed. Her face twisted in a mask of confusion. "From what little I saw and heard, it was clear to me that the Tradition willworkers came here to destroy the clone. They were frightened of it. Or, at least of the being it had become."

"Great," said X344, struggling erect. He could feel the tug of the Deep Universe gate, a steady, insistent pull. Around him, the air of the Collective whistled past as it disappeared into the huge black void. A wind was stirring. It was time to leave. "Damn clone's alive for fifteen minutes and half the universe wants to destroy it. Somehow, I have this terrible suspicion that we've been played for suckers the past year."

"Exactly my thoughts," said Reed. Her eyes burned with hatred. She spoke in slow, deliberate tones. "I am no one's puppet. The fools who manipulated me will be paid back in full. They'll drown in their own blood."

"Sure," said X344. "Very dramatic. Talk is cheap. First things first. Save the revenge crap for later. You woke me up for a reason, Reed. The two of us aren't exactly buddies. I can't imagine you crying at my funeral. Why did you bother? What's the catch?"

The Research Director smiled. "The catch, my dear

metal-headed freak, is that when the Tradition inter-lopers invaded our realm, they brought an unwelcome visitor with them, one who remained after their departure. The beast, though badly wounded, guards the only exit to Earth. I know my limits. I'm a thinker, not a fighter. Besides, time is growing short. Defeating the monster is beyond me. Only with your help do I have a chance of escape before the entire station disappears into the Void Beyond. So, I woke you."

"At least you're honest," he replied. "My boss, Comptroller Klair, barely thought to mention to me that the Deep Universe Beacon might be dangerous. So much for years of loyal service." X344 shrugged, thinking of how Klair's screams had suddenly cut off when the black curtain had touched him. "He paid the price for keeping secrets."

"No time for anything other than the truth," said Reed. She looked at X344 with a critical eye. "The beast on the loading dock is a sabertooth tiger. My pet, Semok," and she waved a hand at the quivering octopoid mass, "damaged it badly. But the monster is far from finished. Killing it won't be easy."

"Do we have a choice?" asked X344.

"The beast or the portal into the Deep Universe," said Sharon Reed. "I prefer the beast."

"I'm not much for mysterious journeys, either," said the cyborg. "Let's go play with this giant cat."

His tank treads whirred noisily as he moved. It was a bad sign. His emergency power was failing already. With so much of his internal equipment off-line, X344 couldn't estimate how much power reserve he had left. But he suspected it wasn't going to be enough to kill a monster from the dawn of time.

"This beast one of yours?" he asked Reed as they approached the tunnel to the loading dock. "I didn't know the Progenitors were playing with prehistory."

"I never saw anything like it before," said Reed. "My senses tell me it's not a product of genetic engineering. The monster's not something made in our labs. Nor is it the creation of any willworker of the Nine Traditions. The Paradox Effect wouldn't allow such a beast to function in the Gray Collective. I'm forced to conclude that somewhere in Static Reality, these gigantic tigers still exist."

"You have a plan?" asked X344, not the least concerned about the sabertooth's origin. "Or am I just supposed to slam the cat on the head until it collapses?"

"Whatever you like," replied Sharon Reed. The wind was growing in strength. It howled, half-drowning out her words. Walking away from the portal was becoming increasingly difficult.

"I'm wearing a poison ring," she declared, waving her right hand. A gold band decorated her index finger. "It contains enough toxin to kill a grown man in fifteen seconds. How much effect it might have on a sabertooth tiger, I don't know."

"All of my sophisticated weaponry was removed when I started work on the AW project," said X344. "Mission Specialist Shade insisted. Didn't want any accidents, he claimed." The cyborg paused. "What happened to Shade? I didn't see his body anywhere. And he was missing when the countdown began."

Reed shook her head. They were in the tunnel now leading to the loading dock. Air rushed past them at near-gale force, its power multiplied by the narrowness of the passage. It was like walking against the wind in a fierce rainstorm. Every step forward was an effort. "He's gone. Vanished. Another mystery."

A roar of animal fury cut off any further conversation. X344 had fought more than his share of enemies of the Technocracy. He wasn't scared easily. Yet the tiger's growls sent cold chills snapping through his body.

"Racial memory," said Sharon Reed, her features white, her voice trembling. "Echoes from our distant past. Primitive man fought and killed these beasts before recorded history."

"So much for progress," said X344. They were at the end of the corridor. Cautiously, he peered out into the loading bay. The platform was a slab of concrete forty feet wide by fifteen feet long. There were spaces for three trucks. Two of the slots were empty. The third was occupied by a ten-ton transport. It looked to be in working condition.

A narrow tunnel, wide enough for one vehicle, stretched a hundred feet beyond the dock and ended in a blank wall. The gate to Static Reality—Earth. The correct code, punched into a transmitter built into the truck dashboard, opened the portal. It seemed simple enough. All they needed to do was get in the vehicle and drive to daylight.

The platform appeared empty. X344's eyes scanned the area. Normally he relied on a highly sensitive heat detection system, but unfortunately, like many of his enhancements, it was off-line now. It didn't matter. It only took him seconds to locate the big cat.

"Our baby's down at the end of the tunnel," he declared calmly. "If we run, we might make it to the truck without a fight. So move!"

Giving Reed a shove in the right direction, X344 rolled out onto the platform. He grimaced as his tank treads skidded on the concrete. For the first time in decades, he wished he still had feet instead of wheels. His companion, experiencing no such difficulties, was demonstrating sprinter speed. She was already halfway to the truck.

A blood-curdling shriek of animal rage shook the concrete walls. Moving with the speed of an express train, the sabertooth tiger hurtled through the tunnel. It had either smelled or seen them. X344 blinked at the size of the giant cat. It was at least a dozen feet long and stood as tall as a man. The beast had to weigh over a thousand pounds, all of it muscle. Two tusk-like teeth, nearly a foot long, jutted from its upper jaw. The monster roared again as it drew closer. It ran like lightning. There was no way either X344 or Reed would reach the truck in time.

The cyborg did what he had to do. One of them had to survive and alert the Technocracy about what had taken place. The pattern-clone represented a threat to the future of all mankind. For all of his anger and hate, cyborg X344, once the man Ernest Nelson, believed in humanity's ultimate Ascension. And he was willing to sacrifice his life for his beliefs.

With a cry of rage all his own, X344 directed his remaining energy into his arms and treads. All other life support systems shut down. Nothing else mattered more than strength in his claws and wheels. Treads screeching on cement, he hurtled forward at breakneck speed directly at the oncoming cat. Crouching close to the pavement, head pulled down between his massive shoulders, X344 aimed himself like a human missile at the tiger. The beast, sensing the sudden unexpected motion, altered direction so that it was on a collision course with its attacker. Fifty feet separated them, then thirty, then twenty.

Eyes blazing red, jaws gaping like the mouth of hell, the huge sabertooth launched itself into the air. If he had been an ordinary man, X344 would have been ripped open. But X344 was a cyborg, a blend of man and machine. Atomic fusion cells powered his body, not muscle. With a surge of power, he accelerated the moment the tiger left the ground. Head bent so that it was only inches off the floor, steel claws scraping the cement for balance, he shot underneath the beast and beyond.

Concrete and flesh collided with a bloody splash as the giant tiger crashed head-first into the loading dock floor. For a second, the beast wobbled about, stunned.

Seizing the opportunity, X344 leapt onto the back of the dazed tiger. Steel fingers drilled into each side of the monster's skull, anchoring into bone. Shrieking in pain, the giant tiger tried to rip the cyborg off its back. But with its overdeveloped upper body and neck muscles, the beast couldn't reach X344 with its claws. Howling, it thrashed back and forth, trying to dislodge him from his hold. But all of the cyborg's strength was focused in his arms.

Knees pressed tightly into the beast's sides, fingers clenched into the tiger's bloody skull, X344 hung on. Like the famous allegorical figure, he was riding the tiger. Letting go would be death.

Wind whistled in the cyborg's ears. Small dust devils whirled in the tunnel as the pull from the Deep Universe gateway grew stronger. Time was running out for the last few inhabitants of the Gray Collective.

Snarling a bloody froth, the beast reared up on its two hind legs. Its claws stretched for the ceiling. X344 cursed. Releasing his grip meant death, but if the massive beast dropped backwards, he'd be crushed beneath its weight. There was nothing he could do. His luck had run out.

A short distance away, a diesel motor bellowed. Like a massive jackhammer, the steel hood of the ten-ton truck smacked into the lower belly of the sabertooth. Bones snapped like peanut brittle. With a crash, the huge beast collapsed across the front of the transport. Clutching the monster's back, X344 tried to draw in a deep breath but couldn't. Still, he refused to let go. The tiger wasn't dead yet.

Massive head only inches from the truck's cab, the tiger swung a huge paw at the reinforced glass of the windshield. Though made to stop a high-speed bullet, the pane was no match for the tiger. X344 caught a glimpse of the startled features of Sharon Reed. Her hands flashed for a second, then she vanished as the badly injured tiger tried to scramble up across the engine housing and into the cab.

The beast's claws sank into the steel hood as it slowly rose to all four feet. Body shuddering, it coughed in pain. Slowly, it took a tentative step forward on the slippery metal. The monster coughed again, its huge body sagging. X344 was forgotten. The tiger wobbled, no longer steady on its feet.

Raising its head, the beast opened its jaws to roar its defiance. It made no sound. Instead, like a balloon suddenly punctured, the tiger collapsed to the hood of the truck. X344, barely alive, clinging tightly to the monster's back, didn't move. He was taking no chances that the sabertooth might have enough energy for one last attack. He had seen others less cautious than himself killed in equally unpredictable circumstances.

"It's dead," announced Sharon Reed, raising her head from behind the dashboard. She reached through the shattered windshield and tapped the tiger on one massive paw, as if reassuring both herself and X344. "Took twenty-seven seconds."

"Twenty-seven seconds?" repeated X344 as he gingerly climbed off the sabertooth's spine. In death, the beast was no less impressive than life. Now, for the first time he was able to see how badly wounded the monster had been when it attacked. One of its eyes was gone, smashed to jelly, and its rear right leg was a shattered mass of bone and muscle. Large black patches across its body indicated that it had suffered massive internal injuries battling the horror Reed had called Semok. The beast had sustained wounds that would have killed anything else living. Even then, it had been a tough customer.

"My poison," said Reed, holding up her ring. "Potent stuff. I stabbed kitty with it when the beast smashed the windshield. After that, it was merely wait and watch."

"We make a good team," said X344, shoving the sabertooth tiger onto the dock floor. "Brawn and brains."

He stared at Reed through the shattered windshield. There was little strength left in him. Keeping his eyes open was proving difficult. The wind was pulling at him, trying to wrench him off the metal and onto the cement. "Now what?"

"You're a wreck," the Research Director declared. "Body badly damaged. Energy almost gone. The pull from the beacon is growing stronger. The Gray Collective's doomed. If I leave, you'll be swept through the portal in minutes. Assuming you survive till then."

"That's the truth," said X344. Reed talked too much. "What's your point?"

"Just want you to remember that your continued existence is due to my intervention," said Reed. "I'm the one who saved you. Never forget that."

She pushed open the passenger door to the cab.

"Get in. You need major repairs and a complete overhaul. I want a Progenitor technician to pull this knife out of my back. We both need time in the regeneration tanks."

The Research Director stepped on the gas. The truck surged forward. Ahead of them, the blank wall wavered and turned opaque. The gateway to Earth was open.

"The Inner Council isn't going to view this mess very favorably," she declared. "They'll want answers. I suspect, we'll be the ones sent to find them."

A cynical smile touched Reed's lips. "You're right in what you said. We do make a good team. Who knows? If we're lucky, we might even discover the truth."

"If that Deep Universe gateway in the laboratory is part of the answer," replied X344, his voice shaking slightly, "then I'm not sure I want to know the truth."

Then they were gone, and with them, the last traces of life in the Gray Collective vanished. It was the first realm to fall in what was to become known among the Awakened as the Horizon War. It was not the last.

Chapter One

"It's time, I think," said the man known only as Seventeen, "for a council of war."

His gaze traveled around the small circle of his companions. They were five in all. Himself, a living question, a mage without a name or past; Sam Haine, the Changing Man; Sam's friend, the healer and shaman Albert; the warrior woman, Shadow of the Dawn; and her mentor, the seemingly ageless willworker known as Kallikos. Together, they had dared the perils of the Gray Collective and returned alive. A dozen Tradition mages held prisoner in the Technocracy hideaway had been rescued. Already, under the guidance of their friend and ally Alvin Reynolds, the captives were on their way back to their homes. But the major thrust of their mission, the destruction of the AW pattern-clone, had failed. That mysterious being had vanished an instant before Shadow's katana would have sliced him to ribbons.

Two days had passed since their expedition into the Horizon Realm. Those forty-eight hours had been filled with frantic activity. After their escape from the Technocracy stronghold, they had traveled north with their rescued comrades to the safety of the Casey cabal. The hideaway was located a few miles outside of the city of Rochester, New York. There, among the sanctity and protection of the sacred grove of power that anchored the mage community, Seventeen and his friends had spent most of a day questioning the ex-prisoners of the Gray Collective. The results had been disheartening.

None of the captives knew anything about the true nature of the pattern-clone. Even Cindy Reynolds, Alvin's sister who had aided Seventeen's earlier escape, was in the dark regarding the actual purpose of the artificial being. Nor, disappointingly, did any of the prisoners have any knowledge of Seventeen's past or real identity.

"Nothing," Alvin Reynolds had reported, with a shake of his head. "I managed a quick tap into the Collective mainframe while the rest of you were freeing the captives. Impossible for me to break into the encrypted files concerning the pattern-clone. But the prisoner records weren't protected. I downloaded all the information available. Everyone we saved was listed there, along with those who had died during the course of the Progenitor experiments." He raised his hands in a gesture of defeat. "Everyone but you, Seventeen. There not a mention of your existence anywhere. No name, no record of your capture, not even a memo detailing the tampering done to your blood and nervous system. It's as if you never existed."

"Or," said Sam Haine, whose thought patterns were as serpentine as any Technocrat, "someone wanted poor Seventeen's identity and background kept a secret. Especially to those who followed afterwards."

"Who?" asked Seventeen, knowing that Sam never advanced an idea without evidence to support his claim.

"Don't rightly know her name," said Sam. "But I suspect we know what the young lady looks like. She was a-leavin' with our friend Mr. Clone when we arrived in that damned Collective."

"The Jenni Smith look-alike," said Seventeen, remembering the mystifying young blonde he had met in the Casey Collective little more than a week ago.

"She's my pick, son," said the Changing Man. "Them girls are up to something tricky. Mark my words, Seventeen. You discover what they plan and that's when you'll learn your real name."

After long hours of question and answer, everyone involved in the adventure, as well as those rescued, agreed there was no more of importance to be learned. The prisoners had been well isolated from the happenings of the Horizon Realm and what little knowledge they did possess added nothing to the picture already assembled. It was time to say goodbye.

The prisoners wanted their freedom. They had spent months in captivity, always faced with the imminent prospect of their demise. Now saved, they wanted out. More than anything, the rescued mages desired to return to their homes, their families, their lives. There was no way that Seventeen and his comrades could deny their wishes.

Alvin Reynolds agreed to handle the details. The members of his Hand of Hope cabal had arranged many relocations and reunions in the past. A few late-night phone calls set the proper wheels in motion. By the next afternoon, all of the prisoners were gone, safely heading home, escorted through a nation-wide, underground runaway-relocation network. In a world without any laws preventing child abuse or wife beating, such a secret organization filled a horrifying but necessary niche. There was little chance of any of the prisoners being traced. Tradition mages fleeing the minions of the Technocracy passed unnoticed among the thousands of women and children desperate to find safe refuge for the night. Harsh reality served as an effective mask.

Reynolds and his sister were the last to leave. "I'll be back," the big man had promised as he made his final preparations to depart. "All I want is to make sure Cindy is safe at home, surrounded by plenty of friends and firepower."

"Can't say I blame you, son," said Sam Haine. "Man's got to protect his family." The white-haired old man grinned. "My problem is that I tend to think all Tradition folks are relatives of mine. You take care. Come back to us when you can."

"That I will," promised Reynolds. He held out his hand to Seventeen. "My friend, you brought me hope when I had just about given up. Without you, I'd never have found my sister. I owe you much. And I'm not one to forget a debt."

Solemnly, the two men shook hands. Then it was Cindy Reynolds's time to say goodbye.

Tears filled the tall woman's eyes as she reached out and grasped Seventeen by the shoulders. She hugged him tightly. It was the first time the two prisoners had ever touched.

"You saved me, Seventeen," she declared, emotion choking her voice. "You made the impossible possible. The night you escaped, I felt certain you were going to your death."

"I had plenty of help," said Seventeen smiling. "Yours most of all."

Gently, he pulled free. Strong emotions made him uncomfortable. "We'll meet again," he said, raising a hand in farewell. "I'm certain of it."

"Hopefully under better circumstances," declared Sam Haine, as the brother and sister departed. "I hate long good-byes. Make me hungry. Let's eat, son."

Now, the meal was done and the five of them were alone in the sacred forest grove not far from the Casey cabal common house. Although it was nearly 10 PM, a small fire and the bright moonlight provided plenty of illumination. Not that it mattered for Seventeen. He could see perfectly in almost total darkness.

"All our cards are on the table, son," said Sam Haine. "Best we examine them and add up the score."

Grimacing, Seventeen folded his arms across his massive chest. A tall man, he wore a pair of jeans without shirt or shoes. Muscles like steel bands stood out in stark relief beneath his chalk-white skin. He gave the impression of being carved from solid rock. His angular face, blunt and square, was entirely hairless. His huge hands, ending in thick fingers, curled into immense fists.

"Easier said than done," replied Seventeen. "I feel like a blind man given a new deck of playing cards and told to deal a hand of bridge. There's meaning somewhere, but not visible to me."

"A thoughtful analogy, my friend," said Albert. The black man, seven feet tall and thin as a rail, rarely spoke, but when he did, his comments revealed a sharp mind. "We have plenty of information. What occurred during our brief sojourn at the Gray Collective is important only when considered in light of everything that took place before. The pattern-clone rests at the center of a huge jigsaw puzzle. We have all the pieces. Now they must be assembled into one unit. To understand the clone's importance, we must analyze all of the events surroundings its creation as a cohesive whole, not as a series of unrelated occurrences."

"Then you're saying the attacks on me, Jenni Smith's wild accusations…" began Seventeen.

"…and more were all related to what happened in the Gray Collective," concluded Albert. "Do you not agree, Sam?"

"Course I do, you African toothpick," said the Changing Man, grinning. "We've spent so much time together, we think the same. Damn right embarrassing at times."

Without the slightest sound, Shadow of the Dawn rose to her feet. Tall and slender, with her hair knotted in a long black braid, she defined grace of motion. Dressed in a loose-fitting blue jacket and matching pants, she wore no shoes. An enigmatic smile curved across her thin lips. "As a pupil," she said, her tone polite and low, "I was taught that to a careful observer there are no coincidences. In our world, nothing occurs by sheer chance. Everywhere there is a pattern, a tapestry woven of many hues. The Wheel of Drahma turns and we dance to its tune."

Seventeen bit his upper lip. He found Shadow of the Dawn extremely attractive. The Japanese warrior woman was the most fascinating female he had yet met. It didn't bother him that she could easily cut him in tiny pieces with her twin swords if she so desired. Her martial arts skills were part of her mystique. Her conversational skills, however, left much to be desired.

"Would you care to elaborate a little?" he asked, smiling.

The young woman nodded. "With your kind permission?"

"Fine with me," said Sam Haine. He lit one of his special cigars, the kind that generated no smoke or smell. "I love hearing a good-lookin' woman speak her mind."

"Sam has a way with words," said Albert, "that makes me wonder if English is truly his native tongue. Please continue. I am certain your insights will prove to be quite valuable."

Shadow glanced at Kallikos. The black-bearded man nodded slightly. Since their return from the Gray Collective, the mysterious wizard had hardly said a word. Much of the time, he had sat in quiet contemplation, his eyes focused on vistas not visible to anyone else.

"*The Ascension Warrior*," said Shadow, her soft voice echoing through the sacred glade. "That name was used by the Technocrats of the Gray Collective to describe the pattern-clone. Alvin Reynolds learned that much from the computer records he downloaded from the Gray Collective's mainframe. Along with the fact that nearly fifty mages of Iteration X and the Progenitors had worked on the design and growth of the clone over the past year."

"I always thought creating a biomech was child's play for Technomancers," said Albert.

"But this baby wasn't your ordinary, everyday clone," said Sam Haine. "Those bastards were damned busy working. We've got Seventeen as proof of that. Look at him. The boy's got blood that heals his wounds and makes him strong. He talks to computers with his hands. Even kills sauroids without weapons. And remember—he was just the experimental, prototype model. This here Ascension Warrior's probably got all of Seventeen's powers and bunches more besides."

"The downloaded files made it clear that the wizards of the Gray Collective were trying to create the ultimate fighting machine in the Ascension War," said Shadow. "They planned to make hundreds of copies of the pattern-clone and transfer the minds of their greatest mages in those forms. Almost immortal, nearly unkillable, these genetic superbeings would put an end to the Nine Traditions and ensure the Technocracy's never-ending domination."

"A frightening picture of the future of mankind," said Albert with a shudder. "Right out of the worst nightmares of H.G. Wells and George Orwell."

"Fiddlesticks," said Sam Haine. "Never could've happened. You should know better, Albert."

"Why not?" asked Seventeen.

"'Cause those folks in the Technocracy ain't all brothers and sisters," said Sam Haine. When he got riled, the white-haired man's speech grew more colorful. "They don't love each other any better than our Verbena and Euthanatos folks. Major rifts separate them Conventions. Metal heads from Iteration X and Progenitor Skin Doctors might've played nice working on the pattern-clone, but you can bet your last wooden nickel they was each planning on crossin' the other and taking full control of the project when it was completed."

"I did sense a rivalry between several of my captors," said Seventeen, trying to think back to his days in captivity.

"Rivalry? Ha!" declared Sam Haine. "Son, I've been spyin' on those poor misguided fools for years." As the Changing Man, Sam Haine possessed astonishing magickal skills that enabled him to impersonate anyone he had ever met. That he had used his talent to infiltrate the Technocracy didn't surprise Seventeen.

Robert Weinberg

Nothing Sam Haine did surprised Seventeen. "The leaders of each branch of the Five Conventions making up the Technocratic Union are convinced they're the only ones who know the true path to salvation. Sound kinda familiar? They ain't much different than lots of mages in the Nine Traditions. Give a man magick powers, and right away he knows the right way to run the universe."

Sam Haine snorted, blowing the tips of his mustache away from his mouth. "Awakened doesn't mean smarter, son. Just more damned stubborn. Anyways, there's no way on God's green earth that those Technomancers would have agreed on sharing the pattern-clone. Remember what the Gray Collective looked like when we made our house call? Not real tidy was it? Seems like our friends might have been engaged in some sort of fracas before we barged in with our pet tiger."

Shadow cleared her throat. Seventeen smiled. The young woman's explanation of the many-colored tapestry had not proceeded very far. Sam Haine had a habit of taking every conversation and bending it to his whim. "I would like to address that issue," she said.

"Sure," said Sam, waving his big cigar. The tip glowed red in the moonlight. "You keep talkin', Miss Shadow. Been making a lot of sense so far."

The Japanese girl smiled and shook her head. "Thank you. There were a number of bodies scattered throughout the main laboratory of the Gray Collective when we first entered. Though I had no chance to examine them closely, it was obvious to me that they included biologically altered and metal-enhanced mages. I feel it is safe to assume that Sam Haine's assessment of the rivalry between the two Conventions is accurate. Obviously, with the anticipated completion of the pattern-clone project, war had broken out between the two rival factions."

"You ain't forgettin' that giant squid-thing that fought with our cat?" interrupted Sam Haine. "And those giant robots cracked like nutshells all over the floor?"

"No," said Shadow sighing, "I have not forgotten those beings. More evidence of the battle that we interrupted." She hurried on before Sam could say something more. "Nor am I discounting the third force in that struggle. The being you named as Empress Aliara, the Countess of Desire. One of the Maeljin Incarna."

"That's what she's called," said Sam, grinning. "I've encountered her once or twice in my travels through the Tellurian. Wisely kept my distance in the past. She's poison, plain and simple. One of the Dark Lords that live in the Deep Umbra. Has her headquarters in a place called Malfeas, on the doorstep of Hell."

"What was she doing in the Gray Collective?" asked Seventeen. "And was it really wise to push her into that gateway?"

"To answer your second question first," said Sam, "no. It was the craziest damned thing I've ever done. You'd think a man of my age would know better." The white-haired man took a deep drag on his cigar and grinned ear to ear. "But I couldn't resist. Not many's the man who can say he sent one of the Maeljin Incarna flying into limbo. I'm sure Aliara's gonna make me regret it for all eternity. But, given the chance, I'd do it again."

"You," said Albert, pride and affection mixed in his tone, "are incorrigible."

"And damned proud of it," said Sam.

"The Technocracy hates and fears the Dark Lords," said Albert as Sam puffed away on his stogie. "The main purpose of the Technocratic Union is to keep Reality safe from creatures like the Maeljin Incarna. Such spirits are the embodiment of uncontrolled lust. Aliara represents the antithesis of science and reason. Beyond any doubt, she wasn't at the Gray Collective by invitation."

"She came to claim the pattern-clone," said Kallikos, catching everyone by surprise. The black-bearded man rose to his feet. He was a tall man of uncertain age, with golden skin, broad shoulders and a tapered figure. Long dark hair curled in a ponytail down his back. A hook nose and large dark eyes gave his features a distinctive hawk-like look. "Like the rest, Aliara desired to use the clone form for her own purposes."

"How?" said Seventeen. "I understand how the various factions in the Technocracy planned to utilize the pattern-clone against the Traditions. But what possible use could it be to one of the Dark Lords?"

"She wanted to fill the empty body with her essence," said Kallikos. "Like all creatures of the Deep Umbra, Aliara has no true material form. She cannot materialize on Earth without the aid of massive blood sacrifices. I feel certain Aliara viewed the pattern-clone as the answer to her wildest desire."

Kallikos glanced at Sam Haine. "Wherever that Deep Universe gateway deposited Aliara, she most likely was not permanently damaged by her intrusion. The Dark Lords are nigh indestructible. I would strongly advise you stay clear of the Umbral Realms for the foreseeable future."

"My thoughts exactly," said Sam. "No place like home, I always say. Especially when there's a raging inferno waiting outside the door."

"The Maeljin Incarna are so consumed with hatred that they cannot remained focused on any individual very long," said Kallikos. "The Countess Desire will forget you shortly. But for the moment, be on your guard."

"I'm watchin'," said Sam. "So's Albert. He's my secret weapon."

"Aliara's interest in the pattern-clone helps define our tapestry," said Shadow of the Dawn. "Her involvement clarifies much that was unexplained."

"It does?" said Seventeen, bewildered. "I'm still lost in the details."

"It is quite simple if you look at the whole picture," said Shadow, smiling at Seventeen. She looked to Kallikos. "May I continue?"

"Of course," said the black-bearded man. "I spoke only to clarify Aliara's possible motive. I did not mean to interrupt."

"I understand," said Shadow, the slightest hint of

annoyance in her voice. "None of you would ever dare speak out of turn. You are much too polite."

Seventeen stifled a smile. His companions, like most willworkers, thought highly of their own opinions, and had trouble remaining silent for more than a few seconds.

"The original purpose of the AW project was clear," said Shadow, her tone neutral and calm. "It was an effort to combine the expertise of the Progenitor Genegineers with the high-tech wizards of Iteration X. Working together, the two groups designed a revolutionary new clone they dubbed the Ascension Warrior. Realizing the tremendous potential of such a being, both groups schemed to destroy their collaborators once the undertaking was completed.

"Meanwhile, Aliara learned of the project through one of her spies in the Technocracy. The Dark Lord, excited by the possibilities the clone offered, made her own plans to seize it. Thus, there were three separate groups all anxious to gain possession of the Ascension Warrior when fully functional."

Sam Haine nodded, puffing on his cigar.

"Seventeen's escape frightened the leaders of both Iteration X and the Progenitors," continued Shadow. "The two factions feared that if he contacted the right people in the Nine Traditions, they might realize the danger posed by the AW project and strike against the Gray Collective. Seventeen was a unique threat because he had been a test subject for many of the project's experimental treatments. He was a living example of the menace being grown in the secret laboratory. The Technomancers had to silence him."

"So they sent out those HIT Marks to find and destroy me," said Seventeen. "And later, the Men in Black." He frowned. "But then, who was responsible for the motorcycle gang?"

"Aliara," said Shadow. "The outlaw bikers were pawns of the Maeljin Incarna. Unaware of the efforts of the Technomancers, the Dark Lord summoned her own forces to deal with your escape."

"Maybe," said Sam Haine. "Maybe not. Trouble is, Shadow, you're not old enough to think crooked. Take it from someone who's been around long enough to be one of your dishonorable ancestors. You're sharp, but it takes decades of doublecrossin' and backstabbin' to see the world in proper perspective."

"Who do *you* think sent the bikers?" asked Seventeen.

"Somebody else," said Sam. "Shadow's explanation is nice and simple. Only problem is that she's dead wrong. Nothin' in life is simple. There's at least five parties involved in this mess. Evidence is clear as this spring water if you looks real close."

The white-haired man chuckled. "Our friends in the Gray Collective, both groups working together, were behind the Men in Black. Like you said, they wanted Seventeen dead. Bikers came for the same purpose, but they weren't workin' for Aliara or the Technocracy. Sorry, but the New World Order doesn't allow screwups like that to happen. Whoever used the outlaws was enemy number three. Their identity is still a mystery."

Sam paused. "Aliara is enemy number four. She sent the crazy woman who ripped the guy threatenin' Seventeen to pieces. The killer's actions sound typical of one of the Dark Lord's slaves."

"But why would Aliara want Seventeen alive?" asked Shadow.

"Because the bitch liked keeping the Technomancers worried," said Sam. "She needed them scared, so they'd work faster. Aliara knew they weren't goin' to shut down the project. She's probably fixed it so they couldn't even if they tried. Alive, Seventeen served as a threat. Dead, he meant nothing. So when she learned that the Men in Black were going after our boy, she instructed her agent to sabotage the attack."

"And five...?" said Seventeen.

"You seen her more than most, son," said Sam. "Jenni Smith. The girl who accused you of murder in this grove a week ago. And who disappeared with the pattern-clone in the Gray Collective. Somehow I'm of the feelin' she's a lot older than she looks. Don't ask me to explain more 'cause I don't know. But she's a player in this game. A damned important one."

"Six," said Seventeen. "You're ignoring the most significant, and yet most mysterious person in this entire tangled web." He turned and looked straight at Kallikos. "Who is the pattern-clone?"

"I-I-I'm not sure," said Kallikos. His voice wavered, a strange, puzzled expression on his face. "Though I can observe the future in visions, I am not capable of seeing inside a human heart. Or question a man's inner spirit, his Avatar. For centuries, I felt certain I knew the identity of the one reborn in the Gray Collective. Now, having finally encountered him in the flesh, I am not as convinced. He may be the one I fear. Or he could be some other, the result of an even darker conspiracy."

Kallikos's features turned grim. The seer had risen to his feet. Standing in front of the fire, his flickering figure appeared ghostly. "His actual name matters little. Whoever he might be, the future he promises remains the same. That vision has not changed."

His head turned as he looked at each of them, as if searching for an answer. "Tomorrow and the days after are not yet set on a single path. I view what might be, not that which already exists. The future rests on choices made in the present. My vision is of probability, not reality. My words are a warning, not a certainty."

Although the night was warm and the stars burned like torches in the dark sky, the grove suddenly seemed cold and dark. The bearded man's eyes bulged, staring at sights beyond mortal perception. His golden skin turned ash-white with dread. Kallikos's words rang like the notes of a funeral bell, tolling death and dissolution.

"The destruction of the Nine Traditions," he intoned, his mouth barely moving. "The corruption and eventual collapse of the Technocracy. An unending curtain of darkness covering the world. The cessation of individual thought. Mankind drowning in a sea of black blood. A crumbling of the barrier separating life from undeath."

Kallikos's face was a mask of utter despair. Trance-like, his bloodless lips pronounced the final doom. "The end of good. The triumph of absolute evil."

Chapter Two

Hours later, Kallikos's horrifying prophecy still echoed in Seventeen's mind. The others had returned to the manor house that served as home for the Casey cabal. Alone, he sat before the embers of the dying fire, contemplating a world of darkness.

After completing his litany of despair, Kallikos had collapsed to the ground unconscious. In an instant, Shadow of the Dawn was at his side.

"He is unharmed," she announced after a quick examination. "Oftentimes these visions come upon him unawares and drain the strength from him. It has happened before. Kallikos merely needs peace and quiet for the rest of the night. Once he has rested, the seer will be fine."

"A sound sleep sounds like the perfect cure," declared Sam Haine. "You and Albert can haul Kallikos back to the manor house. The Casey cabal will make sure he's not disturbed. Not surprisin' that a Time Master passes out now and then. All that doom and gloom. Eternal night's enough to knock anyone off his feet."

The white-haired man shook his head. "Not that I believe in that end-of-the-world sort of stuff, you understand. Predicting the future's a talent I don't possess—nor want to. I'll leave it to the seers and prophets to figure out what's true and what's just a bad dream. Probability and possibilities and multiple time lines give me a headache. I prefer more pleasant conversation. Tonight, I plan to do my talkin' with a certain Mr. Jack Daniels."

He looked to Seventeen. "You join me, son? Albert's a fine friend, but he has his share of bad habits. Not drinking is prime among them. A shot of whiskey goes down a lot smoother with good company. Plus, I knows a spell that cures hangovers before they happen."

"I appreciate the invitation," Seventeen answered, "but I'll pass. This quiet glade suits my mood perfectly. The idea of a few hours of solitude appeals to me. Besides, I suspect my marvelous biosystem wouldn't allow me the pleasure of getting drunk."

"Probably not," said Sam. "Damned shame, being forced to be healthy. If you get tired of being alone, Seventeen, come on back to the manor house. I'll be awake all night. No doubts about that."

"I as well," said Albert, with a wan smile. As Sam Haine's friend and protector, the giant African was obviously accustomed to the Changing Man's sprees. "Rest well, Seventeen. The world will be a brighter place in the morning."

Despite Albert's farewell, Seventeen found no peace in the darkness. Sitting cross-legged before the dying fire, he tried to relax but could not. Kallikos's warning preyed on his thoughts. The pattern-clone, or whatever it had become, had to be destroyed. Again and again, the line *A breaking down of the barrier separating life from undeath* circled through Seventeen's mind.

"Undeath," he whispered. That term haunted him. The seer had spoken not of the boundary separating life and death, but the dark curtain between life and *undeath*. Seventeen knew that Kallikos had not misspoken. His vision contained a warning of horrors that could not be ignored. Rising from the depths of his buried memories came a title of dire significance. *The Kindred.*

Angrily, Seventeen pounded a huge fist against his chest. Frustrated and annoyed, he felt like screaming. His entire life consisted of memories from the past eight weeks. Fifty-six days. Before that was nothing. He had no identity, no past, no name. Bits of data, fragments of information known in his previous life drifted out of his subconscious, but otherwise his past was a blank.

Something moved outside the fire's dim light. Instantly, Seventeen's rage disappeared as his senses cleared. A lone figure stood a dozen feet away, masked by a blurring of the atmosphere that could only be magick. The space had been empty an instant before. Somehow, his visitor had stepped out of nowhere.

"Welcome," said Seventeen, calmly. "Please don't be frightened. I've been expecting you to show up."

A young woman giggled. "Liar, liar, burn on fire," she recited in a high-pitched, sing-song voice.

"Jenni Smith," said Seventeen. He remained motionless beside the smoldering fire. Any sudden movement and the girl might run. He wanted to talk. "I knew it had to be you."

"*Sure* you did, Seventeen," said the girl sarcastically. She stepped forward, the veil of illusion falling away from her features as she moved. "Nobody can detect a teleportation spell before it happens. It's impossible."

"Not for me," said Seventeen. "I'm different."

The girl looked exactly the same as when Seventeen first encountered her a week before. Slender, with blue eyes and flowing blonde hair, she wore a long blue dress decorated with immense pink flowers. A thin shard of clear crystal hung from a rawhide thong around her neck. She appeared to be no more than eighteen years old.

Jenni stared at Seventeen, a thoughtful expression on her face. "No question that you're unique," she declared. "But I still don't believe you. No matter. It's unimportant."

"Are you the Jenni Smith I met here at the Casey cabal?" asked Seventeen, deciding the direct approach was best. "Or the one we spotted in the Gray Collective with the pattern-clone?"

The girl laughed. "Not bothering to be subtle, Seventeen? I'm Jenni. The person you saw in the Umbra was Velma."

"Identical twins?" said Seventeen, a trace of mockery in his voice. "Clones perhaps?"

"Magick," replied Jenni. She didn't specify what type and Seventeen knew asking would be a waste of breath.

"Jenni and Velma," said Seventeen. He didn't think she was lying about the names. There was no reason that she should. "Two of you. Are there more?"

"Ask me no questions and I'll tell you no lies," said Jenni cheerfully. "Besides, I didn't come here tonight to discuss my sisters. I came to talk about you."

"Me?" said Seventeen. "What about me?"

"My sisters and I want you to join us," said Jenni. She sounded sincere, but Seventeen suspected Jenni was an accomplished actress. "Working together in the service of the Master of Harmony, we can remake the world and guide humanity to Ascension."

"Working together?" he repeated. "If I remember correctly, the last time we were in this grove, you accused me of ripping a Gray Man to pieces. That's not exactly a gesture to inspire cooperation or trust."

"Circumstances dictated my actions that evening," said Jenni, not sounding the least apologetic. "After spending most of the afternoon talking to you, I reported my findings to Velma. She and I agreed that you represented a real danger to the AW Project. We couldn't let your actions jeopardize years and years of preparations. Being on the spot, I was given the job of neutralizing you."

"Neutralize as in murder?" said Seventeen.

"Not necessarily," said Jenni. "I knew about the Men in Black, of course. From what Velma told me, it seemed unlikely they would be able to kill you, but I hoped maybe their attack would slow you down. When that scenario collapsed, I improvised. I knew my charges wouldn't stick. You weren't in any danger. But it would take days before an investigation cleared you of any wrongdoing. Buying us precious time to complete our sacred mission."

"What if my mysterious savior hadn't killed the Gray Man?" asked Seventeen. "But I survived his attack anyway. Then there wouldn't have been a murder involved. What would you have done then?"

"Seduced you," said Jenni, giggling. "Don't laugh. I've already kissed you once. My mark is on you, dearest. Maybe I don't look as dangerous as that swordswoman traveling with you, but my magick doesn't need steel to be effective. During the months I spent at the Casey cabal, not once did anyone question my background or reason for being there. They accepted me and my claim that Sam Haine was my mentor. So did you. Deception might be more subtle than swordplay, but it cuts just as deep."

"Who was that woman who killed the Gray Man?" asked Seventeen. "Another sister?"

"Don't be stupid," snapped Jenni. "We're not maniacs. I have no idea who she was. Or why she was there."

Seventeen wondered if he should mention Aliara,

then changed his mind. The less he revealed the better.

"If I'm such a danger, why do you suddenly want me to work with you? What caused the sudden change of heart?" "Now that the resurrection has taken place, the situation has changed dramatically," said Jenni. "You no longer represent a threat. Instead, you've become an important part of our plans. I've come to convince you that joining our crusade is in your best interest. And that it's in the best interest of humanity."

Casually, Seventeen pulled his feet under him so that he was half-sitting, half-crouching. Jenni seemed not to notice.

"The Master of Harmony brings the gift of Ascension to all the Awakened," the girl continued, her entire face glowing with a religious fervor. "He plans to tear down the artificial barriers that separate the Nine Traditions and the Technocracy, putting an end to the Ascension War. Acting together, the united Awakened will destroy the Nephandi and the Marauders, bringing peace to the Tellurian. Under the benevolent guidance of the Master of Harmony, all humanity will prosper. It will be the beginning of a true rebirth of the human spirit."

"It's a magnificent vision of the future," said Seventeen. "But I'm still at a loss as to my part in this fabulous enterprise. Why do you need me?"

"You've been selected for a great honor," said Jenni. Her voice sunk to a whisper. "The Master of Harmony wants you to be his viceroy on Earth. To rule the material world as his anointed second-in-command."

She paused, her eyes wide. "With one word, you can become the supreme arbiter of Gaia, owing allegiance to only one other—the Master of Harmony. Immortal and omnipotent, a god among men. It is your destiny."

Seventeen's throat went dry. "You must be kidding," he managed to utter. "Why me?"

"Your blood is as his blood," replied Jenni. "More than that, I cannot say. I'm only the messenger. If you need more for an answer, ask the Master of Harmony."

"He's on Earth?" asked Seventeen. "You can take me to him?"

"His actual location isn't important," said Jenni, suddenly evasive. "I can transport you there if you desire. The path is open. But only if your answer is yes."

For a moment, just for a moment, Seventeen was tempted. Absolute, omniscient power was not easily rejected. Using it, he could change society, deliver justice to the oppressed, right terrible wrongs, save countless lives. As Jenni said, he could be more than a man. He could be a god.

Then, creeping out of the dark recesses of his mind, came the words. *An unending curtain of darkness covering the world. Mankind drowning in a sea of black blood. The end of good. The triumph of absolute evil.*

"Kallikos the Seer spoke of a future ruled by the pattern-clone, the being you've named the Master of

Harmony," said Seventeen. "It wasn't the utopia you described."

At the mention of the Time Master, the girl's features turned crimson. For an instant, her face quivered, as if made of jelly. Her flesh and bone seemed to melt, merge together into a flat, ambiguous mask. Then, with a snarl of rage, she was once again Jenni Smith.

"How can you believe the drug-induced dreams of a jealous old fool?" she asked, venom dripping from every word. "Kallikos hates my master. The seer remains rooted in the past. He fears change. His visions are clouded by his outdated beliefs."

Jenni Smith took another step closer. "You must believe me, Seventeen. The Nine Traditions are slowly but steadily losing the Ascension War. We need to proceed very carefully. Most people accept science, not sorcery. The Master of Harmony understands. We need compromise, not constant war."

"Somehow," said Seventeen, "I don't see the Inner Circle of the Technocratic Union making peace with the Council of Nine. Not unless they dictate the terms."

"You assume the Technocracy has a choice," said Jenni. "They don't. Nor do the Nine Traditions. The Master of Harmony isn't begging for their participation. He demands it."

"*Cooperate or else*," said Seventeen. "One man dictating terms to the mightiest mages in the Tellurian. Pardon me if I sound skeptical. No willworker, not even the pattern-clone, is that powerful."

Robert Weinberg

"The Master of Harmony is no ordinary being," said Jenni. She spoke as if reciting a religious litany or mantra. "He died once before, centuries ago, trying to warn us of our folly. His words were forgotten, ignored for ages. Only his disciples, a chosen few, believed. Now he has returned, fulfilling a promise made to us shortly before his death. Resurrected by the unsuspecting fools of the Gray Collective, the Master of Harmony controls magicks unlike any seen on Earth in five hundred years. No power in all the Tellurian can stop him. With an unshakable will and indestructible form, he truly is the Ascension Warrior."

"And if I can't make a decision without further facts?" he asked.

"There may be another chance," she replied. "Who can tell? I will warn you, though. Those who do not stand with us, stand against us. There is no middle ground."

She stretched out her arms. "Seize the moment, Seventeen. Join us. Join me."

"Not tonight," said Seventeen and launched himself forward. Powerful legs propelled him like rockets. He moved with lightning speed, faster than humanly possible. But not fast enough. Massive hands clenched on empty air. He sprawled flat on grass. Jenni Smith was gone.

"Damn," he said. With a sigh, he rose to his knees, wiping the dirt off his chest. Then froze, as he caught sight of a figure only a few feet away.

It was Shadow of the Dawn. She stood motionless,

hands resting gently on her hips. A hint of a smile was on her lips.

"How long have you been there?" asked Seventeen, standing. He brushed off the last of the dirt from his shoulders. "Hear any of my guest's proposition?"

"I thought it best for you not to be left unprotected," said Shadow. "Sam Haine agreed. After Kallikos was comfortable, I returned to the glade. Not wanting to intrude upon your thoughts, I remained among the trees. I witnessed your entire encounter with Miss Smith. Once she disappeared, I decided to reveal myself. I did not want you thinking I was spying."

"Not a problem," said Seventeen. He grinned. "I actually believed no one could get close to me without my sensing their presence. Evidently, I was terribly mistaken."

"I am a Dragon Scale," said Shadow with a shrug of her shoulders. "We are trained not to be seen."

"You heard everything then," said Seventeen. "My chance to rule the world. What did you think of Jenni's offer?"

"You were wise to reject it," said Shadow. "This Master of Harmony she worships is a false god. The peace he proposes is the peace of the grave."

"Black blood and eternal night," said Seventeen. His gaze met and held Shadow's. She made no attempt to look away. "Do you think the pattern-clone is allied with the Kindred?"

"The undead?" said Shadow. "Possibly. My knowledge of vampires is small. I suspect I will learn more shortly."

The warrior woman padded to within an arm's length of Seventeen. "Be warned, my friend," she said. "Great forces swirl about you. A war has begun that tears at the very shape of reality. Your destiny and mine and those of our companions are bound in its coils. If we fail, the Tapestry will perish. The Master of Harmony must be destroyed, no matter what the cost."

"Kallikos told you this?" asked Seventeen.

"*I know this*," said Shadow fiercely. "The truth is in my heart. And in my soul. As it is in yours."

She was the most beautiful woman Seventeen had ever seen. Reaching out, he drew her close. She came willingly into his arms. They kissed, and her lips burned like fire against his own.

Chapter Three

Terrence Shade pulled open the door to the apartment building and entered the foyer. It had taken him nearly an hour to reach this spot from the toxic waste dump on the shore of Lake Ontario. Dimensional travel was a lot faster than street traffic. He wasn't concerned. There was no hurry.

The structure's security guard, sitting at his watch-stand while reading the morning paper, looked up with disinterested eyes. Seeing Shade, he frowned. *Joe Steeger* said the gold badge on his shirt. A big, fat man dressed in an official-looking blue and white uniform, the guard had pasty white skin and greasy black hair. He wore a .45 automatic strapped to his belt.

"Can I help you, sir?" asked Steeger, putting down the newspaper. His tone made it clear he wanted nothing more than for Shade to turn around and leave. "This building is off limits to anyone other than residents and their invited guests."

Shade grinned at the guard, revealing a full set of

Robert Weinberg

bright white teeth, but he said nothing. A short, squat man with beet-red face and full black beard, Shade wore a white shirt, white pants, white belt, white socks and white bucks. On his head rested a wide-brimmed white hat. A pair of dark sunglasses hid his eyes.

Sighing loudly, Steeger made a big show of looking down at the note pad on the top of his desk. "No one's expecting a visitor this morning. They gotta call down in advance. So, since you're not a guest, that means you're a resident."

Shade nodded, as if agreeing with Steeger's comments.

"Like hell you are," the officer stated, his voice cold. "You're not one of our tenants. I've handled the front desk at this building for years. Never saw you before. What do you want, buddy?"

Shade, still grinning, reached out and patted Steeger on the cheek. Yelping in surprise, the security guard swatted Shade's hand away. "Keep your fuckin' hands off me, you pervert," he growled. The fat man placed one hand on his service revolver. "I don't take shit from anyone, 'specially not the likes of scum like you. Get moving before I stop acting so fuckin' polite."

"No need to resort to violence, Officer Steeger," said Shade, his voice surprisingly mellow. "I was merely admiring your healthy flesh."

Shade raised a hand and pointed to his own face. "If you look very closely, you can see the scars where my skin was burnt to a crisp. The marks are almost gone. It happened yesterday—an eternity ago—but I'm a fast healer."

Steeger said nothing. He remained unmoving, his fingers wrapped around the butt of his gun. His mouth hung wide open. Tiny droplets of spittle fell to the floor. Only his eyes were alive, his gaze darting back and forth like a bird trapped in a cage.

"Please sit down," said Shade. "And shut your big mouth. After all, we don't want to attract any attention. This is a very proper, safe building. Deadbolt locks, bullet-proof glass, cameras in the elevators, the works. Nice people live here. It won't do to have the chief security officer drooling on the carpet."

The guard did exactly as commanded. He moved stiffly, like a robot. Carefully, he lowered himself onto the edge of his chair. He sat straight up, his back rigid, face forward. His one hand still clutched his .45. The other rested in his lap, thick fingers clenched in a fist. The fear in his eyes had turned to terror.

"That looks better," said Shade. "Nice and friendly. Two friends discussing baseball scores."

The man in white removed his dark sunglasses. The pupils of his eyes were white, his eyeballs blood red. "Seeing them makes you want to scream, doesn't it?" he asked, tucking the dark glasses into his shirt pocket. "Imagine what it's like looking out from inside." Shade chuckled. "The worst part of it," he said, more to himself than to Steeger, "is that Aliara won't let me go mad. She's very very cruel. Extremely cruel."

He patted Steeger on the cheek again. "You wouldn't be in this terrible predicament, actually, if you hadn't been such an arrogant asshole over the past few years. Dumb bastard, you annoyed the wrong person. She mentioned you to someone who's easily offended. Bang, I'm here. Payback time."

Shade shrugged. "There's a lesson to be learned from all this, Mr. Steeger. Never insult a stranger. They might have powerful connections. Unfortunately, for you, school's out for the summer."

Red-and-white eyes stared at the clock on one edge of the security station. "Seven forty-five in the morning." He laughed, a shrill, piercing sound. "Despite the rush hour traffic, I'm fifteen minutes early. Oh well. The early bird and all that. Millicent Hargroves, Mr. Steeger? She's one of your tenants. You know them all. That's what you told me. What's her apartment number?"

"Seven B," said the security guard, able to say those few syllables and nothing more.

"Excellent," said Shade, putting his sunglasses back on, "you still remember. It's quite important that your memory is still functioning."

The red-faced man leaned forward on the desk. "Now, here is what I want you to do, my friend. In a minute, I'm going to walk to the inner door at the end of the hall. When I get there, you will buzz me through. I'll use elevator one to go to Ms. Hargroves's apartment. Don't worry about a key. I don't need one."

Shade paused. His smile widened. "Once I'm out of sight, you will regain full use of your body and your senses. Continue working as before. Don't mention me or this conversation to anyone, but don't forget it either. Check your clock every few minutes. That's very important. Watch until it turns 9 AM. Then, when the next tenant comes to your desk, stand up and draw your pistol. Make sure the safety is off. Why carry a loaded weapon if it's not ready to use? Say in a loud, clear voice, *I should have shown more respect to my betters*. Repeat that phrase now, please. I want to hear how it sounds."

"I should have shown more respect to my betters," said Steeger. His eyes twitched wildly.

"Perfect," said Shade. "Remember, say it nice and loud. Apologies aren't worth much if they're not heard. After speaking, take your pistol and put the barrel into your mouth. Aim upward. Push it all the way in, as far as it can go. I want the metal to be touching the back of your throat. Then pull the trigger."

Shade straightened. "I can't imagine you will survive the first bullet. But if you do, please continue firing until your brain ceases to function."

The white-clad man smirked. "Worst thing about it, Steeger," he said, "is that you can't go mad either. Aliara's rules. Escape through insanity is not allowed."

Shade started down the hall to the security door. "At least," he called over his shoulder, "you'll only suffer for an hour. I'm cursed for eternity. Now buzz me through and get back to work. The clock is ticking."

White shag carpet covered the living room floor of apartment 7B. The furniture was all white. The walls of the room were black. Feeling like a polar bear in the midst of an ice floe, Shade dropped down to a large plush sofa. He didn't mind waiting. He had no place to go.

Twenty minutes passed. A key grated in the lock. "Hell," came a woman's weary voice as she discovered the door was already open. "Damn arrogant thieves don't even bother…."

The woman's tirade came to an abrupt stop as she entered the living room. A tall, gaunt black woman, she was dressed in a plain, conservative gray skirt and blouse. "Who the fuck are you?" she asked. "And what the hell are you doing in my apartment?"

"Say hello to your new assistant," said Shade, removing his sunglasses. His red eyes provided an interesting contrast to the sea of whiteness. "I bring greetings from the Great Beyond."

"An assistant?" said Ms. Hargroves, astonished. "What the hell do I need an assistant for?"

Shade shrugged. "Mine is not to reason why," he declared. "If you want to complain to Aliara, be my guest."

"No thanks," declared Ms. Hargroves. "I may be ignorant, but I'm not stupid. I need a beer."

Kicking off her shoes, the gaunt woman walked into the kitchenette. "You want a beer, redeye?"

"Sure," said Shade. "My name, for your information, is Terrence Shade. Formerly Mission Specialist Terrence Shade of the New World Order. Call me whatever you like. You're the boss."

"Shade will do just fine," said Ms. Hargroves, returning to the living room with two bottles of beer. Handing one to Shade, she dropped into a sturdy armchair directly across from the sofa. "What's going on, Shade? Why are you really here?"

Shade lifted the beer bottle to his lips and drained the contents in a single gulp. "Aliara said nothing about keeping secrets," he declared. "I'll tell you everything I know."

He paused. "But first, could I have another beer?"

"Sure," said Ms. Hargroves. "Get it yourself. Then start talking."

"I take it you're familiar with the AW Project?" asked Shade after downing his second drink. "Good. No need for me to detail all the work that went into that endeavor. Actually, this was the fourth or fifth time Iteration X and the Progenitors have attempted to create the perfect clone. None of the other efforts succeeded. The technical problems always proved insurmountable. This try, everything meshed. Every challenge was faced and overcome. Technological breakthroughs became routine. Despite intense personality conflicts between the leaders of the two Conventions at the Collective, work proceeded smoothly towards a satisfactory conclusion."

Shade hesitated, frowning. "Thinking about it, I realize now that events were *too* stable. Considering the volatile tempers involved, there should have been more conflict. Obviously, I was not the only one in the Collective following the orders of an unseen mentor." The red-eyed man shrugged. "Even the best of us are merely pawns in a multi-player game of cosmic chess. Aliara's been my patron for decades. Somehow, she learned of the project and wanted me involved. I pulled a few strings and became Mission Specialist for the Construct. It wasn't until a few weeks ago that I learned the reason for the Dark Lord's interest. She planned to channel her essence into the pattern-clone and walk the Earth in physical form."

"One of the Maeljin Incarna among the masses," said Ms. Hargroves. "Astonishing."

"Terrifying, actually," said Shade. "A preview of Armageddon."

"The world's unchanged," said Ms. Hargroves. "Obviously she didn't succeed. What went wrong?"

"Aliara came to the station a few moments before the clone became self-aware," said Shade. "As a reward for my faithful service, I was sent to the Dark Lord's palace on Malfeas. The Queen of Lust proceeded to the main laboratory on her own."

He thought it best not to mention how Aliara's touch scorched his flesh...or the mind-shattering horrors he'd encountered in the Void Beyond. No matter. He suspected Ms. Hargroves guessed what remained unsaid. His red eyes were message enough.

"The best-laid plans of even Those Beyond sometimes go astray," said Shade. "Entering the lab, Aliara was immediately attacked by advanced mechanoids emerging from a dimensional gateway. Worse, she sensed another being had already taken possession of the clone's brain."

"Who?" asked Ms. Hargroves.

"Aliara never learned," said Shade. He chuckled.

"Before she could do more than disable the robots, the Dark Lord was *pushed* through the gateway from which they came. Caught in a dimensional rift, she twisted reality and materialized safely on Malfeas. Her displeasure with this outcome made even that realm tremble."

"So the Technocracy retained control of the pattern-clone," said Ms. Hargroves. "Enzo Giovanni won't be pleased. He wanted the biomech destroyed."

"You assume too much," said Shade. "Her brief mental contact with the pattern-clone convinced Aliara that the being possessed no ordinary human mind. She could not define how it was different, just that it *was* different. I truly think she believes that her arch-rival among the Maeljin Incarna, Lord Steel, is manipulating the creation."

"What nonsense," said Ms. Hargroves loudly, then instantly clamped her mouth shut. Disagreeing aloud with Aliara was bad policy. "I serve as a spy for Aliara. My employer, Enzo Giovanni, one of the Kindred, and his closest friend and ally, Ezra, a renegade mage, plot to rule the world. They intend to do this by gaining complete control of the Pentex organization and Clan Giovanni. Their mentor is Lord Steel."

The gaunt woman drained another beer. "Enzo thinks to keep secrets from me, but nothing he says or does goes unreported. He fears the pattern-clone. As does Ezra. Their worries reflect those of their sponsor. In the past few months, they have done everything in their power to sabotage the AW Project."

"With no tangible results," said Shade. "How odd

for such a deadly duo. Still, you may be right. Aliara sees the steel glove of her rival behind every curtain. Remember, though, that the Dark Lords are masters of misdirection. Enzo lusts for power. Ezra thirsts for revenge against the world. Such fools are easily manipulated."

"You seem to know quite a bit about my business," said Ms. Hargroves.

"Aliara thought it best that I come to you well prepared," said Shade. The color drained from his ruddy cheeks. "Intense pain serves as an effective teacher. I learned extremely fast."

"So I gather," said Ms. Hargroves.

"Do you know a man named Sam Haine?" asked Shade, seeking to change the subject.

"No," said Ms. Hargroves. "Should I?"

"He's a Reality Deviant, belonging to the Nine Traditions," said Shade. "Called the Changing Man. Aliara sent me here for two reasons. To help you keep track of Enzo and Ezra's grand scheme, and to locate Sam Haine and give him a push."

"A push?" Ms. Hargroves asked.

"Sam Haine was the mortal who shoved Aliara into the dimensional gateway at the Gray Collective," said Shade. "She wants me to repay the favor. The Dark Lord wants the Changing Man pushed through a doorway into Malfeas. Where she will deal with him at her leisure for the next thousand years."

The cool, unemotional Ms. Hargroves shivered.

"That reminds me," said Shade. "What time is it?"

Ms. Hargroves glanced at her watch. "Nine fifteen."

"Perfect," said Shade. "May I use your intercom to the lobby?"

"Why not?" She pointed to a voice box and buzzer on the wall of the kitchenette. "Over there."

"Thank you." Shade smiled.

He pressed the buzzer for a minute. No one answered. He pressed again, holding down the button for a long time. Still no reply.

"Apology accepted," said Shade.

"What are you talking about?" asked Ms. Hargroves.

Shade only smiled.

Chapter Four

"Officially," said the man who claimed his name was John Doe, "you are now listed in all records, documents, and Technocracy databases as dead. You will be pleased to know that you died heroically fighting the enemies of Enlightenment."

"Sorry I missed my own funeral," said X344. "Was it nice?"

"Your remains, along with those of your companions on the Gray Collective, were unfortunately lost with the destruction of the Construct," said Doe, a sad expression in his blue eyes. "The memorial service, I am sure, was quite moving."

"Don't worry, Ernest," said Sharon with a sardonic smile, "if we don't satisfy our colleagues on the Inner Circle, you might still have the privilege of hearing the exact same invocation. From inside a coffin."

"A ridiculous accusation," said Doe, chuckling. He sounded exactly like Terrence Shade. Sharon wondered if the New World Order even taught their Mission Specialists how to laugh at a certain pitch.

It wouldn't surprise her in the least. "We would never terminate two such important members of the Union for not complying with the wishes of the Inner Circle. Though, with serious doubts as to your loyalty, assignment to a remote outpost in a developing nation would be a distinct possibility."

"That doesn't sound so bad," said the cyborg cautiously.

"Think Nepal, metal-head," said Sharon, acid in her voice. "Or Borneo. As a Research Director, I transferred troublesome underlings to both locations. Imagine trying to blend in with the local population. You wouldn't be able to hide your body modifications beneath that trenchcoat so easily."

"Nepal?" repeated X344. "Isn't that near Tibet? It's the edge of nowhere."

"Bingo," said Sharon Reed.

John Doe frowned. The Mission Specialist obviously found her flippant attitude distressing. Sharon didn't care. For months and months, obeying the dictates of her superiors in the Progenitor hierarchy, she had held her temper in check on the Gray Collective. Keeping peace with Ernest Nelson and his boss, the insufferably smug Comptroller Klair of Iteration X, had not been easy. Never the most patient person, she had exhibited incredible restraint.

Now, after surviving an ordeal that would have killed any lesser being, she found herself forced to endure yet another round of compromises. Sharon had her limits. Not even the Inner Council could ask her to be polite forever. Conciliation went only so far.

Once they'd left the Gray Collective, she had driven the truck straight to the nearest Technocracy headquarters. With her wounds desperately needing attention and the cyborg hovering between life and death, Sharon had no time to be selective. They both needed immediate treatment. Dynamic Security was the largest Union base in the northeastern corridor of the United States. It was also controlled by the New World Order.

Paranoia, fortunately, had its benefits. A week before, the Specialist running the base, as well as his top Gray Man, had been killed during Terrence Shade's disastrous raid on the Casey cabal. His replacement, only on the job three days, was a short, aggressive man with jet-black hair and eyebrows named Russ Kinross. He'd reacted instantly when he learned Sharon and her passenger were the only survivors of the Gray Collective. Fearing he would be blamed if the two passengers didn't survive to tell their stories, Kinross had frantically slashed red tape and regulations. Medical care was immediate and intense.

Rest and recovery, however, were not part of Technocracy regimen. Less than an hour after Sharon emerged from the regeneration tank, she was visited by an inquisitor dispatched by the Inner Council. Still groggy from biofeedback procedures, she offered little resistance to the blank-faced individual's piercing questions. The interrogation had lasted nearly two hours. Afterwards, to her chagrin, Sharon discovered she couldn't remember anything she had been asked, what she had said, or even the gender of the representative.

Whatever information she and X344 had revealed during their questioning brought swift reaction. The next morning a short, slender bald man with limpid blue eyes and a wide, friendly smile came calling. He introduced himself as John Doe. His sincere concern for her well-being oozed out of every pore. That he was a Mission Specialist for the New World Order was quite clear. Sharon, who considered the NWO a group of intrusive spies set on minding everyone else's business, distrusted him immediately.

His features creased with worry, Doe told Sharon that the Technocracy needed her to return immediately to active service. Though she had more than earned the gratitude and thanks of her comrades, there was no time for relaxation. The Ascension War, the ongoing battle for creation, never ceased.

The destruction of the Gray Collective had shaken the leaders of the Five Collectives badly. The Inner Council wanted answers—explanations for the disaster—and they wanted them as soon as possible.

"Since you and Nelson are the only known survivors of the Gray Collective," declared Doe, "it seems eminently logical for the pair of you to handle the follow-up investigation. No one else has ever seen the mysterious pattern-clone. Nor are we sure what miracles this bizarre Frankenstein's monster is capable of performing."

"Didn't Terrence Shade, in his reports to the Inner Council, describe the exact purpose of our modifications to the clone's biosystem?" said Sharon. "He took detailed notes on every enhancement we made."

John Doe's pleasant voice turned icy. His friendly blue eyes froze. "Mission Specialist Shade's reports on the AW Project are being re-examined as we speak. The communications he sent to the Inner Circle were sadly lacking in detail. The Council and the Symposium were not fully aware of the biomechanical breakthroughs achieved by the Technocrats of the Collective. Shade never made it clear to anyone that the clone was so powerful."

"Surely no one suspects Shade was a traitor?" said Sharon, a sinking feeling in her stomach answering the question before John Doe.

"The Inner Circle did not communicate their feelings on the subject to me," said Doe. "However, Shade's undivided loyalty to the New World Order seems highly doubtful."

"But if he wasn't following your orders," said Sharon, "who was he working for?"

"That is one of the things we would very much like to know," said Doe.

"Shade's dead," said Sharon. "The Gray Collective's destroyed. Suspect and evidence gone. Case closed."

"We are not convinced Mission Specialist Shade numbers among the departed," said Doe. "According to your debriefing as well as that of Ernest Nelson, Shade was not present when the clone gained awareness. His absence raises further questions about his actions. So does the unexpected arrival of the Deep Space alien entity known as Aliara, Queen of Desire.

We have many questions, but no answers. The Technocracy wants you to find them."

"Do I have a choice?" asked Sharon.

"Of course," Doe had responded, his tone making it clear that she did not. "There is always a choice."

"I'm not Shade. I'm loyal to the Technocracy," said Sharon. She also had no secret patron with vast powers to ensure her survival if she said anything different. "I'll do whatever is required of me."

"I expected no less," said Doe, smiling once more. "We will discuss your mission in detail later today."

Now it was later. Sharon and X344 were in a small office filled mostly with a large steel desk. John Doe sat behind it. On the desk were two thick manila envelopes marked TOP SECRET. PROPERTY OF DYNAMIC SECURITY. Sharon, who had been at many such meetings, knew that a new identity rested within each folder.

"Stop worrying about transfers," said Doe, a broad smile replacing his frown. His eyes were not laughing. "Nothing like that is going to happen. I'm confident that working together as a team, the two of you will quickly unravel the mystery surrounding the destruction of the Gray Collective. You'll be heroes."

Sharon felt no such surge of confidence, but thought it best not to tell Doe that. He proclaimed them as future heroes. She suspected he actually meant scapegoats. Again, she knew better than to disagree openly. Despite his big smiles and sparkling blue eyes, John Doe was not a pleasant man. And he definitely was not a happy one.

"You can remain here and recuperate for another forty-eight hours," declared the Mission Specialist. "That's all the time we can spare. Normally you'd not be pushed out of here that fast. But the Inner Council fears any further delay could have far-reaching consequences. The pattern-clone must be located, and if identified as a threat to the Technocracy, neutralized. Shade's possible treachery must be researched and evaluated. And the mysterious behavior of Velma Wade needs to be explained."

"Finding the answers to that particular riddle will be my pleasure," said Sharon savagely. "I owe Velma a knife in the back. One twisted slowly while she squirms."

"Of course," Doe said after a moment. As a Mission Specialist, his hands were tainted with blood, but the expression on Sharon's face when she swore revenge was enough to make even the most dangerous killer uneasy.

"I'm ready for war," said X344. Twelve hours of time-compression surgery had resulted in major changes to the cyborg's appearance. His artificial limbs had been modified and redesigned. Wearing dark gloves, heavy-duty work boots and a black trenchcoat, he could pass for human. More importantly, the surgeons had reattached his weapon systems—removed when he was transferred to the Gray Collective. The cyborg was once again a walking high-tech arsenal of mass destruction.

"As I mentioned, you are both listed as dead in all of our data banks. There's no guarantee that Shade or Wade aren't part of some secret conspiracy against the Union. Quite possibly, their cohorts may still be actively involved in Technocracy affairs. The Inner Council thus thought it best that no one know you are still alive."

"How do we know the programmers making the changes can be trusted?" asked Sharon. "I considered Velma above suspicion. And she betrayed me."

"I did all of the computer work myself," Doe said dryly. "Your original files have been flagged. We'll be alerted instantly if anyone tries to download information from them. Meanwhile, your fingerprints, eyeprints, internal scans, brainwave patterns, and all other identification codes have been switched to new identities."

The Mission Specialist shoved the thick manila envelopes across the desk towards them. "Here are your papers, identification cards and revised biographies."

Doe looked at X344. "When you first joined the Technocracy, all traces of your previous life were wiped clean. To keep things simple, since you will be dealing mostly with the Masses while in Static Reality, you will again use the name Ernest Nelson."

Sharon stifled a grin. There was justice in the world. The cyborg hated his original name.

Nelson shrugged. "Call me what you want," he growled. "Names don't matter much. Inside, I'm still X344."

Doe beamed. "A proper attitude." He turned to Sharon. "Your new name is Susan Rand. Your home remains California, but I lopped thirty years off your age. Now you're almost as young as you look."

Sharon didn't know if Doe meant the remark as a compliment or an insult, so she said nothing. Like all Progenitors, she realized that physical age meant nothing. Only conditioning mattered.

"Both of you now have security clearance Alpha-Alpha," said Doe. "That's the highest rating below Inner Circle membership. You can access classified information on any computer in the Technocracy network. When necessary, you can request aid and assistance from the leader of any nearby Construct. No one will question your decisions—as long as they produce results. In this investigation, you speak with the voice of the Technocracy."

"Finding answers is going to be the trick," said Sharon, already trying to think of herself as Susan. "Neither Ernest nor I are Operatives trained in espionage and spying. We don't have a clue where to begin this investigation."

"You have numerous possibilities," said John Doe. "All that is necessary is for you to change your outlook. *Question everything, trust nothing.* That's a basic credo of the New World Order. Remember it on this mission."

"Velma Wade," said Ernest Nelson. "We start with her and the pattern-clone. They're definitely alive and on the loose. After having her in your service for years, you know how she thinks. We'll start by examining your previous assignments. Somewhere, she made a mistake, left a trail we can trace. Once we discover the truth about her, maybe we'll find a clue to where she's hiding. Find Wade and I'll bet we find the pattern-clone."

"It's worth a try," said Sharon. "Though Velma always impressed me with her thoroughness. It's hard to believe she would have made any mistakes."

"Look for contradictions," said Doe, "or sudden unexplained shifts in her personality. Events in the past take on new significance when viewed from the present. No one in the world is perfect. No one."

"You don't know Velma," said Sharon.

"Ain't that the truth," said Nelson. "Damned shapeshifter was obsessive about details. Still, everybody makes mistakes. Besides, we already got an angle to explore."

"An angle?" said Sharon.

"Wade worked for you for years," said Nelson. "Loyal, trustworthy, the works. Doing all your dirty jobs." He laughed. "Just like me and Comptroller Klair. Don't try to look innocent, Reed. I'm not dumb. She liked what she did, same as me. Wade was sitting pretty as second-in-command to a powerful leader. For Ops like her and me, it's a damned good life. But she literally stabbed you in the back for a pattern-clone. There's got to be a reason. A really special reason for her doing that.

"More importantly," continued Nelson, "it's not a decision she made overnight. You don't throw away your entire life on a whim. Wade knew exactly what she was doing. She was obviously with you at the Gray

Collective for one reason—to create the pattern-clone and leave with it once the being came to life."

Sharon stared at the cyborg. She loathed admitting it, but Nelson had stumbled across something important. "I always thought of myself as the boss," she mused, her thoughts speeding in strange directions. "The one in charge. But now I'm wondering. We need to find out why I was assigned to the AW Project. I always assumed it was by sheer chance, or due to my previous work in genetic manipulation. Now, I'm not so sure."

John Doe was no longer smiling. "Your conclusions are most disturbing. They require immediate attention. After this meeting, I will do some investigating on my own. I should have the results before you leave this construct. An undertaking the size and complexity of the AW Project needed approval from the Symposium. There should be detailed records regarding the entire proposal. Including the name of the person who initiated the program. That individual may be entirely innocent. Just a brilliant Technomancer with a new concept for clone development." John Doe paused. "Or Velma Wade's co-conspirator."

If Doe's suspicions were correct, and Sharon suspected they were, that person had probably quite effectively covered his tracks months ago. It was equally likely that he had flagged the Symposium's records when the project was discussed and approved. Doe's investigation might actually alert the mastermind. Dangerous men do dangerous things when threatened. Doe could be sticking his head into a noose.

Saying nothing of her suspicions, Sharon turned her head slightly and glanced at Ernest Nelson. As if reading her thoughts, the cyborg looked in her direction. He nodded. They needed to stay alert and keep close watch on John Doe.

"Sooner or later," said Sharon, wanting to warn Nelson of another possible danger, "Velma is going to learn I'm still alive. That's when things will get messy."

"Why is that?" asked Doe. "Why would your ex-assistant care that you didn't perish with the Gray Collective? She obviously got what she wanted with the pattern-clone."

"Because every clone I help design," said Sharon, "I program with an automatic shutdown sequence. One sentence spoken aloud by me in the pattern-clone's presence, it dies. The trigger is built into the being's DNA structure. It cannot be deactivated or disabled. My existence puts the pattern-clone at risk. Velma knows that. That's the reason she tried to kill me at the Gray Collective. And that's why she'll keep trying. Until she's successful or the clone is destroyed."

Chapter Five

In bold, red neon letters, the sign proclaimed SLEAZY SAM'S BAR AND GRILL. Below it, in smaller script, were the words OPEN ALL NIGHT, EVERY NIGHT. The bar itself, a wooden tombstone two stories high, was set back a few hundred feet from the highway, an offshoot of I-491 west. The only other structure in sight was the gas station across the street. Its solitary occupant was an old man reading a magazine in a steel-and-glass change booth. A sign on the booth wall proclaimed he was "armed and dangerous."

Though it was almost 3 AM, the parking lot was nearly full. A dozen big rigs took up most of the space, but a scattering of passenger cars were also present. Surprisingly, several were recent luxury models. Despite its name, Sleazy Sam's attracted a very mixed clientele.

Police blotters throughout upper New York State listed Sleazy Sam's as a major trouble spot. No sane cop went near it after dark. Sleazy Sam's saw more murders in a month than most towns saw in a year. It was, Madeleine Giovanni decided as she steered her mini-van into a parking spot, a perfect investment for someone with more money than conscience.

Opening the van door, Madeleine stepped out into the night. In the bright lights of the cold parking lot, she presented a striking picture: chalk-white skin, devoid of all but a trace of color. Black eyes, matched by shoulder-length jet-black hair. Sensual killer's lips, red as fresh-spilled blood. Seductively slender, the woman wore a short black tank dress, midnight silk stockings and low, practical heels. Her only jewelry consisted of a silver necklace decorated with the Giovanni family crest.

Like a wolf cub's, Madeleine's features held a curious blend of innocence and savagery. Strange lights danced in her eyes, and she moved with stylish grace. Though obviously unarmed, Madeleine seemed self-assured. Nothing would bother her. Nothing would dare to.

Footfalls echoed on the concrete a dozen feet away. Feet scuffled on asphalt. Someone coughed. Another laughed. Shadows flickered in the moonlight.

"Field mice," murmured Madeleine. "Human ones. How perfect."

She stared into the darkness with eyes sharp as a cat's. A quick search revealed a half-dozen scarecrow figures hiding behind the massive interstate tankers. Teenagers, dressed in rags despite the chill. Boys and girls. The usual runaways and dropouts from a society that preached moral virtue but practiced corporate greed. Madeleine sympathized with them, but the world was a cold place; always had been and always would be.

Hunter's instincts pinned a barefooted girl moving quietly, several yards to her left. A *curious* mouse, then. Good. With inhuman speed, Madeleine whipped about, closed the distance, and snapped the girl's wrists together in a vice-grip. The mouse squeaked as the Dagger of the Giovanni dragged her into the harsh spotlights. Squeaking was about all the girl *could* do; tall and skeletally thin, the teenager couldn't weigh more than ninety pounds.

The mouse found her voice: "Bitch, what's your *problem?*"

Stringy blonde hair caught the light, falling like greasy straw across bright blue eyes. Torn denim framed white spots of skin. Cold glare shone on a pretty, dirty face, as pale as Madeleine's own. The girl planted her heels and dragged against her captor's grip. No use. The light speared a navel ring, glittering defiantly from a pale, thin belly. The girl's voice was equally defiant, and equally thin: "Let the fuck *go* of me, you psycho cooze, or I'll fucking scream!"

Madeleine cinched the mouse's wrists together. The words slid into a gasp of pain.

"Who are you, child?"

Another gasp as the bones grated. "Fuck off."

"Tell me your name, girl, or I will be forced to cripple you."

"Eat me." A *spirited* mouse.

Madeleine's eyes glittered in the halogen light. The

girl stared back, terrified but rebellious. A thin vein pulsed in her throat. The monster smiled. There weren't many mortals who could look her in the eye. This one would do nicely. "Stop wasting my time, child. I merely asked your name. Do not harm yourself for pride. Believe me, it is not worth it."

The girl relented. "Lucy," she whispered. The word sounded more like a threat than a name.

"Thank you." Madeleine let her go at once. Lucy stumbled backward, catching herself before she fell. "You see? Very simple."

"Crazy bitch." The girl drew back, rubbing her wrists. A short boy, also barefooted and dressed in ragged denim, moved toward her, protectively.

"So many have said." Madeleine's smile widened. "I imagine that we have both heard the phrase before. Am I correct?"

"Yeah," Lucy growled. "You're a goddamned genius. What's your point?"

Madeleine raised her free hand and pointed at her van. "My name is Madeleine, and that is my vehicle. I am going inside this establishment for a few hours. It would be very inconvenient for me if, when I left, my van was not here. So I am appointing you as my deputy. Guard my vehicle closely, Lucy. Make sure it remains undisturbed. *Do you understand?*"

"I understand you're fuckin' crazy." Lucy's voice quivered with uncertainty.

"If my car is damaged in any way," said Madeleine, stressing the *any*, "I will hold you personally responsible, child. If it is protected, I will see to your compensation." For an instant, the monster's eyes blazed blood red. "I am Madeleine Giovanni, of the House of Giovanni, and I do not make idle threats. Obey me and you will be well rewarded. Act the fool and you will be given a fool's reward."

No one needed to ask what she meant. Without another word, Madeleine turned away and strode toward the bar's entrance. Behind her, she heard Lucy whispering to the other scavengers. Old shoes scraped on the blacktop. Four teens, all thin and ragged, emerged from the shadows. One boy, three girls, none of them older than seventeen. Some held clubs of salvaged pipe; others clutched bottles or blades in their pale fists. An unwashed smell carried on the autumn breeze. The four moved to block Madeleine's path. Lucy and her "bodyguard" padded up behind her.

The monster slowed and met each child's eye in turn.

The words came all at once:

"What'cha doin' here, lady?"

"You a narc?"

"You got somethin' goin'?"

"Looking for those fucking cannibals?"

"Are you an angel of the Lord, come to punish the wicked?"

The last question—phrased in a hollow, haunted voice—caught Madeleine by surprise. She stared at the waif, no older than fourteen, who had spoken. This girl wore a faded black dress and sweater, and carried a thin-bladed knife. Her eyes held a fanatic's shine.

"What makes you think that?" Madeleine asked.

"Mama told me angels were beautiful—" the girl's voice was too deep for her tiny frame—"and that they always wore black."

"Her mama was a crack fiend with a hard-on for Pat Robertson," snapped a young lady in cutoffs, Keds and a faded yellow T-shirt. She didn't seem to feel the cold. Her arms were flecked with old track marks and her face bore more lines than any girl's should have. This would be the leader, Madeleine guessed. The one with the age and experience her packmates lacked.

Madeleine's voice softened. "I am no angel, I'm afraid."

The leader stepped in close to the child, shielding her with one arm. The other crooked a rusty bayonet. "Stupid bitch went on and on about God and angels and shit, till one day she decided to go to go take a permanent tour. Jumped off the roof, and tried to drag Sarah with her. Stupid toad went splat right in front of her little girl, and Daddy sobered up just long enough to throw her into rehab for shit she was never doing. Not like me. She's clean." The red-haired leader stared right into Madeleine's eyes, daring her to argue. "When I ran, I took her with me. She's been living with us ever since."

"Us?"

Aware she'd said too much, the leader snapped her lips shut and lowered her chin to a fighting stance. She raised the bayonet and backed away. A chain clinked behind Madeleine's back as it dropped into swing-position.

"Please," said Madeleine. The soft word carried a hint of command, backed up by a strong, subtle wave of mind-control. "I will not report you, nor harm you unless you cross me. I believe we have more in common than you imagine. Perhaps I can help you."

"No one helps the Rat Pack," the redhead spat. "We've had enough 'help,' thank you very fucking much."

Behind the conversation, Lucy held the chain easily, ready to swing it at Madeleine's head. The monster turned. "I am not your enemy unless you make it so. Lucy, put the weapon down. Please."

Lucy growled but assented. The chain coiled to the ground. "Thank you," said the Dagger of the Giovanni, and she meant it. Despite herself, the assassin admired these human field mice. Broken homes had not broken their spirits. "I did not mean to insult you," she said, turning to the leader. "If I have, I am sorry." Again, the words rode on a stream of soft domination. Manners alone would not smooth these urchins' rough edges. After a moment, she reached for the redhead's hand. "I am Madeleine, as I said. Who are you?"

The leader stared silently for a moment, then offered her own hand in response. "Allyson. These are my brothers and sisters, my family. We may not look like much, but we'll fuck up anyone who messes with us. You already met Lucy. That's Sarah. Sybil's the skinhead—"

"I'm not a skinhead," replied a slight black girl in

army castoffs and tennis shoes. Her head was absolutely bare; even her eyebrows were missing. Her voice was soft but edgy.

"Okay," Allyson apologized. "It's not a fashion thing, she was just born that way. Not too pretty, but she's fast as shit. Brian and Pete, they're brothers. Ran away from home. Neither of them talk too much. Seein' the scars on their backs, I can't say I blame 'em."

"Where do you live?" asked Madeleine. "How do you survive?"

"We got this cabin out in the woods," Allyson replied. "Hunter's place we found last year. It hadn't been used in a long time, so we cleaned it up and it's ours. Location's a secret. Too many fuckin' weirdos around here lately."

"You mentioned cannibals?" Madeleine turned to Lucy. Were there Lupines nearby? "What sort of cannibals?"

"Fuckin' Texas Chainsaw cannibal dudes," the defiant girl replied. "They'll chop you up and eat you raw." Lucy's voice strained suddenly. Her shoulders tensed. "Fuckers got Jamie last year…I thought he was never gonna stop screaming…." In spite of herself, Lucy let silent tears spill. She swiped a hand across her face. "Almost got me, too, but I'm too fast." Lucy knelt and scooped up her chain, then hugged the links to her chest. "And too chickenshit." The girl's shoulders trembled, but she refused to cry again.

The Dagger of the Giovanni touched Lucy's shoulder, brushed her hand softly across the girl's cheek and stroked her hair. "Sacrificing yourself would have been foolish," said Madeleine. "You made the right decision. Do not mourn your slain friend. Wait until the time is right. Then avenge him."

Lucy whined a small, hurt cry and settled against Madeleine's arm. The short boy reached out awkwardly and took Lucy's hand. Madeleine hugged the girl with real compassion.

"You meant what you told Lucy?" Allyson ventured. "About some sorta reward if she keeps your van safe?"

Madeleine nodded. "I pay for services rendered. Does the Rat Pack need funds?"

"Yeah, we're kinda short these days," Allyson admitted wryly. "I try to keep these kids clean, so we're not into any fucked-up shit. That makes it tough. There's lots of money if you're willing to deal and turn tricks, but fuck you if you try to make an honest living. Leo—that's the dude inside—passes us scraps sometimes and pays us to straighten up the lot, but that's about it. Brian and Pete wash windshields in the city, but people's so-called 'generosity' sucks. Lots of days, they come home with nothing."

Allyson's gaze wandered. Her voice did likewise. "Summers past, this used to be a good place to stay. People would come out to the forest for office picnics and stuff like that. We'd end up with lots of food, and usually got some other stuff they forgot. So much for that now, though. Folks are scared of the woods. Fuckin' cannibals and carjackers and shit like that. Cops don't do a damn thing, so we starve."

"You know this area well?" asked Madeleine. If

possible, she wanted to aid these outcasts. Odd, she knew—charity from a blood-drinking corpse. Still, the desire to help was there. Perhaps it came from the girls' defiance, or the angel remark, or the sheer weight of tragedy these children bore. Perhaps it came from Madeleine's own…unsatisfactory… childhood. No matter. As Lucy nestled in Madeleine's arms, freely and without any form of compulsion or command, the Dagger of the Giovanni resolved to help the Rat Pack. Her motivations were her own, and she did not consider them important enough to question. Besides, if the children *worked* for Madeleine, her aid was not charity.

"Sure, we've been everywhere," said Allyson, "and most of us grew up around here. City really isn't that big. Not many suburbs. Everything else is a fuckin' farm."

"How do you get about?" asked Madeleine. With a final, hard hug, she disentangled herself from Lucy. The girl pulled away a bit sheepishly and looked down at her bare, cold feet.

"We got bikes," Allyson replied. "Nothing fancy. No gears or hand brakes, crap like that. Still, they're a lot faster than walking. And we know all the short-cuts."

"Guard my van," said Madeleine, reassuming her air of dignified command. "When I leave the bar, we will talk further. Depending on what I learn inside, I may have some work for the Rat Pack. A dangerous assignment, but profitable."

"Fuck danger," said Allyson. "We're hungry."

"I will be back," Madeleine promised. "Wait for me."

The club was about what she expected—a rectangular room, twenty-five feet by fifty, with a low, wood-beamed ceiling and dim, hazy light. Clouds of smoke, stirred by sluggish ceiling fans, wove across the barroom like neon-poisoned ghosts. A sticky CD juke blared out Willie Nelson. It was not a new song, but there was little new about Sleazy Sam's. Very little new at all.

Once, the bar itself might have been considered elegant. It sat like a dog near the entrance of the room, all gold and ivory trim on a supple oak finish. Years of smoke, beer, piss and puke had dulled that finish to a muddy brown, however, and the cheap neon didn't help appearances. Scattered throughout the room sat a half-dozen round tables with chairs, their surfaces cratered by cigarette butts. Three booths in the rear offered slightly more privacy; two of them were occupied. Behind the bar, a single picture—a cheap painting of three naked women in a bed—lived up to Sleazy Sam's name.

Madeleine estimated there were forty people present. A dozen clustered by the bar, while the rest packed around the rickety tables. Most of the patrons were men, but there was a scattering of women as well. Most of the guys chose their wardrobes from biker magazines and C&W videos; the women favored denim, black leather and skimpy white cotton. No one gave Madeleine a second glance. That suited her fine.

In a nearby booth, four men huddled together, their eyes fixed on the center of the table. One held a small metal spoon in his trembling fingers. Madeleine couldn't see what they were using—coke, crank, heroin—nor did she care. The only rule at Sam's seemed to be that all rules were bullshit.

The monster slid into a high chair at the far end of the bar. A few seats away, two men in Hell's Angels jackets guzzled beer and compared conquests. The nearer of the two—a three-hundred-pounder with drooping mustache and beady dark eyes—casually glanced at Madeleine. She crossed her legs and smiled a hunter's grin. For an instant, a trace of her true nature flashed across her features. Shocked, the big man grabbed his friend by the arm and scurried to safety at the other side of the room.

"I think you scared poor Ralph," said a tall, dark-haired bartender. "He's not used to having beautiful women smile in his direction."

"Then he's all talk," said Madeleine with a shake of her head. "How disappointing. From his remarks, he sounded quite virile."

The bartender squinted at her for a moment, as if trying to guess if she was fooling. Finally deciding she had to be, he grinned. "His conquests are legendary. And like many myths, based on very little truth. You want a drink?"

"A Bloody Mary," said Madeleine.

"You're new at Sam's," said the man as he prepared the concoction. "Just passing through?"

"I am here on business," said Madeleine. "Do you know everyone who comes in by sight?"

"The ones who matter," he replied, putting the drink in front of Madeleine. "These days, a barkeep's got to be careful about his customers. Never can tell when an undercover cop might try to make a name for himself. Dead lawmen are always a pain in the butt to explain. It's a lot easier keeping them out."

"You are Sleazy Sam?" asked Madeleine.

"Nah," he said. "I'm Leo. Sam's been dead for years. Two drunks got in a really vicious fight one evening and slammed into the juke box. Got Sam pissed. Machine's damned expensive. So he came out from behind the bar and pulled the two bozos apart. Wasn't a smart idea. One of the pair was carrying a bowie knife. He sliced Sam up something terrible before somebody managed to put a bullet in the asshole's brain. Poor old Sam bled to death on the floor right over there. If you look close, you can still see the blood stains. Marks like that don't wash out. I'm Sam's nephew. Been running the place ever since. Doesn't make much money, but I figure I gotta keep it open. You know, as sort of a tribute to my dear uncle."

"Very touching," said Madeleine. She wiped her cheeks, as if rubbing away imaginary tears. "Did you cremate his body and scatter the ashes over the parking lot?"

"No," said Leo, "but that sounds right touching. Be back in a minute. Gentleman at the other end wants a refill."

Madeleine raised the Bloody Mary to her lips. She

turned slightly, so the glass was out of sight. A whispered word and the liquid disappeared. Madeleine neither ate nor drank. But she liked to maintain appearances.

Leo returned as she placed the empty glass on the bar. "Another?" he asked. "Third one's free."

"Not right now," Madeleine replied. "Sleazy Sam sold out three years ago and moved to Florida. He cheats old people at cards and spends his afternoons at the horse races. You manage the place for the absentee owners."

"Right," said Leo, with a shrug of his big shoulders. "Though the other explanation's a lot more colorful. How'd you know?"

"*Honor over death*," said Madeleine softly. "Your employer, Pietro, sends his greetings. I am his granddaughter, Madeleine Giovanni."

Leo whistled. "I take it then, that the photos I took proved to be interesting?"

"The ones of Ezra?" said Madeleine. "They are why I am here."

"Shit," said Leo, looking over Madeleine's shoulder. "Here comes trouble. The Hellblazers. Little Willy Smith and the Riley Brothers. Sorry. I can't interfere," he muttered. "People would wonder. I never get involved."

"No problem," she replied and slowly turned around. "I fight my own battles."

Three men faced her. Two looked to be twins. One stood a few inches taller than Madeleine, the other a few inches shorter. Wide toothy grins split their faces, beneath large hook noses, dark brown eyes and curly, thick hair. They were in their late twenties. Squat, heavyset individuals, with wide shoulders and barrel chests, they wore jet-black jeans and black leather jackets. The leather was decorated with a crude devil's head just above the heart.

The third man stood nearly seven feet tall and weighed well over four hundred pounds. Most of his bulk lay in his belly, which hung exposed over his belt. His face was blood red, with pig-like eyes and a mouthful of yellowed teeth. He was completely bald. Madeleine thought he was the ugliest man she had ever seen.

None of the trio appeared very intelligent. They were all extremely drunk.

"We wanna screw around," said the fat man. His voice was high and shrill. "With you."

"That's right," said the taller of the twins. "The three of us, same time. Really get it off."

"No thank you," said Madeleine, aware that the room had suddenly grown quiet. "Please leave me alone."

"Nope," said the fat man. His eyes said the rest.

"Willy," said Leo. "Get lost. Remember what the cops said. One more complaint about rape and they'll throw you and Cain and Abel in jail. Whether they can find witnesses or not."

"We ain't raped nobody," Willy replied. He shuffled a step closer to Madeleine, his mouth twisted in a lopsided grin. "Never been convicted uh nuthin'."

Madeleine slid along the bar, away from the fat

man. The last thing she wanted was to draw attention to herself. But anything she did in this situation was wrong.

Salvation came from an unexpected source. Abel, the shorter twin, had just stepped forward to cut off Madeleine's further retreat when from the front door a woman's voice cried, "Death! Death rides the highway!"

A young blonde woman, no more than twenty, stood in the entrance. Tall and slender, with baby-blue eyes, red lips and dimpled cheeks, she appeared the soul of innocence. She wore a black halter top and black bike shorts. Directly beneath her breasts were two long scars, forming a huge X. In her hands, the girl held a .20 gauge sawed-off shotgun. "It's Sister Susie," said Leo, astonished. "The nuts just keep coming through the door."

"Enough is enough," shouted the blonde, marching up to the three Hellblazers. She seemed to be in a daze or a trance. The woman's words, Madeleine suspected, were not her own. "Rabid animals cannot be allowed to live."

"What the fuck is *your* problem?" said Willy, turning away from Madeleine to stare at Susie. He shook his head. "We ain't no animals."

"No mercy for them," declared Sister Susie. Moving with surprising quickness, she stepped close to the red-faced giant. Before the fat man could react, the blonde swung her shotgun into his face. The twin steel barrels caught him flush in the nose. Bones broke. Blood spurted across her pale skin but she didn't seem to notice. Her finger squeezed tight on the trigger of the shotgun. The slightest twitch and Willy's brains were on the ceiling.

"*No mercy*," intoned Susie. She stared with bright eyes into the fat man's face. "*No forgiveness.*"

"Easy, Susie," said Leo. "Easy."

Cain and Abel stood a half-dozen feet away from the third Hellblazer. It could have been miles. Frozen in place, they dared not move an inch.

"Inform your fellow cannibals that some of us are tired of their attacks on the helpless," said Susie, pressing the shotgun deeper into the ruin of Willy's nose. Her voice turned shrill. "*Enough is enough.*"

"Right, right," Willy whispered, his eyes wet. "Whatever you say."

"Enough, Susie," said Leo. "You've passed on the message. Now let Willy and the Riley brothers go so they can spread the word. Okay?"

Slowly, ever so slowly, Sister Susie nodded. Carefully, she pulled the gun, its twin barrels red with Willy Smith's blood, away from the man's face. Her finger remained steady on the trigger. Whimpering, the big man clutched his smashed nose with both hands.

Susie waved the shotgun at the Riley brothers. "Go and warn your friends."

The Riley brothers needed no urging. Grabbing the blubbering Willy Smith, they dashed out the front door in an instant. Nodding, Susie lowered her shotgun and turned to Leo. Her face glowed with the light of fanaticism. "Justice is slow, but it is relentless," she declared.

"Ain't that the truth," said the bartender. He waved a hand in the air. "Show's over, folks. Back to reality. Next round's on the house."

Fifteen minutes later, Madeleine was finally able to talk with Leo. "Has she always been like this?" Madeleine asked, glancing at Susie.

The young woman sat alone at a round table, nursing a glass of white wine. The shotgun rested on her lap. She muttered to herself, oblivious to her surroundings.

"Susie found religion about a week ago," said Leo. "Up till then, she hung out with a pretty nasty bunch. Hijackers, maybe worse. Evidently, they fucked with the wrong people. Of the six, Susie was the one who made it. And her brains were fried.

"She came in here late that night, spouting off the stuff you heard. All about justice riding the highway, no forgiveness, and enough is enough. Weird. Like someone imprinted those words on her brain."

"Perhaps someone did," said Madeleine. "The police investigation turned up no clues?"

Leo snorted. "What investigation? The cops were happy to see those fuckers dead. Officers poked around for ten minutes, listened to Susie's speech, then drove off laughing. Blondie's stopped in here every night since, preaching the gospel. 'Sister Susie,' the regulars call her. Tonight's the first time she ever got violent."

Robert Weinberg

"I owe her a favor," said Madeleine. "Now let us talk about Ezra. Did he see you take the photos?"

"Not a chance," said Leo. "As instructed, I was real careful. Stayed inside the whole time. I used the outside security monitors for the apartment building to spot him. Recorded his arrival on them. No surprise, though—the tapes were blank. Not so the camera I set up on automatic timed advance on the second floor. Photos I sent to Venice came from there."

"Still," said Madeleine, "he arrived by automobile. And left by the same method."

"Your boy showed up at 2 AM," said Leo, "and left at 3:30 the same night."

"Very interesting," said Madeleine. "I should be going. It is getting close to dawn and I need to be off the road by sunrise. I will return, though I am not sure when. Meanwhile, there is a small gang of teenagers living in the forest nearby."

"Yeah," nodded Leo, his voice turning suspicious. "The Rat Pack. What about them?"

"Feed them," said Madeleine. "Make sure they receive some supplies. Use whatever funds are necessary. You have my authorization. I want those children healthy. They are under my protection."

"Sure," said Leo, relaxing. "The kids are okay. Outcasts, all of them. It's a tough life for the brats."

"I know," said Madeleine. "I will be back."

She found the Rat Pack grouped around her van. Allyson, bayonet in hand, squatted on the bumper. The others, armed with kitchen knives, pipes and switchblades, lurked behind cars and trucks nearby.

"Looks like you stirred up some serious shit in there," Lucy remarked, grinning. "One of those dumbshits dropped his wallet jumping into his truck." She held up a handful of bills. "You mind if we keep this?"

"It is yours," Madeleine replied, dismissing the money. "Truthfully, however, I was not the one who frightened them. A woman Leo called 'Sister Susie' made any action on my part unnecessary."

"Huh." This from Lucy. "Check that shit out. Two weeks ago, that psycho was eating people. Now she's a nun."

"Go figure," said Brian. "I guess seeing your friends turned into cole slaw makes a believer out of you."

"Oh?" Madeleine looked quizzically at the short boy. Bashfully, he glanced away.

"We saw them get diced a couple of weeks ago," Lucy said. "Nasty. Sister Susie's one of those fucked-up cannibals I was talkin' about. Or at least, she *was*. She played decoy for them on the side of the road..." The girl shook her head. Blonde hair flashed. "You believe that shit? She'd act all hurt and innocent. Totally Julia Roberts. People'd stop to help and the gang would jump 'em. This time, they got jumped instead. Cool, huh?"

"How did you happen to see this take place?" Madeleine asked. "You said that you avoided the cannibal tribe."

"Lucy's been keeping an eye on the cannibals for a while," bald Sybil offered. "Sometimes she'd sneak into their camp to see what she could swipe. I guess you could say she's got issues with them."

"Fuck you too, Sinead O'Connor," Lucy shot back.

"Chill, Sybil," Allyson growled.

Madeleine shook her head in disgust. Children forced to spy on cannibals waylaying travelers, hoping to steal supplies. And mortals called the Kindred monsters.

"What happened?" Madeleine asked Lucy.

"The assholes fucked with the wrong car." Lucy grinned as she pulled her chain taut between her bony hands. "These two older folks got out—an old man with a beard an' fancy clothes, and an Oriental lady. Chinese, I think, but I'm not sure...."

"She sliced them up with a pair of knives," Brian added. "Really big, sharp knives. They tried to shoot her, but their guns jammed."

"It was because she is an angel," Sarah added in her weird, deep voice, "blessed by the power of God."

"There we go again with that angel shit," muttered Sybil.

"Swords," said Madeleine, hoping to get the conversation back on track. "She killed them with two swords."

"Yeah," said Brian. "Whatever."

"A gang of them, one of her?" said the Dagger of the Giovanni. "She must have been very dangerous."

"She was fuckin' *incredible*," Lucy declared, rising up on her toes. "Man, she spun like this..."—the chain whooshed—"...and this..."—again, in an arc—"...and came across like this...."

"Jesus, Luce!" Allyson cried, cringing. "Watch what you're doing!"

Madeleine grinned. It was not a pleasant sight. "I believe I get the picture."

"Man," breathed Lucy, obviously disappointed, "I wish I could've done that to 'em. This woman was like magic, I swear."

"Perhaps she was, at that" murmured Madeleine. "Do you remember what she looked like?"

"She was tall," said Lucy. "Real pretty, with long black hair. Like I said, she looked Chinese. Kinda like that chick in *Supercop*."

"An oriental swordswoman," said Madeleine, thinking aloud. "Accompanied by a man in fancy clothes. A fascinating combination. Especially considering Sister Susie's condition…."

She motioned the Rat Pack closer. "My van has been well guarded. You have earned my trust. As of this moment, consider yourself in my service. You are agents of the family Giovanni. As such, you need to be in the best possible physical condition. Leo, the bartender, will feed you. Eat well, exercise, regain your health. Prepare yourself for battle. I will be gone for several days. While I am away, keep sharp watch for the mysterious swordswoman Lucy observed. I would very much like to meet her. As well as her companion."

"You got it," Allyson replied, checking the others for agreement. The Rat Pack, as one, nodded and whispered confirmation. "Cool. Let's do it."

"Who're we gonna fight, Madeleine?" Lucy asked.

An excited flush reddened her pale skin. The monster could smell the blood. "When are we gonna fight?"

"As for whom, I am not sure," said Madeleine, turning away from her new wards. "As for when, I can only say it will be too soon."

Chapter Six

"We must travel to Horizon," declared a fully restored Kallikos the next morning. The five of them sat clustered around the kitchen table in the Casey cabal farmhouse, having just finished breakfast. "We must warn the Council of Nine about the Master of Harmony. I'm sure they will refuse to act until it is too late, but an attempt must be made nonetheless. Our only hope for the future is somehow to change the present."

"Something's going to happen at Horizon?" said Sam Haine. "You sure?"

Kallikos nodded. "Quite sure. What Jenni Smith told Seventeen last night merely confirms my own suspicions. Our enemy's ego knows no bounds. He sees himself as a messiah, reborn to lead the Awakened into a new golden age. Like all megalomaniacs, he believes his own lies. Thus, before waging war, he will offer peace."

Seventeen licked his lips, remembering Shadow of the Dawn's words just hours ago. *The peace of the grave.*

He looked at her from across the table. Her gaze met his and she nodded.

"Takes a heap of guts walkin' into the stronghold of your opponent and telling everybody to lay down their weapons or else," said Sam Haine. "But then again, I ain't a fighting man. This Master of Harmony don't sound like he lacks for courage."

"Fear means nothing to one who has been resurrected from nothingness," said Kallikos. "Besides, as a construct of the Technocrats, the Master of Harmony cannot physically enter the Tradition realm we call Horizon without setting off numerous alarms. Instead, he will send one of his disciples." He glanced at Seventeen. "Perhaps that was why he desires your assistance. He may want you to act as his proxy to Horizon Realms in which he is powerless."

Seventeen shook his head. "I don't think so. Jenni Smith spoke of her master controlling powerful magick not used in centuries. I had the distinct impression that the Master of Harmony doesn't need my help. Or anyone else's. There's something else about me he wants. Or fears. But I don't know what."

"Seems to me," said Sam Haine, looking at Kallikos, "that you might not be entirely welcome in Horizon these days. Been quite a while since you made an appearance there."

Kallikos's dark eyes narrowed. "You know?"

Sam shrugged. "I got a notion. Came to me while I was sharing a glass of cheer with Mr. Jack Daniels. I remembered once upon a time hearin' about a certain Time Master who had these here astonishing visions.

Did me a little research in the Casey cabal library. Found the proper reference right away. Scary stuff, for sure. Visions of the future, seen a long time ago, that are coming closer and closer to truth every year. The seer who foretold such stuff was pretty amazing."

"In my youth," said Kallikos, his voice low, his tone grim, "I dreamed great dreams. An idealist, I envisioned a future in which all humanity would strive towards Ascension. In my folly, seeking to further that noble aim, I studied with the great sages. I read the secret books, the forbidden tomes. The more I learned, the greater my hunger to learn. Engaged in my quest, I experienced the ultimate pleasures. I endured frightful agonies. My skills grew, changed, evolved. And after long years, my dreams turned real. I discovered the secrets of prophecy."

Kallikos shuddered. "I thought it to be the greatest gift. The power to see the future, to know in advance what was going to happen, and have the opportunity to change history. Only gradually I realized that this talent was not a gift but a horrible curse."

"Big difference knowing an avalanche is gonna happen," said Sam Haine, "and being able to stop it with your bare hands."

"Exactly," said Kallikos. "I see what *might* happen. Events can be changed, but rewriting the future is almost impossible. Most important events result from a vast combination of factors taking place over years, often decades. Temporal nodes, when a specific action twists history, are few and far apart. The awakening of the pattern-clone was one such point. We failed, and now thousands will die. If we fail again, millions will perish. A third disaster and the Tellurian is doomed."

"Gotta be difficult living with the weight of the future on your shoulders," said Sam Haine.

"The knowledge is enough to drive a man mad," said Kallikos, his voice trembling. "Think of it. Living for decades, for centuries, knowing that someday you will be forced to make decisions that will affect the fate of mankind. That each step you take is on a path that leads to the same final choice. The moment of decision is quickly approaching. Life or death? After five hundred years, I am still not sure of the answer."

Sam Haine rubbed a finger across his lower lip. "According to the author of a book I consulted, the mage who made those horrible predictions died centuries ago. Sittin' here in this room, listenin' to what you're saying, I suspect that ain't the truth."

Kallikos shrugged. "What is truth? The antithesis of dreams. My name is Kallikos. I use no other."

"It's your call," said Sam Haine. "A man's defined by what he does, not by a bunch of syllables."

"There are only three portals leading to Horizon," said Albert, steering the conversation in a new direction. "The nearest one, the Lachesis Portal, is located in a backwater section of Kansas. Sam and I have entered Horizon through that gateway several times. It is not a pleasant journey. And to get past the guardian, you need an invitation and the proper passwords."

"I have an invitation," said Kallikos. "I know the proper passwords."

Seventeen frowned. Conversation was swirling around him but he had no idea what any of it meant. "Excuse me," he said. "I'm lost. *Where* are you talking about? Three portals whose destination is located *where?*"

Sam Haine grinned. "I think I understand your confusion, son. Oftentimes, willworkers inherently *know* stuff, so the names they pick for certain talents, places, or ideas isn't always the best. You understand Horizon Realms, right?"

"Alvin Reynolds explained their existence to me when we were visiting…" said Seventeen, discovering he could no longer speak the name of Vali Shallar. "According to him, there is the material plane and the psychic plane. Together, they form the Tellurian. Earth, where humanity dwells, is the center of existence, and the hub of static reality. Surrounding our world are the spirit realms—the Near Umbra and the Deep Umbra.

"The Near Umbra lies closest to the material world. It's a reflection of the Earth, but more spiritual—psychic—in nature. Alvin told me very little about it.

"Beyond the Near Umbra lies the Deep Umbra. It's the outer edge of the spirit world, a region that stretches out to infinity. Little is known about it other than that it is home to the Nephandi, Marauders and worse. Creatures like the Maeljin Incarna exist in the Deep Umbra.

"Separating the two regions is the Horizon. In essence, this area serves as a barrier, a dividing zone, between the Near Umbra and the Deep Umbra. It keeps the Nephandi and the more alien, monstrous inhabitants of the Deep Umbra from invading static reality."

"Get on with it, son," said Sam Haine, waving about his ever-present cigar. "We know all this stuff."

"Existing in the Horizon are places called Horizon Realms. They are artificial lands, islands of reality created by powerful willworkers. Using quintessence drawn from nodes on the Earth—static reality—groups of Archmages build special worlds of their own. In such places, the laws of nature obey the belief systems of their creators. Thus, in the Gray Collective, Technocracy science was able to work miracles. In the realm we traveled with Alvin, the magick of the Nine Traditions held sway."

"Sounds like you understand the concepts well enough," said Sam Haine. "The one thing you don't know, though, is that the largest Horizon Realm ever created by the Nine Traditions, the meeting place of the High Council, is named—*Horizon*." Sam chuckled. "That's the place we're discussin'. Kallikos wants us to travel to Horizon, the Horizon Realm, located in the Horizon. You got that?"

"And we have to go somewhere named Kansas to get there?" said Seventeen.

Sam grinned. "Son, it's amazin' how your memory can be sorta selective at times. You remember all sorts of neat stuff but Kansas remains forgotten. Not that I blame you much. Even Dorothy wasn't entranced by

Kansas. And look what she went through to get out of that state."

Seventeen shook his head. "Dorothy?"

"I also am unaware of this person, Dorothy," said Shadow of the Dawn. "Is she someone of importance?"

"Forget it," said Sam Haine, shaking his head, his expression astonished. "Forget I ever mentioned her. Let's return to the point of discussion. Kallikos wants to go to Horizon to warn the Council of Nine about the pattern-clone. Personally, I think it's a waste of time and effort. Once the clone starts trouble, the Nine will find out about him quick enough. But I'm ornery, so I'll go along whatever the decision."

"I follow in Kallikos's footsteps," said Shadow of the Dawn. "His wishes are mine."

"Much as I like Horizon," said Albert, "I agree with Sam that a visit there would serve little purpose. By nature, willworkers are men and women of strong opinions. In Horizon, like Doissetep, the other great stronghold of Tradition magick, the Archmages spend more of their time involved with petty intrigues and politics than with more important matters. They squabble like spoiled children. Your fame may force them to take notice of what you say, Kallikos, but no amount of fame can make them admit their peril."

"Two for, two against," said Sam. He peered at Seventeen. "As usual, son, the decision rests on your shoulders."

Seventeen didn't hesitate. "I say we go. Like Kallikos, I feel certain the Master of Harmony plans to issue an ultimatum to the Council of Nine. From what you say here, it sounds equally certain that such demands will be rejected. I'm convinced our enemy is no fool. He expects such a reaction and is prepared to act immediately. Jenni Smith made it quite clear. There's no grays in this fight, only blacks and whites." Seventeen drew in a breath. "If there's to be a war between the Master of Harmony and the mages of the Nine Traditions, I want to be there when it starts."

"The Horizon War," said Shadow of the Dawn.

"War in Heaven," said Sam Haine. "Even to an old cynic like me who's seen more than his share of trouble, it's a frightening thought."

"We are agreed, then, to travel to Horizon?" asked Kallikos.

"Seems to me that it's probably the only Horizon Realm safe for me to visit these days," said Sam Haine. "Besides, I'd like to have a word or two with this Jenni Smith if she shows up. Girl used my name in vain and I'd like to make it clear to her I don't approve."

"When do we leave?" said Seventeen.

"I believe right about now," said Kallikos, with a trace of a smile.

The bearded man snapped his fingers. Seventeen blinked as the world suddenly turned black. It was as if Kallikos had shut off all light. For an instant, Seventeen felt lightheaded, almost ethereal. His mind seemed to be floating free from his body. Then, with a mental click, light returned. They still sat clustered around a table, but the furniture was old and worn. They were definitely not in the Casey cabal.

Chapter Seven

"Nicely done!" exclaimed Sam Haine. "We're somewhere in Kansas, I take it?"

"Not far from the Portal," said Kallikos. "Not so near as to be noticed, either. It's a deserted old shack less than a mile from our destination. Sleepers in the area avoid it, claiming the place is haunted." He nodded. "A spell of unease makes trespassers distinctly uncomfortable if they approach too close."

"You've been here before," said Albert.

"More than once," said Kallikos. "My teleportation skills are limited. I can only travel to a few spots whose exact locations I have memorized after long years of effort. This place is one of them."

"Damned impressive spell," said Sam Haine. "Still, we left awfully sudden. I suspect the members of the Casey cabal are gonna worry what happened to us."

"I wrote them a note," said Kallikos, "explaining that we would be gone for days and asking them to guard our possessions."

"A note?" said Sam. He chuckled. "Pretty sure we were going, huh?"

"I have great confidence in my powers of persuasion," said Kallikos. He smiled. "At worst, if the group had decided otherwise, I would have walked into the parlor and ripped up the message."

"Fair enough," said Sam. "Well, we're here. I think it's time to stop jawing and head over to the graveyard."

Kallikos took the lead. It was hot as an oven outside. As they walked, Sam explained to Seventeen and Shadow of the Dawn what to expect at the gateway, and Kallikos told them the password and sigils they needed for admittance. How he knew, he did not explain.

The cemetery was located in a hollow a few hundred feet back from the road leading out of town. A dented old metal sign proclaimed MOOSE JAW CEMETERY. The burial ground consisted of perhaps fifty graves. At the center of the graveyard stood a circle of stone monoliths. They stopped just outside the huge slabs.

In the middle of the circle was a large open grave. Seventeen could see a set of worn stone steps leading down into the ground. This black hole was the entrance to the Ways, the Portal leading to Horizon.

An immense black raven sat perched on top of the headstone directly behind the pit. The bird cast no shadow. "Kakraw," said Kallikos, "the guardian of the gate. A very powerful spirit."

The bearded man turned to them. "We must enter

one at a time," he declared. "Each of us must give the correct passwords and signs. Afterwards, at the bottom of the pit, we will regroup and travel the Ways together. I will enter first."

Without another word, Kallikos stepped between two monoliths and walked straight to the open grave. Standing on the first stone step leading down, he stared at the huge black bird resting on the tombstone. After a few seconds, Kallikos began to speak. Though he was less than a dozen feet away, his words to the raven could not be heard. Nor did the gigantic bird seem to answer. Yet a conversation of some sorts must have taken place. The seer nodded, raised one hand and touched his forehead. Again, a pause. Then, the guardian evidently satisfied, Kallikos descended into the pit and was gone.

"You're next, Shadow," said Sam Haine. "Nothing to worry about. Just remember the passwords and answer the raven's questions honestly. This is the easy part."

Again, the same scenario. This time, after speaking for a moment, Shadow touched her two swords, Whisper and Scream. A moment later, she too entered the darkness.

"Your turn, son," said Sam Haine, and Seventeen stepped into the circle.

The air inside the ring of stones was cold and damp. The chill of death and dissolution. The blackness within the open grave was absolute. A wave of apprehension swept through Seventeen. Kallikos had called the gateway a place of truths. Seventeen wasn't sure if he was prepared for the truth. Especially about himself.

Gathering his courage, he walked up to the pit. Standing on the first stone step, he looked across the opening at the huge raven perched on the tombstone. For the first time, Seventeen could see there were words engraved on the slab. *And the truth shall make you free.*

"Ethan Phillips, *bani* Euthanatos," said a voice in his mind. The voice sounded weary, heavy with age. "Ye come to the Lachesis Portal seeking entry to the Ways. Tell me then the passwords."

"Truth is a sacred flame," said Seventeen. "Honor without justice is meaningless. Great art is passion with form and style."

The raven's eyes glistened. It gazed at Seventeen with unblinking stare. "If truth is a sacred flame," said the raven, "where does it burn, Ethan Philips?"

Without conscious thought, Seventeen raised his left hand and placed his open palm on his chest. "In my blood," he answered. "In my heart."

"Beware, child of Euthanatos," said Kakraw, "that in your quest for remembrance, you are not consumed by that fire. Now, go. You may descend to the Ways."

As Seventeen began his descent, he was struck by the raven spirit's words. The mage had been intent on the passwords. Only now did he realize that—if Kakraw spoke truth—the spirit had revealed not just Seventeen's real name but his Tradition as well. "Ethan Phillips, *bani* Euthanatos," Kakraw had said.

But Seventeen was forced to put these thoughts aside as the darkness overwhelmed him.

The pit was black, totally devoid of light. Even Seventeen's night vision could not penetrate the gloom. The moist, dank air stank of rotting fungus and other, less distinguishable smells. Ancient stone steps were worn smooth by the passage of many thousands of feet. Down, down, down, the tunnel continued, far beneath the surface of the graveyard. The steps seemed to stretch on forever. Ever conscious of time and direction, Seventeen soon realized he could no longer sense either. He had no idea where he was going. Or how long he had been walking.

Light, when it came, was soft and multi-colored, filling the air like a warm mist. There was no floor, no ceiling, no walls. The angles were all wrong, with shadows cutting through shadows, forming odd displacements of space. Distance was neither linear nor circular, but twisted like a corkscrew, turning and turning in ever-increasing spirals that continued towards infinity. Yet Seventeen felt completely at ease. He continued to move, though he was not sure if he was going forward or back or even to the side. All he knew was that he was going somewhere.

"Seventeen," said Kallikos, his hand appearing seemingly from nowhere. "Take hold."

Reaching to his left, Seventeen gripped strong fingers. And found that he was holding onto Shadow of the Dawn. Kallikos stood behind them both, his arms around their shoulders.

"Reality constantly shifts within the Ways," said

Kallikos. "Your five senses mean nothing here. Only your inner eye can guide you through the maze."

"Keep a grip on one another," said Sam Haine, his gnarled old fingers wrapped around Seventeen's right hand. "Even when you think you've lost touch, don't let go."

"Are we prepared?" asked Kallikos, from Seventeen's left.

"Yes," said Shadow of the Dawn, her arms around Seventeen's waist, her lips warm against his neck.

"You're the leader, Kallikos," said Albert, a few steps ahead of them all. His right hand rested on Sam Haine's shoulder. Sam stood directly behind Seventeen.

"Take three steps forward," said Kallikos. He stood only a foot ahead of Seventeen, facing him. Shadow of the Dawn was behind them both. "Now."

Seventeen, realizing his vision could no longer be trusted, closed his eyes and moved his feet in what he thought were three steps ahead.

"Two steps to the left," said Kallikos, his voice coming from behind and in front of Seventeen. Shadow of the Dawn clutched his right arm, yet her breath was hot on the back of his neck. Far in the distance, Sam Haine cursed.

=Heat= and =cold= declared the seer. =Red= and =green= and =yellow.=

Concentrating, Seventeen stopped hearing, feeling, smelling and touching. Freed of all physical distractions, he could sense Kallikos's directions perfectly. *Five steps backward*, the seer commanded. *Then two steps upward*.

This is a dangerous location, warned Sam Haine. *We are in the heart of darkness. Do not be deceived by false visions*.

A figure moved through the Ways, a being of such incredible powers that his passage blazed right through Seventeen's isolation from his senses. The intruder's body was clad in silver-blue gun metal, his face covered by a black steel mask. His eyes burned red.

He rode a gigantic mechanical steed, with vast iron wings that dripped oil and sweat and blood. In one hand, he held a huge serrated sword, glistening with liquid fire. The smell of burnt human flesh filled Seventeen's nostrils as the monstrous figure drew close.

"You belonged to me, once," shrieked Lord Steel. His voice was high and shrill, like a knife scraping bone. The Duke of Hate's crimson eyes blazed with madness. "Soon, very soon, you will be mine again."

Rage boiled through Seventeen's veins like liquid fire. A defiant reply surged through his mind—then abruptly stopped, as he realized that answering an illusion would make it real.

Four steps down, came the next command.

Lord Steel vanished. In his place stood a young woman. Short and slender, with short, curled red hair, she had thoughtful features and a boyish figure. She wore a green shift of purest silk and a green stone on a gold chain around her neck. Her eyes were deep green and swirled with secrets; her complexion was as fair as the dawn. To Seventeen, she seemed the most desirable woman in all creation. A willworker of astonishing power, she called herself Scarlett Dancer. Long ago, she and the man named Ethan Phillips had been lovers. Light and dark, day and night, they formed a perfect match, each complementing the other's weaknesses and strengths. Until she had suddenly disappeared.

"Come to me, my love," she said and her voice was sweet and warm and intense. "I wait for you still. You know my secret. Only your love can rescue me from my eternal torment. It is in your power to save me from damnation. We could be together forever. Please, please. If you love me as you once did, join with me."

One word would be his doom. Scarlett was no more real than the Duke of Hate. She existed only in his memory. And with that realization, the illusion vanished.

Take five short steps forward, came Kallikos's mental command. *Then turn sharply to the left and return to your senses. Danger is very close.*

Obeying, Seventeen found himself standing on the edge of a high cliff. The swirling colors were gone. Instead, though no sun was visible, the landscape was bathed in a dim, twilight glow. Shadow of the Dawn, her hand holding his, waited to his right. Beyond her stood Kallikos. To the left, forming the other end of the human chain, were Albert and Sam Haine.

Less than a foot in front of them was what appeared

to be a bottomless gorge. Dark thunderclouds swirled far below. A narrow stone bridge, no more than three feet wide and thirty feet long, spanned the abyss. On the other side, on an identical crag, stood a solitary figure, dressed from head to toe in a heavy black cowl that completely hid its features. Only the being's hands were visible. Long and narrow, white as bleached bone, they grasped a long oak stave ending in a curved blade. A scythe, used not for harvesting wheat, but souls. Like some demonic tollkeeper, the guardian of the Ways waited on the end of the stone bridge, blocking passage to the meadow beyond.

Fear like a cold wave emanated from the being, causing Seventeen to shudder. Here stood the embodiment of dissolution and decay.

"Beyond this bridge lies Horizon," said Kallikos. "However, we still must pass one final test."

"The Lord of the Ways can take many forms," said Kallikos. "It never assumes a guise without a purpose." He paused. "Though I do not recall the spirit ever appearing in such ominous raiment. It is, of course, the classical Reaper."

"Come." A voice spoke in Seventeen's mind, in tones like ice. He could see from the others' lack of reaction that he was the only one who heard the Reaper's call. "Come to me. Your destiny awaits."

As if in a dream, Seventeen dropped hands with his companions and stepped out onto the bridge. Despite traveling through the maze with the others, he knew this last challenge was meant for him alone. Looking neither right or left, he walked slowly across the stone

Robert Weinberg

span. Winds howled beneath his feet. Thunder bellowed. Lightning flashed. Strange, frightening red shapes moved in the black clouds. Seventeen ignored it all. His gaze remained fixed on the cowled guardian.

Scythe held in front of its chest, the Reaper could have been carved from marble. It remained motionless as Seventeen came closer and closer. Ten feet separated them, then five, then less than an arm's distance.

With the slightest of motions, the guardian shook its head. The hood covering its face dropped back, revealing a skeletal countenance. A mouth filled with ivory teeth split in a hellish grin. Black eyes, like pools of absolute darkness, stared deep into Seventeen's.

"Your heart's desire is madness. Embrace it, and your destiny is death and damnation," said the same ice-cold voice in his mind.

"The destiny of all men is death," said Seventeen, without hesitation. Still acting entirely on instinct, he reached forward and placed his hands on the scythe's wooden staff. It was freezing cold. Seventeen's miraculous body immediately made adjustments. The Reaper tried to wrench the weapon back and away, but Seventeen refused to budge.

"Night descends," said Seventeen, the words welling up from his subconscious. "Darkness comes. The Wheel turns for each of us. Death should not be avoided, but embraced. For with each ending, there is a new beginning. It is the way."

With that, Seventeen ripped the scythe from the

Reaper's grasp. Mouth agape, eyes flashing white, the guardian stepped back. The touch of the wood, the sense of the balance, the weight of the steel blade sent shock waves hurtling through Seventeen's mind. In a moment of epiphany, he understood the truth. The scythe was his destiny. The guardian had spoken in riddles, testing him, preparing him for the struggle to come.

With a twist of his hands, Seventeen raised the scythe high in the air and brought it whistling down in an arc aimed at the guardian of the Ways. But the steel blade encountered only air. The black cowl dropped to the stone bridge, empty.

"Nicely done, son," said Sam Haine. "Don't know exactly what you did, but seems like it worked."

Seventeen turned. Standing behind him were his four companions. Closest was Shadow of the Dawn. In her hands she held Whisper and Scream. He smiled as his gaze meet hers. She flushed slightly, then sheathed her swords.

"Me, I always like a forward woman," said Sam Haine, chuckling. "Especially one who carries two swords around with her and knows how to use them."

"Horizon beckons," said Kallikos. "We must not delay. The Wheel turns."

"I'm ready," said Seventeen. Uncurling his fingers, he dropped the Reaper's scythe to the stone. "Nicely made, but not mine."

He stepped forward, off the stone bridge, then stopped, astonished.

The Ways were gone. The light was strong and

powerful. The air was clean and pure and filled with the scent of flowers. A flock of birds flew overhead. Far in the distance he could see a huge mountain range, rising into a deep blue sky. In front of him stood an immense stone wall, carved with unusual and intricate designs.

"Impressive, ain't it?" said Sam Haine. Again, they were five. "It's called the Diamond Wall. Not exactly sure why, but who cares."

"And there is the Gate of Time," said Kallikos, pointing to a portal thirty feet to their left. Constructed of a silvery metal, the huge gate was elaborately decorated with strange symbols that seemed to twist and turn upon themselves. "We have arrived in exactly the right location."

"Kallikos!" It was a woman's voice, strong, sensual, full of life.

"Marianna," said Kallikos. "That was quick."

"When a beacon lights the sky," said the young woman walking towards them, "finding the source is simple. When Kallikos returns to Horizon, I sense his presence instantly. Your fire burns as bright as ever, my friend."

"And you are still the fairest of all," said Kallikos.

The seer wasn't lying. The woman he addressed as Marianna was astonishingly beautiful. A few inches over five feet tall, she had an hourglass figure, skin white as pearl, and long golden hair falling in thick ringlets to her waist. Her eyes were a brilliant shade of blue, with the longest eyelashes Seventeen had ever seen. Her lips, curled in a casual, sensual smile, were red as rubies. Her cheeks flushed vivid with health and life. A dazzling wreath of bright purple flowers crowned her head.

She wore very little. A strand of gold beads hung around her neck, a second around her waist. Several long mesh veils were her only garments, and she walked barefoot on the crisp green grass.

"Believe nothing you see," whispered Shadow of the Dawn, her tone making it quite clear exactly what she meant. "This woman is a shapeshifter. She changes her appearance merely to entice men."

"...*And* women," Marianna added. "I don't play favorites."

Seventeen nearly replied that Marianna did an exceptionally good job of enticing *anybody*. The look in Shadow's eyes, however, told him to keep his mouth shut.

"Marianna of Balador represents the Cult of Ecstasy on the Council of Nine," said Kallikos. "She also oversees Balador, the greatest Chantry House of the Cult, as well as Shivakti, the Ecstatic subrealm on Horizon. Her magickal powers are overshadowed only by her beauty."

The blonde woman laughed. "Flattery," she said with the slightest tremor of passion in her voice, "will get you everywhere, my dear Kallikos."

Her smile encompassed their entire group. "Let there be no mistake. I hold the seat on the Council because only a privileged few know Kallikos still lives. He is the true master. Now, tell me who you are so I can play the proper hostess."

"I am Sam Haine, *bani* Verbena," said Sam. "This giant is my friend and associate, Albert du Clair, *bani* Verbena. The young lady is Shadow of the Dawn, *bani* Akashic Brotherhood. The big, hairless brute looking like his eyes are ready to pop out we call Seventeen. Poor boy's minus his memory, but there's no doubt he's a Tradition mage of some significance. We're hoping maybe in Horizon we might finally discover his true name and heritage."

Seventeen resisted the urge to mention Ethan Phillips and Scarlett Dancer. For some undefined reason, he wanted to learn more about his previous life, his true identity, before he proclaimed it to the world. Enough strange, inexplicable events had happened in the past few weeks to make him very cautious.

"How intriguing," said Marianna. She flashed Seventeen a dazzling smile. "A man without a memory has so much to learn. And he has no long-standing prejudices or dislikes to overcome."

"Enough idle chatter," said Kallikos, sounding impatient. "Marianna, stop flirting with Seventeen. You're making Shadow of the Dawn nervous and I need her alert. Did you follow my instructions?"

"Of course," said Marianna. "I petitioned the Council for an emergency meeting this evening. Without revealing anything—particularly since I know nothing—I hinted a major disaster was brewing. One that could affect the balance of power in the Ascension War. Since I am not prone to exaggeration, my words got their attention. At least five or six of the Nine are on Horizon and I expect they will all attend. That is double the number of Council Members who were at the 58th Council. And your old acquaintance, Porthos of Doissetep, also indicated he planned to be present."

"How appropriate," said Kallikos, his tone grim and bitter. "How very, very appropriate."

Chapter Eight

"Wake up," whispered the voice in Sharon Reed's inner ear. "Get dressed. It's time to leave."

Instantly awake, Sharon glanced at the glow-in-the-dark clock in her room. It read a few minutes before 3 AM. Swiftly she rolled off the bed and pulled on her shoes. Normally she slept nude. Tonight, she had gone to sleep fully dressed, lying on top of the covers. Neither she nor Ernest Nelson knew for sure there would be trouble, but they both believed in being prepared.

"What's happening?" subvocalized Sharon. Several hours after their meeting with John Doe, Nelson had come by her room for a brief visit. During the course of their idle conversation, he passed her a miniaturized transmitter and receiver swiped from the Construct's supply depot. Minor frequency adjustments guaranteed that they could communicate without fear of being overheard. "Is something wrong?"

"I'm not sure," said Nelson. "Earlier in the evening,

I scattered microchip sensors in a number of hallways. For the past ten minutes, none of them have reported motion."

"So?"

"Do you know of any Construct where Technicians aren't busy, day or night?" answered Nelson. "Someone's knocked my sensors off line. Some person or some group. If they eliminated *my* detectors, you can bet every other monitoring device in the building is offline as well."

"It must be an attack," said Sharon, getting off the bed and standing up. She reached beneath her pillow. "In force."

"My feeling as well," said Nelson. "I'm on my way to your quarters. I should be there in fifty-seven seconds."

"Better hurry!" shouted Sharon as the door to her room burst inward. Three huge figures carrying butcher cleavers stood framed in the opening, the light from the hallway pouring into the dark chamber. Laughing maniacally, they started forward. "I've got company."

Her first burst of shells caught the man on the left in the chest. With a howl of surprise, he slammed back into the wall. As part of her re-outfitting, Sharon had asked for and received an Uzi machine gun pistol. An expert marksman, she had slept with it, fully loaded, beneath her pillow.

The second blast hit the middle man as he was halfway across the room. A dozen bullets pounded into his face, exploding his head like a rotten pump-

Robert Weinberg

kin. Blood and brains sprayed across the walls and floor as he collapsed in a heap at the edge of the bed.

"No fear!" shrieked the third attacker, leaping forward. Desperately, Sharon swung her machine gun. Bright steel glistened as the cleaver slashed. Sparks flashed as metal clashed on metal. The sudden impact numbed her hands. Knife and gun went flying.

Roaring in triumph, the huge figure grabbed Sharon by the neck. Huge sausage-sized fingers wrapped around her throat. Massive muscles bulged in the man's arms and chest as he pressed his thumbs into her windpipe and started to squeeze. "Gonna twist your fuckin' head off!" he roared, his features twisted in insane fury.

Sharon spit in his face.

The madman screamed, not in anger but in unexpected agony. Hissing, acid etched holes in his nose and cheeks. His skin blackened and dissolved like paper in flames. A second heart was not Sharon Reed's only biomodification. Years ago, she'd installed acid sacs inside her mouth. Close up, she was as venomous as a cobra.

"How about a kiss?" Sharon snarled, spitting the remaining fluid into the man's open mouth. Screeching in pain, the maniac fell back, clutching his throat. Blood frothed on his lips. Staggering about wildly, he slammed into the bed and collapsed across the sheets. His body jerked spasmodically and then was still. There was quick-acting poison mixed in with the acid.

A dark shadow wiped the savage grin off Sharon's

face. The first man, his torn shirt revealing the flak jacket beneath, had climbed to his feet. The blade of his machete gleamed in the hallway lights. Sharon's gaze flicked around the room. Her machine gun lay on the floor, directly in front of her foe. Giggling dementedly, the man kicked it far out of reach.

"Game's over," he declared, swinging the machete back and forth in front of his chest. Slowly, he advanced, carefully avoiding the pools of gore. His eyes stayed fixed on Sharon's face. She tensed, gathering the full force of her will.

The floor shook as a dull hollow boom echoed along the corridor. Cursing, the big man stumbled forward as the lights outside flickered. Seizing the moment, Sharon twisted reality, bending coincidence to her purpose. Her enemy's feet hit a patch of blood on the slick floor. With a cry of surprise, he lost his balance and tumbled backward. The machete went flying as he dropped to the floor. Instantly Sharon was on him, her fingers slashing for his eyes. Her supply of venom was gone but her nails were strong as steel.

The floor buckled again as a second explosion shook the building. Rocked back, Sharon momentarily lost her grip on her foe. Growling, the big man slammed his fist into the side of her head. Half dazed, Sharon tried to fight back. She swiped at the man's chest, but she'd forgotten the flak jacket. Her nails couldn't penetrate the woven mylex fiber.

Eyes burning, the madman punched Sharon in the throat. Gasping for breath, she tumbled off the man and back to the base of the bed. Rolling onto his

Robert Weinberg

hands and knees, the big man lunged forward, his forehead crashing into Sharon's stomach. Her eyes filled with tears of pain. Ineffectively, she tore at the back of the man's head, trying to rip off an ear. Anything to stop his attack.

"You're dead, bitch," grunted the madman. "Right now."

He drew back a giant fist to smash Sharon's face. And froze in place.

"*Not now*," came a voice directly behind him. Steel fingers held the maniac's fist in an unbreakable grip. Ernest Nelson had finally arrived.

The madman shrieked as Nelson's digits constricted, snapping bones like dry twigs. With a jerk of sheer power, the cyborg wrenched Sharon's attacker into the air. Nelson's other hand caught the man in mid-flight, slapping him hard across the face. The maniac dropped to the floor, dead, his features a smashed red ruin.

"Sorry for the delay," said Nelson, helping Sharon to her feet. "Power's gone in all the lifts. I had to make my way to this level by the stairs."

"Those explosions?" asked Sharon, shaking her head, trying to clear her thoughts. Her body could take a lot of punishment, but she was unaccustomed to hand-to-hand combat. "Where?"

"Where'd you expect?" replied Nelson. "John Doe's office. That was the main focus of the attack. Grunts like these were just used as shock troops, set loose to cause trouble. The main target was Doe. Guess someone didn't want him checking into the records. He's history. Fortunately, whoever's in charge of the attack doesn't know about us. At least, not yet."

Dressed in a dark trenchcoat, a slouch hat pulled down to shadow most of his face, Nelson looked like a refugee from a detective movie. Only the sparkle of his steel fingers betrayed his brotherhood to the machine.

"We better get moving," he said, gesturing to the corridor. "This pace is blitzed. We stick around, we'll be dead too."

"Who?" asked Sharon as she grabbed her Uzi off the floor. Stepping over the bodies of her three attackers, she made for the door. "Not the Traditions. This isn't their style."

"Nephandi," said Ernest Nelson. "Abominations against science. Reality Deviants from hell."

Sharon licked her lips. Suddenly, she felt cold all over. "I thought we'd kicked those bastards into outer space!"

"Only in our propaganda reports," said Nelson. "There's no sure method to detect mental corruption. Evil never dies. Nephandi blend in fine with the Masses. Not to mention the Enlightened. They stay undercover until necessary. Only when they turn, do you realize your best friend's actually a homicidal maniac."

He grinned. Nelson actually appeared to be enjoying himself. "You ready?"

"As ready as I'll ever be," said Sharon. They stepped into the hallway. It was deserted. In the silence,

Sharon could hear the faint sounds of automatic weapons fire. And voices raised in terrible pain.

"You have a plan?" she asked.

Nelson pointed to a door in the wall thirty feet down the corridor. "Of course. I downloaded a map of this place into my memory bank. We take the emergency stairs three levels up," he said. "They'll bring us to a hallway just like this one. Follow it another fifty feet. It branches. We go left. Take it to the end. There's another stairwell. Up one more flight and we're at the garage. Once there, we grab an armored limo and drive for daylight."

"Sounds do-able," said Sharon, as they warily started for the door. "What do you calculate are our chances of escape?"

Nelson grinned again. "Taking all factors into consideration, I figure it's around one in a thousand. Remember, we're in the middle of a major incursion. There's a horde of Nephandi pawns cluttering up the Construct, aided by a bunch of Technician turncoats. They're vulnerable to our techniques and weapons, but we can't defeat them all. Must have sent a few shaytans to insure they took out John Doe. If they're following usual procedures, they've got a fairly powerful Random Element leading the pack. Best if we don't meet up with him."

They had reached the door. Nelson motioned her back. "Cover your ears," he said.

He pulled something small from beneath his trenchcoat. Cautiously, he wrapped the fingers of his right hand around the doorknob. Slowly, making no noise, he turned the knob. Then, with a quick wrench, he yanked the door open, tossed the small ball into the stairwell, and slammed the door shut. An instant later, the steel plate buckled as if slapped by a mallet.

"Percussion grenade," explained Nelson. "Soundless but effective. Plays havoc with the inner ear. You see anybody moving on the steps, shoot first and ask questions later."

"They could be on our side," said Sharon.

Nelson shrugged. "Think of them as casualties of war. No time to check identity cards. Assume everyone's an enemy."

Opening the door, Nelson entered the stairwell, Sharon right behind him. The cyborg was arrogant and single-minded, but Sharon knew he was right. Their survival depended on ruthless action. No mercy.

The stairs in the hall were set in a zig-zag pattern. There was a landing on each floor as well as a smaller platform where the stairs turned. They ascended the metal stairs as quickly as possible. The half-way point was deserted. On the next level, they came across a lone woman lying right in front of the exit, her hands pressed to her ears, mewling in pain. She was dressed in a black jumpsuit and carried three knives stuck in her belt. All three were stained with blood. Sharon shot her in the head without regrets.

The second mid-point was empty, so was the landing on the second level up. Sharon had her foot on the stairs leading to the next mid-point when Nelson laid a restraining hand on her shoulder. "The door on the level above us just opened," he whispered. "Sounds like three or four people. They're starting down. Best we use a crossfire. Lie flat on the floor close to the wall. Fire as soon as they reach the bend in the stairs. Aim for their legs. I'll manage the rest."

Sharon stretched out on the steel floor, her elbows planted on the steps in front of her. She aimed the Uzi at a spot a few feet above the base of the next landing, ten steps up. Nelson huddled at the top of the stairs they had just ascended. He held what appeared to be a snub-nosed pistol in both hands.

She could hear their foes descending now. A thin line of sweat trickled down her back. They were talking, but it sounded like gibberish. *The Dragon's Tongue*, secret language of the Nephandi. Sharon's finger tightened on the trigger.

Four of them rounded the bend in the stairs at the same time. Two men, two women, they wore blue NWO Technician uniforms. For a second, Sharon hesitated—then opened fire when she caught sight of the machetes they carried and the grisly trophies hanging from their belts. The quartet had been busy. A half-dozen heads—eyes wide in shock, still dripping blood and brains—bounced against their hips.

From less than a dozen feet away, Sharon couldn't miss. The bullets cut into the legs of the four, ripping their knees and thighs to shreds. Sharon kept firing, spraying bullets back and forth across the landing until the Uzi ran out of ammunition. Two headhunters staggered back into the wall; the other pair collapsed to the ground. Still, all four were reaching for their weapons when a plasma bolt from Ernest Nelson's pistol fried them like hot eggs on a skillet.

"Never forget," said the cyborg, hurrying up the steps to the still smoldering corpses, "Nephandi die hard."

Savagely, he kicked in the skulls of all four head-hunters. "Don't ever leave behind anything that could possibly move. It's amazing what those From Beyond can reanimate. Take it from me, it's no fun trying to kill a corpse."

Suddenly, the air in the corridor thrummed with a high- pitched wail of incredible agony. Like an electric drill, it echoed unmercifully through the hallway, pounding against Sharon's eardrums.

"Hell," snarled Nelson, as the sound died away. "We're screwed. We gotta get out of here. Fast."

"Who was that?" asked Sharon. She had never seen the cyborg so distressed. Nelson was already scrambling up the next flight of stairs. Dropping the empty gun on the steps, Sharon chased after him. "Or should I ask, *what* was that?"

"Operative files list him as the Wailer," said cyborg. His face was dead white. "Over the past decade, he's killed at least a dozen of our best. That long, drawn-out scream is his trademark. It means he sensed our presence. He's got a talent for locating and eliminating high level Technicians and Administrators. People like you and me."

"What's he look like?" asked Sharon, desperate for more information. They were on the third level.

Nelson was already reaching for the door leading to the hall. "What technique does he use?"

"Damned if I know," said the cyborg. "He's destroyed every agent who's ever come in contact with him. Monster leaves his victims in a puddle, their bones smashed to splinters. But no one knows any details. His wailing disrupts all bands of data transmission."

The second scream lasted longer than the first. Sharon clamped her hands to her ears. Her head throbbed from the intense vibrations. The noise was maddening.

When it ended after a few seconds, her gaze met Nelson's. He nodded, his features twisted in a combination of hate and fear, as if answering her unstated question. The Wailer was getting closer.

"No more wasting time," said Nelson, his plasma gun ready. "Down the hall, branch left. Up the stairway one flight to the garage. Grab anything we can drive."

The cyborg wrenched the door open. Sharon caught a quick glimpse of a crowd of people perhaps fifteen feet away. Nelson gave them no chance to react. His plasma gun belched fire. The air crackled with energy and the smell of burning flesh.

"Come on," growled the cyborg, grabbing Sharon by the arm and dragging her into the hall. "Move."

Behind them, muted by the closed door, the Wailer howled again. The monster was in the stairwell, getting closer by the minute.

Shaking off the last vestiges of panic, Sharon

vaulted over the smoking bodies that jammed the corridor. Nelson, his trenchcoat flapping like a gigantic cape, reached the branch in the passage. He paused, his head swiftly swinging right and left, as if listening. The cyborg cursed and started to raise his plasma gun. Before he could, a new threat hit.

It came barreling out of the right corridor, a huge figure seven feet tall, with immense shoulders, four ape-like arms and a huge barrel chest. The creature's face consisted of a huge gaping mouth filled with yellowed fangs, and a blinking cyclops eye over two shallow nose holes. With a bestial roar, it grabbed Ernest Nelson around the head and chest, pinned his arms at his sides, and squeezed.

Fomori. Insane human disciples of the Dark Lords, warped and reshaped by corruption and decay into grotesque monsters. Slavering drool, the red horror tightened its double bear hug on the struggling cyborg. Even Nelson's machine-enhanced strength couldn't break the monster's grip.

For an instant, Sharon considered abandoning the cyborg. From here, she could probably manage on her own. Then, as though the thought tempted her, she rejected it. Escape brought no guarantee of survival. She needed Nelson's skill and strength to stay alive.

That decision made, Sharon needed to find a method to free Nelson quickly. The Wailer couldn't be far behind, and the four-armed freak that held the cyborg was slowly but surely crushing him.

Sharon was out of venom. Her poison ring was empty. The empty Uzi was gone. Left with no choice, she used the only weapons she still controlled. Her hands.

She leapt onto Nelson's back. Momentum shook the monster but it refused to topple. Sharon didn't care. Using the beast's crossed arms as stepping stones, she climbed up onto Nelson's shoulders. The red thing roared its defiance at her, but the fomor dared not let Nelson free.

There was no time for finesse. Ruthlessly, Sharon rammed the three inner fingers of her left hand into the monster's one eye. Hot blood spurted across her arm. She dug deep, nails clawing at the soft tissue. With a shriek of pain that rivaled the sound of the Wailer, the creature flung its arms wide open, dropping Nelson and sending Sharon flying. Staggering about blindly, the fomor disappeared back into the right tunnel.

"Let it go," said Sharon, helping Ernest Nelson to his feet. The cyborg looked dazed and confused. "Our future's nearly over."

Behind them, the door to the stairwell banged open. Sharon refused to look over her shoulder. Half-carrying, half-dragging Nelson, she stumbled into the left passage. The Wailer's shriek set the walls vibrating. Sharon's teeth felt like they were going to explode. Motes danced before her eyes. The blood in her veins flared white-hot. Sharon dropped to her hands and knees. The world turned black.

Then, as she felt the last threads of consciousness slipping from her, the air in the corridor rippled, seemed to twist in agony. As if cut by a knife, the

Wailer's howl ceased. Groggily, Sharon raised her head. The silence was deafening. A few feet distant, leaning wearily against the wall of the corridor, stood Ernest Nelson.

"My last concussion grenade," said Nelson. Sharon could barely make out his words. She suspected it would be hours before her hearing returned to normal. Assuming she lived for hours. "I threw it as far as I could. The Wailer saw it coming and ducked back into the stairwell. We better hurry. The explosion bought us a few seconds, no more."

"Did you see him?" Sharon asked as they limped along the tunnel leading to the last stairway. "Did you?"

"Just a glimpse," said Nelson. "He's human. Short but wide." The cyborg hesitated, as if trying to articulate a difficult thought. "He was…strange. I can't explain it, but the Wailer didn't look right. His face, his mouth, they were distorted. Twisted. Inhuman."

Sharon nodded, not really understanding, yet bothered by Nelson's remarks. The Wailer's screams, the gruesome description of his victims, and Nelson's vague description all sounded frighteningly familiar. Too familiar to be déjà vu. Buried somewhere in her past was a clue to the Wailer's identity.

They were on the stairs leading up to the garage when they heard the Wailer yet again. Distance and the stairwell's insulated walls lessened the impact of the scream to agonizing but bearable. Like a lash, it spurred them on, drawing the last dregs of energy from weary muscles.

"Gotta hurry," declared Nelson. He and Sharon supported each other as they forced themselves up the endless steps. "Gotta hurry."

Half-dead, they arrived at the landing leading to the garage. "It's clear," said Nelson. "Nobody's around."

The cyborg guided Sharon past a dozen black Cadillac limousines before pointing to what appeared to be a telephone company repair truck. "We're in luck," he declared, reaching under the seat for the keys. Seconds later, the engine roared to life. "Paranoid sonsabitches in the NWO booby-trap their cars. Disabling the explosives would take too much time. Besides, I like this baby better. It's designed for surveillance and espionage. Can take a lot of punishment."

Nelson flicked a switch. "Twin chain-guns," he declared, smiling. Putting the truck in gear, he steered out of the parking space and into the lane marked *Out*. "Complete with tracers and explosive shells. We've got teeth."

"Unfortunately," said Sharon, pointing at the security stop at the end of the ramp, "so do they."

Two heavy-duty vans, their front bumpers wedged together, blocked the checkpoint. Behind the vehicles waited nearly a dozen men and fomori, armed with rifles, shotguns and machetes. Past them, the steel overhead door of the garage was down.

Spotting the repair vehicle, the Nephandi started firing. A rain of bullets plunked off the hood and windshield of the truck. Sharon flinched, but the glass held. "Reinforced with primium filaments," said Nelson, "Hold on tight."

He shifted the truck into neutral and stepped on the gas. The engine roared, the wheels whining against the pavement. The vehicle shook with suppressed fury as the cyborg pushed the pedal to the floor.

Behind them, a hideous wailing rose from the stairwell. Nelson cursed as a thin spiderweb of cracks shivered across the windshield. "Keep low," he commanded. "Shield your eyes."

Moving with machine-like precision, the cyborg tripped a series of switches on the dashboard. The bellow of dual chain-guns filled the garage. Twin lines of fire slammed into the vans blocking their way. Steel buckled as the vehicles rocked with the force of the incendiary bullets. With an audible *woosh*, both vehicles exploded in a sea of flames. In response, the windshield of the truck disintegrated in a hail of glass fragments.

Crouched behind the steering wheel, Ernest Nelson thrust the gearshift into overdrive. Like a rocket, the repair truck shot forward. Sharon's eyes bulged as they hurtled straight at the burning wreckage of the twin vans. She had no time for fear. Moving with incredible acceleration, the truck smashed between the two vehicles...and burst through. The Nephandi were down, dead or dying. The Wailer was too far behind to be a problem. Only the heavy steel security door blocked their exit.

Nelson slammed on the brakes and gave the steering wheel a half spin. Sharon had no idea what he was doing. Nor was there time to ask. The front of the truck was now aimed at a spot five feet to the right of the garage entrance. The dual chain-guns chattered. Plaster and bricks dissolved in a cloud of dust. His left hand gripping the top of the steering wheel, Nelson slammed the gas pedal to the floor. The truck leapt forward. Energy belched from the plasma gun held in the cyborg's right hand, aimed straight through the missing windshield.

The reinforced steel door blocking the exit might have withstood the onslaught, but no ordinary wall would. With a triumphant screech of rubber on cement, the repair truck crashed out the front of the Dynamic Security corporate headquarters garage and onto the streets of early morning Albany.

"I told you I checked the computer diagrams of that place," said Nelson, laughing, as he shifted the truck into high gear. "Figured they'd have the damned door closed. We gotta dump this buggy quick and find some alternate transportation."

Twenty minutes later, driving in a late model Ford stolen from a used car lot, Sharon exhaled for what felt like the first time in hours. Nelson was cheerfully hunting the airwaves, searching for a radio station that played Techno-Industrial.

"Incredible," said Sharon, with a shake of her head. "We're still alive. Plus we know for certain that whoever first proposed the AW Project does not want to be found. Now all we need do is discover the traitor's identity and present location."

"Dr. Lauri Coup," said Nelson, smirking. "She's based in Indianapolis, Indiana. That's where we're going."

Sharon stared at the cyborg. "How?" she asked, astonished.

"I sent a bug to Doe's office during our interview," said Nelson. "TV transmitter the size of a mosquito. It works just fine with my digitalized vision. Lauri Coup. According to the computer search and scan, she's the one who came up with the original idea for the pattern-clone."

He grinned. "I ain't so dumb after all, huh?"

Sharon had to admit he wasn't.

Chapter Nine

"Charles Klair," said the voice, "open your eyes." Sluggishly, Klair did as he was told. His mind felt as if it were sheathed in cotton. Thinking was difficult and he had little memory of what had occurred in his recent past. Vague shadows, dreams of motion, a troubling vision of a sheet of absolute blackness, flickered then disappeared in a whirlpool of confusion.

He found himself lying in the middle of a large bed, his head propped up on two fluffy foam pillows, his arms resting on top of a light-blue blanket. He wore a light-blue hospital gown, loosely tied in the back. The room surrounding him was not large, its only furnishings a small chest of drawers, a large mirror behind it, and a single chair at the side of the bed. Everything was white—sterile, colorless, antiseptic white.

Moving his head slowly back and forth, Klair searched for a clock. There was none. Nor was there anyone present, or any sign of an intercom system.

Where the voice had come from that woke him, he had no idea. No art or pictures of any type decorated the bare walls. There was no television or radio. This was a chamber designed for healing, not relaxation. The only door faced him. Strangely enough, there were no windows.

He drew in a deep breath and exhaled. Again. Then once more. The mist surrounding his mind slowly receded. Klair shook his head, feeling alert and completely awake. A glimmer of his possible location struck him, but he refused to acknowledge the possibility. He had practiced logical thinking for decades and he saw no reason now to begin wasting time on mere speculation. Facts, not fancy, mattered to Charles Klair.

Cautiously, carefully, he probed his face, his torso, and his limbs with his hands. He felt the same as ever, seemed to be the same as ever, yet deep in his mind, the knowledge that he was somehow different worried him. His artificial eye functioned perfectly, as did his biomechanical hand. The skin of his chest felt tender, but there were no marks on his flesh, no scars, no signs of tampering. Still, the thought lingered that he would not be in a hospital without good reason. He considered getting out of the bed and trying the door, then decided against it. In situations without answers, better not to ask questions.

The door opened a minute later. A tall, slender man with dark-brown hair, a bushy beard and horn-rimmed glasses stood in the entrance. He wore blue medical scrubs and white sneakers; in one hand, he carried a clipboard and pen. The visitor seemed familiar, but Klair could not place him. Behind the doctor, in the hall outside, figures moved, conversed in low tones, but Klair couldn't get a clear glimpse of any of them. Again he felt troubled but could not pin down an exact reason why.

"Well, well, Charles," said the man, walking over to the side of the bed. The plastic badge above his heart identified him as Dr. Castillio. "How are you feeling? Sitting up at last. You look better, that's for sure."

Klair nodded, not saying a word. His mind raced, trying to place the doctor's name, his voice. Finally, frustrated and annoyed, he gave up. He couldn't remember.

"Still hampered by memory loss?" said Castillio, as if reading Charles' mind. The doctor made a mark on his board. "We had hoped by now the neural pattern would have healed. Even using the most advanced techniques, repairing brain damage is extremely difficult. I will return...."

"You're Dr. Otto Castillio," interrupted Klair, the name rising out of the depths of his subconscious. "You treated me for bronchial pneumonia when I was ten years old. That was four decades ago, in a hospital in Baltimore, Maryland, that probably no longer exists. You are either dead or long retired. And this room is nothing more than a basic fabrication of the recovery area, pulled from those same childhood recollections."

The doctor chuckled. "Nonsense. Merely déjà vu,

Charles. The ravings of a man who's suffered a major head injury." Castillio waved a hand about, as if demonstrating the reality of the white room. "If you're not in Sisters of Mercy Hospital, as you claim, then where are you?"

Klair frowned. Closing his eyes, he tried desperately to patch together the shadowy images that lurked just beneath the threshold of memory. "I am in," he began, grasping for the word that would pull everything together, "Autocthonia."

"Very good," said the doctor. His face was no longer that of a middle-aged bearded man. The features were melted, fused, transformed into a much different visage. It was a composite image, an everyman, a blending of the features of a thousand different faces. Klair had seen it many times before. "Who am I?"

"You are *The Computer*," said Klair, "the artificial intelligence that leads Iteration X."

"Excellent," said the holographic image that had been Doctor Castillio. The room had changed as well. Gone were the white walls, the dresser, the mirror. Klair lay in a steel chamber, filled with huge machinery, complex circuitry and a dazzling array of medical and biomechanical equipment. Three drone robots hovered in the background, checking system readouts and adjusting incomprehensible devices. Klair was still reclining, but no longer rested in a bed. A reconstruction tank encased his entire body except for his head and upper chest. Such devices were used only in the most serious emergencies.

Robert Weinberg

"What happened to me?" asked Klair, his voice growing shrill. *"What has happened to my body?"*

"The Horizon Beacon," said the smooth, neutral voice of the hologram. "When the passage opened between the Gray Collective and Autocthonia, you were caught in the center. Half of your body was transported here, while the rest remained there. In effect, you were sliced into pieces. Fortunately, you were cut across the middle instead of from top to bottom. Your vital organs remained intact.

"The HIT Mark VI's in the transfer zone detected your presence instantly. Physical laws operate differently here, so you were still alive, though near death. My guardian robots identified you and, at my command, brought you here. Over the past several days, your body was reconstructed and enhanced using the most advanced techniques in the universe. The only doubts were whether your intelligence survived the trauma. Thus, the careful handling of your awakening."

"What have you done to me?" asked Klair, feeling he was trapped in a nightmare from which there was no awakening.

"I believe," said the hologram, "you will find the results most satisfying. Your new form embodies the supreme goals of Iteration X. You are a true composite of man and machine."

"Why did you bother?" asked Klair. *The Computer,* unable to understand human emotion, possessed neither tact nor diplomacy. Though Klair had dreamt of becoming one with the machine, he had not envisioned such drastic measures. Nor did he entirely trust the motives of the AI. *The Computer* was sentient, and in the past few weeks, Klair had learned that it had ambitions beyond the Enlightenment of mankind. "Why make this effort for me? What makes me so special?"

"You served me well at the Gray Collective, Comptroller Klair," said the hologram. "Though you failed to complete your mission. The pattern-clone body was not delivered to me. However, it quickly became clear that events conspired against you. The pattern-clone awakened with a fully developed identity, one evidently programmed into the construct's DNA. The being vanished with Velma Wade instants before it could be destroyed by an invading team of Tradition Willworkers. The Gray Collective no longer exists."

The hologram twisted into an expression not remotely human. Staring at the image in horrified fascination, Klair realized *The Computer* was angry. "I want you to locate the pattern-clone as quickly as possible. And once you have found it, destroy it."

"Velma Wade," repeated Klair. "Then the Progenitors must control the construct?"

"No," said the hologram, speaking with mechanical precision. It no longer seemed even remotely human. "That supposition is incorrect. The situation is much more complex than you realize. New factors, reality variants, have joined the fray. Nothing is as it seems."

"I don't understand," said Klair.

"Everything will be explained shortly," said the

hologram. "First, your new body must be tested. Nothing could be done until you were fully aware and functional again. The amalgam is a highly experimental technique. There may still be flaws in the system."

"So I'm the guinea pig?" said Klair, bolder than usual. He was beyond caring.

"Think of yourself as the prototype," said the hologram. It attempted a smile, but only succeeded in looking sinister. "The first of a new generation of man/machine bioconstructs. If the technique proves successful, all future Comptrollers will be required to become such amalgams."

The hologram waved to the computer drones. "Release Comptroller Klair from the reconstruction tank."

Five minutes later, the huge container drained of green fluid. Klair stood naked on the laboratory's steel floor. Looking down at his body, he experienced a flutter of doubt. Was the AI trying to trick him? Except for his skin appearing slightly whiter than usual—possibly a result of the strange lighting in the Realm—he appeared exactly the same.

"I'm no different," he said, voicing his thoughts. "I can sense the coldness of the floor beneath my feet. My body feels fine, perfectly natural. I see no evidence of any damage like you described."

"If you did," said the hologram, "then the amalgam would be a failure. Walk about. Lift your arms, raise one leg. Stretch. Attempt several different exercises. Do those actions seem normal?"

Klair did exactly what he was told. His limbs moved

easily, comfortably. He felt stronger, healthier than ever before. Only after completing a dozen pushups did he realize a difference.

"My fingers," he said, feeling the flesh carefully. He raised a hand to his face. "My eye. I had biomechanical implants." He stared at the hologram. "These can't be real. New limbs cannot be regenerated overnight."

"All robots in this work area attack human subject GH23765," the hologram commanded the three drones, ignoring Klair's remarks. "Pull him to pieces."

Klair cursed, caught off guard. Before the hologram finished speaking, he was surrounded. Death looked at him from three directions.

The drones were worker machines, resembling giant inverted tops with four long tentacle arms. They were capable of lifting objects weighing several tons. In the past, he had seen the robots twist six-inch-thick titanium steel bars with ease.

A dozen whip-like limbs lashed out at Klair. Purely by instinct, he raised his arms to protect himself. Three tentacles wrapped themselves around each wrist, each ankle. Klair screamed as the robots pulled.

Then, in astonishment, he went silent. Though the drones were pulling with all of their strength, he was not moving. His feet remained firmly on the floor, his hands held straight up to his face. He could feel the steel against his flesh, but felt no pain.

Slowly, he meshed his fingers together and lowered his arms. Metal screeched on metal as the two drones holding his limbs shifted forward. Klair laughed and flung his arms wide apart. Steel tentacles lashed about in a frenzy, clattering on the floor.

Grasping the rope-like arms, he tugged one of the drones close. Klair slammed it on the top with a fist. The robot collapsed to the floor, steel plates buckling. Savagely, Klair did the same to the second drone. Then the third. He grinned with maniacal pleasure at the hologram.

"I'm strong," said Klair. "Incredibly strong."

"Your body is powered by a low-level nuclear device," said the hologram. "Your bones are Primium, and there are lasers built into your fingers. Your vision and hearing have been enhanced. Your flesh consists of a liquid metal alloy developed and produced on Autocthonia. While it feels like normal human skin, it is not. Damaging it will take great effort. You are by no means indestructible, but can withstand incredible amounts of punishment. Do not be fooled. The pattern-clone is your physical equal and more. You are not self-healing. You can be damaged, even destroyed. Also, be very careful of your actions. Though you appear to be mortal, you are actually an amalgam. Accidentally revealing your powers and abilities to the masses will surely attract the Deep Universe entities who guard the laws of Paradox."

"I understand," said Klair. "From what you say, I gather that I am going to return to Earth?"

"Yes," said the hologram. "Come with me. You must observe what occurred in the Gray Collective after your accident."

Klair, following the hologram out of the laboratory, grimaced at the word. His dismemberment had been no accident. He had foolishly warned X344 about the possible dangers of the Horizon Beacon. And had been rewarded by the cyborg throwing the gateway mechanism directly at him.

Fifteen minutes later, they arrived at a second laboratory, having traversed a maze of seemingly endless steel passages filled with an uncountable number of robots and drones rushing from one place to another. Klair felt oddly out of place. As best he could tell, he was the only human—or partly-human being—on this level of Autocthonia.

The chamber was huge. Scattered throughout the room were dozens of large coffin-shaped glass tanks, filled with an amber liquid. Floating in each of the tanks was a body, or remnants of a body. Many of the corpses appeared to have been horribly mauled, clawed or crushed. Walking about, Klair mentally ticked off the identities of the dead. All of them came from the Gray Collective. However, nowhere did he find Sharon Reed, Velma Wade or X344.

"The entire contents of the Gray Collective were pulled through the Horizon gate into Autocthonia," said the hologram. "The clone equipment and files are being examined elsewhere. As expected, the data in the memory banks does not reflect any signs of tampering. Velma Wade covered her subterfuge extremely efficiently. Again, there is a ninety-seven percent probability that this scheme was started years, perhaps centuries, before the AW Project was conceived."

The hologram waved a hand in the air, gesturing at the glass coffins. It was a remarkably human-like gesture. "Using direct electrical stimulus of the cerebral cortex, the final images seen by these victims can be analyzed and recreated by thought processors in this laboratory. Using a central data bank, the multitude of perspectives are linked together, much in the same manner a motion picture is created from many thousands and thousands of still photos. In this situation, instead of a cinema, we have a fairly detailed vision of the final few minutes of the Gray Collective."

Klair almost expected a small motion-picture screen to descend from the ceiling. Instead, the hologram beckoned him over to a nearby laboratory table and chairs. Sitting on top of the table was a huge steel helmet, connected to several nearby computers by hundreds of thin, silver metal strands. The hologram gestured for Klair to sit down.

"Put on the headgear," said *The Computer's* surrogate. "You will experience through the eyes of the dead what occurred in the doomed Collective."

It was an eerie sensation. While the scene remained constant, the picture flickered larger and smaller, darker and lighter, more intense and less, as the events unfolded through the eyes of the more than two dozen technicians present at the conclusion of the AW experiment.

Klair witnessed the opening of the Horizon gateway. He saw the Hit Mark VI mechanoids from Autocthonia emerge, only to encounter the Deep

Universe being known as Aliara, Queen of Desire. Watching her smash the seemingly invulnerable robots to junk made him suddenly aware that despite his new powers, he was not indestructible.

Fascinated, he caught a glimpse of Velma Wade stabbing Sharon Reed, her long-time mentor, in the back. Saw Wade vault over the railing into the pit where the pattern-clone was awakening. Then, in a change of perspective, observed the arrival of a huge beast, followed moments later by a disparate group of strangers he assumed were the Tradition willworkers mentioned by *The Computer*. Notable among them was Prisoner Seventeen.

Again, the viewpoint switched. The picture flickered faster, the action less clear. Klair knew he was seeing the fading images from the eyes of dying technicians. A woman leapt forward, a blade flashed like a lightning bolt, but the pattern-clone and Velma Wade were gone. The picture darkened, then disappeared.

"I saw Sharon Reed die," said Klair as he removed the helmet. "X344 perished opening the Horizon beacon. Yet neither body was retrieved from the Gray Collective. What happened?"

"Your assumptions are unjustified," said the hologram. "My representative on the Inner Circle reported yesterday that both Reed and X344 survived their ordeal. Though badly damaged, the pair escaped the Construct and arrived at the Albany headquarters of the New World Order. They have been repaired and regenerated. The Circle has already assigned them the task of discovering the truth behind Velma Wade's treachery."

"Sharon Reed and X344, still alive," muttered Comptroller Klair. The Progenitor Director who had made his life miserable for months at the Gray Collective along with the cyborg who had tried to kill him. It seemed quite appropriate to Klair that they should be working together. Their new assignment made his own quest so much easier. He was going to find them. And make them suffer horribly.

"Who is Velma Wade?" he asked the hologram. "Who is the pattern-clone? What bond ties them together? And why is it so important that the clone be destroyed?"

"There is not enough information yet to answer those questions with a high degree of probability," said the hologram. "The identity of the clone remains uncertain. As originally envisioned, the construct was designed to be the ultimate fighting unit in the centuries-old battle between the forces of logic and reason and the Reality Deviants known as the Nine Traditions. It featured the most advanced techniques known to both Iteration X and the Progenitors. The pattern-clone should have been entirely devoid of sentience, an empty body waiting to be filled with the proper intelligence."

Klair mentally noted that *The Computer* did not mention that it had planned to seize control of that body for itself. He remained silent. He had become bold, but not stupid.

"The clone awoke, possessing a mind and intelligence of astonishing power," continued the hologram. "Velma Wade, a seemingly loyal member of the Technocratic Union, turned Reality Deviant, attacked her mentor and helped the mysterious construct to escape. The implications are not clear, but they appear ominous."

The hologram once again spoke with machine-like precision. Klair knew he was listening to the actual voice of *The Computer*, hearing the actual fears of one of the most powerful beings in the universe.

"The pattern-clone is perhaps the most powerful artificial being ever created. It has powers over machinery and computers that are only slightly less than mine. Because of its nanobyte blood, it is nearly unkillable. It possesses a mind of incredible power. Supporting the being is a group of shapechangers of unknown numbers, who have skillfully infiltrated the Union. If certain possibilities turn into probabilities, the clone may control techniques not seen in the universe in over five hundred years. Such powers could be extremely dangerous to even the strongest of the Enlightened."

The hologram's features shifted, gradually becoming a smooth, silvery-metal face, with saucer-shaped eyes and a voice-box mouth. "Unchecked, this Random Element threatens the very existence of the Technocracy. If a worst case scenario occurs, man and machine will collapse into a web of eternal darkness."

Chapter Ten

Five people sat clustered around the small table, chatting among themselves and listening to the country singer crooning on the bar's small stage. Two men and three women, they appeared to be perfectly average young adults out for an evening's entertainment. But Terrence Shade knew differently.

The quintet was definitely not ordinary. They were willworkers, members of the Nine Traditions. They came from the Verbena Chantry house located some miles outside of Rochester known as the Casey cabal.

Shade had good reason to remember the place. Several weeks ago, an attack force of Men in Black under his command had assaulted the Chantry, seeking to destroy Prisoner Seventeen. The mission had ended in total disaster, with nearly all of Shade's associates being killed. In a strange twist of fate, Ms. Hargroves had torn apart the Gray Man leading the attack. Now, in an abrupt change of fortune, Shade found himself assisting the person responsible for his greatest failure. Aliara had a sardonic sense of humor.

Shade didn't know the names of his five enemies. Nor was he sure of their powers. Mages appeared perfectly ordinary under most circumstances. From his previous encounter with the Verbena willworkers, he knew they could be dangerous when provoked. Still, he wasn't concerned. Aliara had gifted him with a small measure of her incredible will. He doubted that any of them could match his psychic powers. More important, he was unafraid of death. In truth, he would welcome oblivion, if it came swift and without much pain.

Ms. Hargroves, always a font of information, had provided him with directions to the Casey cabal. Shade did the rest. Trained in the arts of espionage and infiltration by the New World Order, he had spent the entire day scouting various nightspots and bars in the communities surrounding the Chantry house. A few casual questions gave him all the information he needed. The young adults of the Chantry house frequented several hangouts close to the cabal headquarters. Even willworkers need a break from routine. A small but loyal group of them were fans of Tex Wilson, the singer performing here tonight at Cowboy Bob's Bar and Grill.

Shade found country music repetitive and dull, but he was no critic. Nursing his drinks, he had waited patiently for the quintet to arrive. Once they finally appeared, he waited still longer, making sure they were not joined by any unexpected guests. Five of the willworkers he felt he could handle. Seven or eight would test even his augmented powers. Now, a little after eleven at night, he was ready to strike.

The music stopped as the set came to an end. The crowd applauded politely though not enthusiastically. Evidently, many of the patrons shared Shade's lack of enthusiasm for the singer's voice. "Thanks, folks. Many thanks," said Tex, sounding much more from Brooklyn than Texas. "I'll be taking a short break. Back in ten."

His head bobbing up and down as if answering some inner question, Shade strolled over to the five's table. Wearing blue jeans, a white shirt, arrowhead string tie and dark glasses, he appeared totally harmless. "Pretty good singer, huh?" he said to no one in particular.

Surprised, curious eyes turned and stared at him. Invisible fingers picked at his thoughts. He projected innocence, the mind of a cheerful drunk not sure what he was doing.

"I'm Terrence Shade," he said, grabbing an empty chair from a nearby table and dropping down onto it. "Here in the Rochester area on business. You folks from this part of the country?"

"Um, sorry Mr. Shade, but this is a private party," said one of the men, tall and blond, dressed in blue jeans and a muscle T. "Glad to make your acquaintance, but we're not looking for company. So beat it."

"Nice city, Rochester," said Shade, disregarding the man's words. Tony was the speaker's name. Shade snatched that much from his mind. His friend was John. The girls were Erin, Kathy and Jill. Shade liked names. They made things so much more personal.

Names made his victims people instead of mere objects. "My first trip to the region. It's so pleasant I'm thinking of relocating here permanently. Really. I love the climate. Hot in the summer, cold in the winter. And the people are so friendly."

"How interesting," said the girl named Kathy, sitting next to him on his right. Short, with plain features and drab brown hair, she stared right through Shade. "Are we supposed to care?"

"Hey, can I buy you all a drink?" asked Shade, absorbing their emotions like a sponge. In his present state, he thrived on anger, fear and mistrust. He wanted their passions; he no longer possessed any of his own. Before anyone could answer, he raised his hands in mock protest. "Please, please, I insist. My treat. I'll charge it to the company credit account."

"I'm sorry, Mr. Shade," said Tony, "but we're not interested in free drinks. Please, as I said already, my friends and I aren't looking for company. Either leave or we'll be forced to call the management."

"Tony, Tony, Tony," said Shade. He stared at the blond man. "How rude. You should know better than to speak for your companions. What do you say, John? Erin? Kathy, are you turning down my offer? Jill, Jill, are you a pill?"

John frowned. Kathy stared at Shade with sudden concern. "How do you know our names?" she asked.

Shade giggled. Oftentimes in the past few days, he found himself laughing for no reason. Ever since his encounter with Aliara, he'd had little control over his actions. He laughed, he moaned, he giggled and he cried at the oddest moments. Most of all, he wished he had never been born. But there was nothing he could do about that. Aliara's mental web made suicide impossible.

"Oh, I know lots and lots about all of you," he declared, keeping his voice level. Too loud, he knew, and he might attract attention. And he definitely did not want attention yet. "You weren't expecting me, so I was able to skim your surface thoughts without any problems."

"Who are you?" asked Jill. She had deep blue eyes, freckles, and was by far the most powerful willworker of the group. But already he could tell that her talent was no match for his. "What do you want from us?"

Like her companions, she was curious but not afraid. Tradition willworkers, just like those in the Technocracy, possessed incredible confidence in themselves. Five against one, they felt no fear. At present, they considered Shade strange but not dangerous. He wanted them to think that as long as possible.

"As I already told you, my name is Terrence Shade. Once, I was a person of great importance," said Shade, with a sigh and a shake of the head. He was in no rush. "When I snapped my fingers, people jumped. When I wanted something done, it was done immediately. Like all of you, I thought I understood the mysteries of the universe. Nothing worried me. I considered myself immortal. Death was just a word, holding no fear. It was wonderful to be alive."

"Cut the crap, Shade," said Jill, tapping her fingers on the edge of the table. She stared at Shade suspiciously. "You're a mage. I can sense your powers. Who are you with?"

"I belong to the Sons of Ether," said Shade, with a wide smile. Around the table, the five willworkers relaxed. Suddenly, they thought they understood his weird behavior.

Mages belonging to that particular Tradition had a reputation for oddness. Involved in strange science and seemingly impossible projects, they were viewed by their fellow Tradition mages as being distinctly off-beat, with minimal social skills. Which was exactly why Shade claimed membership in their order. During his many years with the NWO, he had interrogated several Sons of Ether; if necessary, he could even imitate their ridiculous patter about quantum waves and vibrations in the ether. He doubted that would be required. His plan called for a brief but meaningful visit tonight. He merely wanted to make a lasting impression.

"Why are you really here?" said Tony. "What do the Sons of Ether want with us?"

"I was getting to that," said Shade. "Just give me a chance. I'm not comfortable surrounded by so many people. The noise, the music, the dancing. It just overwhelms me."

"Okay," said Jill, "I guess I can sympathize with your discomfort. This sort of place isn't for everybody, especially not an Etherite. But don't blame us for being suspicious. We just came here tonight for a good time.

We weren't expecting to encounter company…especially not company we've never seen before."

She looked to the small stage in the front of the club. Tex Wilson had just returned and had retrieved his guitar. His three member back-up group were adjusting their instruments.

"Singing's going to start again in a second," said Jill. "If you have anything important to tell us, better do it now. Otherwise, you'll be drowned out."

"Then I'll be quick and to the point," said Shade. Still smiling, he rose smoothly from his chair. Reaching beneath his coat, he pulled out a six-inch-long razor-sharp stiletto. The blade gleamed silver in the bright lights. Before anyone realized what he planned, Shade grabbed Kathy by her hair, wrenched her head back, and plunged the knife into her throat. Hot red blood gushed from the wound, across her chest, and splashed onto the table. Savagely, Shade ripped the knife blade from one side of the girl's neck to the other, almost decapitating his victim.

"Give my regards to Sam Haine," said Shade, shoving the dead girl's limp body forward. In response to his words, a curtain of inky darkness descended over the room. Every light in the club went dark. "Tell him Aliara always repays her debts tenfold."

The other four mages scrambled for him, but Shade had planned his escape long before sitting down. A mental shield clamped down on his thoughts, making him telepathically invisible. Moving with supernatural stealth and grace, he skated smoothly through the lounge in a zig-zag pattern aimed right for the stage. He wasn't foolish enough to try for the door. That was too obvious. Instead, he rushed past Tex and his boys and made for the service exit behind the stage. As expected, the only one there was a puzzled night watchman.

The guard, a big burly figure futilely clicking the switch of a flashlight that no longer functioned, stood with his back to the door. Though unable to see anything beyond the tip of his nose, he somehow sensed Shade's presence. "Sorry," he said, gruffly. "This here's an emergency exit. Sets off an alarm at the fire station. Use the front door, please."

"Unfortunately," said Shade, "I'm in a terrible rush."

His second knife, shaped like a spike, penetrated the guard's right eye with a satisfying gurgle. The watchman collapsed to the floor, screaming. Stepping over the body, Shade pushed the door open. Reality shifted slightly. A wire overheated, fused. No alarm sounded.

Quickly he scurried across the parking lot to Joe Steeger's automobile. A broken-down old Chevy, it provided all the transportation Shade needed. And he wasn't worried about the security guard reporting it stolen.

He dared not dawdle. In this age of beepers, cellular phones and microwave transmissions, one never knew exactly when the police might arrive. Gunning the motor, he slammed the car into gear and headed for the exit.

In the rear-view mirror, he glimpsed a horde of

Robert Weinberg

people pouring out the club's front doors. Someone, probably Jill or Tony, had finally negated his darkfall technique. Concentrating, Shade sent a wave of panic rippling through the crowd. A woman screamed. Then another. Someone started pushing, clawing desperately to escape. Fear spread like wildfire. In seconds, a disorganized but harmless exodus degenerated into a mad rout. There were would be injuries for sure, perhaps even a trampling or two. A fire in the club would have been a nice touch, but he couldn't think of everything.

Shade smiled. He still possessed the magic touch. Meanwhile, tonight's murder should give the Verbena scum an interesting mystery to ponder. Three or four more attacks should finish the job. Sooner later, the leaders of the Casey cabal would contact Sam Haine. They'd have no choice. And when the Changing Man came to town, Terrence Shade had a very special surprise waiting for him.

An hour later, he parked the car a few blocks away from Ms. Hargroves apartment. The security guard on duty barely glanced at Shade when buzzing him through to the elevators. Behind the man a dark patch on the wall indicated the exact location where Steeger had committed suicide. Bloodstains were difficult to remove, and the building's owner was too cheap to buy new paneling. So the splotch remained.

Every time he walked past the mark, Shade felt like screaming, "I did it, I did it," claiming full credit for the crime. He enjoyed sharing his triumphs with the masses. But, slaving for Aliara, he was bound by her desire for no publicity. The only person Shade could brag to was Ms. Hargroves. And she made it quite clear that she found her new assistant's activities uninteresting.

Opening the door to Ms. Hargroves's apartment, he spotted the gaunt woman standing in front of the refrigerator, taking out a beer. "Lucy, I'm home," he called out cheerfully.

"Your mission ended in success, I gather," said Ms. Hargroves, not sounding amused.

"Perfect," said Shade. "Anything about it on the television? Or the radio?"

"A single murder on a Saturday night?" replied the gaunt woman with a laugh. "You must be kidding. Burn down the entire club and maybe you'd get a minute or two. Otherwise, the killing's just another police statistic."

Shade shrugged, then dropped onto the sofa. "Well, I thought it was executed quite nicely. How goes it at Everwell Chemicals?"

"The same," said Ms. Hargroves. "Enzo's visitor has been going through books, checking out the operation of the plant, but it's all for show. Montifloro couldn't care less how his cousin's running Everwell. He's only interested in one person—Hope, that bimbo Enzo introduced him to when he first arrived. Enzo might be crude and arrogant, but he's not stupid. He understands lust, and he knows how to exploit it to his advantage."

"Your employer and his friend Ezra have something important planned," said Shade. "This situation with Montifloro is just a small part of a much greater scheme. Ezra is mad and Enzo is ambitious. When an elder vampire and an archmage combine forces, anything is possible. We have to find out what they have in mind. Aliara demands it. And her desires are not easily denied."

Ms. Hargroves sighed. "What Aliara wants, Aliara gets. But so far, there's nothing to report. It's almost as if they're waiting—waiting for some event to happen. I don't know what, or when, but I'm certain that soon all hell is going to break loose."

Shade removed his dark glasses. His red eyes burned with unholy fires. "All hell sounds just fine to me," he declared. "Just fine."

Chapter Eleven

After an elaborate lunch presided over by their ravishing hostess, Seventeen and Shadow of the Dawn decided to go sightseeing. Sam Haine, restless as always, agreed to act as their guide. A frequent visitor to Horizon, he promised them an interesting afternoon. Albert, as usual, tagged along. Kallikos did not object, as he and Marianna planned to spend the next several hours plotting their strategy for the Council meeting that night.

"Return before nightfall," he told them, flashing a rare smile. "Enjoy the wonders of Horizon. After tonight, who knows when we will encounter such pleasures again?"

"Cheerful soul, that Kallikos," remarked Sam Haine afterwards. They stood on the street outside of Marianna's headquarters. A steady flow of people swirled by them, dressed in an astonishing range of outfits, ranging from very little to most elaborate. The color, the motion, the excitement that seemed to fill the air had Seventeen's head spinning.

Robert Weinberg

"He carries the weight of the world on his shoulders," said Albert. "After centuries, it must be a terrible burden."

"Well," Sam put in, puffing contentedly on one of his smokeless cigars, "I like my futures to be a mystery. Rather not know what's gonna happen next. Who the hell wants to wake up and know you're going to die that afternoon?"

He flicked a non-existent ash off the end of his cigar and pointed the stogie at Seventeen. "Well, since you got no memory, son, this place is all new to you. What miracles you want to see first?"

Seventeen shook his head. "I have no idea. How much is there to see? And where? How big is this Realm? It seems to stretch on forever. There's mountains in the distance. The only place I can compare it with is that Realm Alvin Reynolds took us. And I didn't have a chance to go exploring there."

Sam chuckled. "Horizon's huge, son. Incredibly big. It's about the size of a small moon. We're in Concordia, the capital city of the Realm. It's fifteen miles in diameter, shaped like a circle. Surrounding it is Orbis Finiens, a continent around twelve hundred miles wide. And on the other side of Horizon lies another continent called Posht. That's a lot of land to explore."

"For today," said Shadow of the Dawn, "I think a tour of a few locations in the city would suffice."

"I kinda figured you would think that," said Sam. "Enough wonders to see in Concordia, anyway, to keep you busy for weeks. Remember, this entire world was built by vast numbers of mages working together. It's a magickal place, filled with surprises and mysteries."

"Some of which are still being discovered," added Albert. "Weaving through the rock far beneath the Council Chambers located in the center of Concordia, there exists a vast underground labyrinth. The maze, much of which still remains unexplored, leads to a number of distant sites on Horizon. According to stories, two Dreamspeakers found a tunnel that led them to Posht. Others claim to have journeyed to the mystickal islands of Triton's Deep. One explorer claims that he once stumbled upon an entrance to the faerie realms. Another report says that strange, magickal beasts, long vanished from Earth, live in the center of the maze. No one is sure of the truth of any of these tales, but all agree that the labyrinth was not created by the founders of the Realm. How it came into being and who formed it are questions that have never been answered."

Sam Haine snorted. "Enough with the spook stories, Albert. Seventeen wants to see some sights, not a bunch of caves."

"During my stay at the Fukuoka Chantry House," said Shadow of the Dawn, "the wise master spoke of a mystic temple known as Songgwang-sa. He said meditating within this fabled place heals the soul. Might not this legendary structure exist here in Concordia?"

Albert smiled. "Where else but on Horizon?" he declared. "I have spent many hours there myself.

Whether meditating there heals the soul, I cannot say. But it is a place of spiritual peace. The temple, a magnificent flame-shaped building, is carved from the wood of the blue bodhi tree that grows only in Horizon's forests. Do you wish to visit it?"

"Yes," said Shadow. "If possible. It would be a great honor to ponder the infinite within its legendary walls."

"Songgwang-sa is located about a half-hour from here by foot," said Albert. "If you prefer, we could ride there in a buggy. I'd advise we walk. Concordia is a city of many unique delights, and it should be savored by close contact. Besides, Sam could use the exercise."

Despite howls of protest from Sam Haine, they chose to proceed on foot. For Seventeen, whose memories seemed to consist primarily of running and fighting, the next few hours were the most relaxed interlude of his life. For the first time since his escape from the Gray Collective, he was not in a rush. With Shadow of the Dawn at his side, Seventeen felt at peace with the world. And he found himself entranced by the majesty and mystery of Concordia.

The serene Temple of Great Awakening was only their first stop. Sam Haine and Albert alternated showing them the incredible sights scattered throughout the metropolis. Sam delighted in the spectacle, Albert in the spiritual. Their party wandered aimlessly through the five-mile-wide Sruth na Mblath, the stream of flowers. Seventeen walked across the water of the Miracle Pool. Shadow of the Dawn peered deep in the Fenestra Inferorum, the "Spectral

Window" that supposedly enabled users to look into the Low Umbra and communicate with the spirits of the dead. Whether Shadow saw anything or not, she refused to say. And they all marveled at the Museum of Living Artifacts, a modern museum that featured exotic specimens living in bizarre and unusual ecosystems impossible anywhere on Earth.

It was late in the afternoon when they came to a spot of special significance to Seventeen.

"That huge building you're seeing," said Sam Haine, "is the Council Chambers of the Nine Traditions. As you might expect in a world of magick, it's a pretty damned impressive place. That dome in the center rises six hundred feet right over the meetin' table of the council. That's where we'll be tonight, listenin' to Kallikos present his case to whomever shows up. Not that I think it's gonna do any good. But it should be a good show, especially when Porthos recognizes who's talkin'. Might be some fireworks like this Realm hasn't witnessed in centuries."

Seventeen was hardly listening. His gaze was fixed on an immense wooden building that ringed the Council Complex. "That's the Archives, isn't it?" he asked. He knew without waiting for an answer that he was correct. Just as he knew he had to speak to someone within its walls.

"Sure is," said Sam. "Over a billion volumes in that library. Kinda impressive, even to an illiterate like me."

"The archivist's name is Nicodemus Mulhouse," said Albert. "Stories claim that he is more than five hundred years old. If so, he predates the founding of Horizon itself. He's a crusty old codger, not an easy man to get along with."

"I'd like to talk with him," said Seventeen. "There's something I need to ask him alone, if you don't mind? Do you think it could be arranged?"

"We're in Horizon, son," said Sam Haine, "not Earth. Less people live on this whole world than in a large town. There's some formalities observed, but not many. Me and Albert and Shadow ain't worried if you need to have a private conversation or two. Keeps us on our toes, wondering, is all. You want to visit the Archives, it sounds fine with me. No reason you shouldn't. And I assure you, once we step into the hall of records, you'll encounter Master Nicodemus quick enough."

Sam Haine wasn't exaggerating. Though it was one of Mulhouse's great-great-grandchildren who met their party at the entrance to the Archives, it was Master Nicodemus himself, arriving a few minutes later, who agreed to Seventeen's request for a private interview. Alone, he and Seventeen sat in a small office, surrounded by walls of books stacked to the ceiling.

The archivist looked as worn and old as his most ancient volume. Entirely bald, with deep-sunken eyes, he was bent at the shoulder, his body twisted with arthritis. He wore a dark-brown robe and leather sandals. When he spoke, his voice creaked with the weight of centuries.

"Well," he said to Seventeen, "what do ye want of

me? My time is precious, and I have little of it with which to humor the requests of strangers."

"I'm searching for answers that I suspect exist only in this great library," said Seventeen. "Working on my own, I know such a task would take an eternity. Unfortunately, I am only mortal and my time is short. Only with the help of the greatest archivist in all the Tellurian can I possibly succeed. That's why I have come to you."

Nicodemus stared at Seventeen suspiciously. "And what is this quest for truth that pushes ye so?" he asked. "A new love potion? Or an elixir to grow back your hair?"

"No," said Seventeen. "I'm searching for my identity. And I'm afraid of what I might discover."

"I dinna understand ye," said the Archivist. He licked his lips, a flicker of interest in his dark eyes. "Ye be a mage and yet you know not your own name. How'd ye pass the guardians to the Realm?"

"They knew me," said Seventeen. "Or at least, they gave me a name. But other than brief flashes of knowledge, I have no memory of my past. It's a complete blank. Except for visions of a monster from hell itself."

"And ye believe that somehow your story might be in the Archives?" Nicodemus remarked. "Even in a billion volumes, not every event that has occurred in the Tellurian is recorded."

"I have a feeling," said Seventeen, "that the information I want is in this building. I can't explain, but sometimes memories buried deep within my mind,

Robert Weinberg

thoughts I cannot fully comprehend, rise to the surface. As soon as I saw the Archives, I recognized them. I knew that I had been here before. I knew that I had spoken to you, in a room like this, perhaps in this very chamber, years ago. That's why I'm sure that the secret of my identity is locked in these Archives."

Master Nicodemus's eyes narrowed. For the first time since they had entered the room, he actually seemed to see Seventeen. "While not as young as I might like to be, my memory is still better than most," he declared. "Ye dinna appear familiar to me."

"My name," said Seventeen, slowly, not sure if he was doing the right thing, "is Ethan Phillips."

"Phillips?" repeated Nicodemus. "Ethan Phillips."

The ancient Archivist remained motionless for a moment, staring intently at Seventeen. Then, slowly, ever slowly, he began rocking back and forth in his chair, repeating the name, "Ethan Phillips, Ethan Phillips. Now I remember."

Nicodemus twisted his head to one side, as if looking at Seventeen at a different angle might reveal some secret otherwise hidden. "There is a resemblance. Not much, but now that ye have said the name, I see it. Your face and his be very similar. But he was young and handsome and not built like you at all. He was a wand, tall and slender, a man who could bend in the wind and not break. Ye are a rock, a pillar of granite to be shattered, not bowed. It will take more than a name and a hint of sameness to convince me that ye be him. Have ye no other proof? No other name?"

"Yes," said Seventeen. "I have another name. Ethan Phillips came here, *I came here*, searching for information about his lost love. Her name was Scarlett Dancer."

Without a word, the Archivist rose to his feet. Turning from Seventeen, he ran his fingers along a collection of immense, leather-bound ledgers on a long bookshelf directly behind his desk. Muttering to himself, Nicodemus squinted at the cryptic markings on the side of each volume. Finally, after several minutes of searching, he pulled out one of the books and dropped it on his desk.

"I am an archivist," he declared. "It is my job not only to know the location of every volume in this library, but also to record and remember how and why each book is used. Me memory is not what it once was, and I am not so foolish to think I will live forever. Thus, every request, every search, every visit made to these Archives, no matter how important or how menial the task, I record in my own personal diaries." Nicodemus's lips twisted into the slightest of smiles. "I archive the Archives."

"Then you have a record of Ethan Phillips's mission to this library?" asked Seventeen. Though he felt certain that *he* was Phillips, he could not bring himself to think of himself in those terms. Ethan Phillips had been another life, another person. Now he was Seventeen. Until he remembered, he would remain two separate, distinct persons. One in the past, one in the present. "You know why he came, and what he found?"

"I remember," said Nicodemus. Wheezing, he opened the massive volume. Ancient fingers, crippled and bent into claws, flipped the pages. "Here are the exact details. While I trust my memory, an archivist knows not to depend on recollections. Records don't lie."

Seventeen leaned forward. "When was I here?"

"You came to see me, to hunt through the Archives, on August twenty-ninth," said Nicodemus, "nineteen hundred and forty-six."

Seventeen's jaw dropped. For a moment he stared at Nicodemus, his mouth wide open in surprise. "More than fifty years ago," he finally managed to whisper. "A half-century in the past."

"Ethan Phillips, *bani* Euthanatos," read Master Nicodemus, "came to the Archives seeking information about his missing lover, Scarlett Dancer, an Archmage of the Order of Hermes. The woman had disappeared several weeks earlier and all efforts to find her had proven unsuccessful. Searching for any possible clue, Phillips remembered that Dancer once mentioned spending several days in the Archives. He arrived here determined to investigate what she had researched. It was a tenuous thread, but it was his only hope."

"Were you able to help?" asked Seventeen. Unbidden, an image of the woman he had seen in the Ways rose phantom-like before his eyes. It was difficult to realize that he was remembering someone he had last seen more than fifty years before.

"Of course," said Nicodemus, annoyed. "Are ye

implying I couldna manage my records? The lady read three books during her visit, and consulted six others. Rare ones they were, filled with the darkest lore ever put on paper. But I make no judgments. I am an archivist, not a censor."

"Sorry," said Seventeen. Master Nicodemus's mood changed as quickly as he turned pages in his ledger. "I meant no disrespect. Please don't mistake my bewilderment for lack of manners. Everything is so strange to me. My life, my memory, began only a few weeks ago. Please continue with what you were saying."

Nicodemus nodded, his features softening. "Aye, I know what it is like to forget. Ye have my sympathy. Sometimes, all a man has left is his memories. All of the volumes Mistress Scarlett consulted dealt with one topic. She wanted to know all there was to know about the Realm called Malfeas."

"Malfeas," repeated Seventeen. He was not surprised. "And were there any particular inhabitants of that unholy Realm in which she expressed particular interest?"

"I think, from the tone of yer voice," said Nicodemus, "ye already know the answer to that question. Mistress Scarlett sought to learn all she could about the dread rulers of that land, the Maeljin Incarna."

With a sigh, Seventeen rose from his seat. "Thank you for your patience, Master Nicodemus. I must leave. My friends are probably wondering what's taking me so long. For now, please do me a favor and don't mention our conversation to anyone. I prefer it remain confidential."

"Of course," said Nicodemus. He stood up and escorted Seventeen to the door. "A strange affair, I must admit. Telling ye twice the same information, a half-century apart. Do the facts serve your purpose?"

"I don't know," said Seventeen. "I just don't know."

His companions were waiting for him in the foyer of the Archives. Sam Haine was engaged in a heated discussion with Albert on the benefits of cigar smoking, while Shadow of the Dawn sat on a bench in lotus position, her eyes staring into nothingness.

"About time, son," said Sam Haine. "We best be getting back to Kallikos and Marianna. Always a good idea to look your finest when addressing the Council of Nine. Don't want them bigwigs thinkin' we're a band of ragamuffins."

"I strongly doubt they will," said Albert, chuckling. "But Sam is right. We should be going."

As before, Sam and Albert led the way, with Seventeen and Shadow of the Dawn following close behind.

"Was your conversation with Nicodemus a success?" Shadow asked Seventeen as they walked briskly through huge gardens of red roses. "Was he able to answer your questions?"

"He provided me with answers," said Seventeen, "but they merely raise new, more troublesome, questions."

Shadow nodded. "The Wheel of Drahma turns. It

never ceases moving. One cycle ends, another begins."

They continued to walk, Seventeen's thoughts deep and dark. Finally, he could no longer contain his worries.

"Tell me, Shadow," he asked, his voice low so their companions couldn't hear, "do you truly care for me?"

The warrior-maiden glanced at him and smiled. "Do you think I am some Tokyo girl, quick to give her kisses to the first man she sees?" she asked, sounding amused.

"No, of course not," said Seventeen. "But you don't really know me. My past is a mystery. Even I'm not sure of myself anymore. It seems possible, perhaps probable, that before I lost my memory, I made some evil bargains."

"Who you were before," said Shadow of the Dawn, her tone turning serious, "does not matter to me. That person no longer exists. If you must seek out the truth, let me travel with you. If you must face evil, let us face it together."

With her words, Seventeen realized that no matter what happened, he was no longer alone.

<u>Chapter Twelve</u>

Alone in his office, deep in the bowels of the Everwell Chemical Plant, Enzo Giovanni sat on a massive chair made of fine mahogany covered with purple velvet and stitched with gold thread. He liked to think of the seat as his throne. Not yet, he knew, but someday, he would wield power greater than any king had ever imagined.

Four flights down beneath the streets, Enzo's sanctum was a large square room with ceiling, walls and floor made of gray cement. Its only furnishings consisted of his throne, a wide mahogany table and several other wooden chairs covered with black leather. The lighting was low and dim, bulbs recessed in the low ceiling. A single door accessed the chamber. Enzo disliked unannounced visitors. As president of Everwell Chemicals and a member of the Board of Directors of the secret Pentex Corporation, Enzo highly valued his privacy. Others who had been less cautious had paid the ultimate price.

It was shortly before midnight and he awaited the arrival of his cousin, Montifloro, due at the hour. Enzo's lips parted in a knowing smile. He suspected Montifloro might be a little late. Though one of the undead, a vampire like himself, his cousin still retained a passion for mortal women. It was a fatal flaw in his character, and one that Enzo had exploited to the fullest over the past few days.

Montifloro had been sent by Pietro Giovanni from their family headquarters in Venice to spy on Enzo, and to discover if he had turned traitor to Clan Giovanni. One of the most cunning and devious members of the family, Montifloro was a skilled investigator who rarely missed a clue. However, his unnatural desires betrayed him. Instead of searching for the truth about Everwell Chemicals and Enzo's acquisition of the company, Montifloro had spent all of his waking hours with Enzo's new assistant, Ms. Hope. A dark-haired beauty, the stunning young woman had captivated his cousin. Just as Enzo had expected.

There was a knock on the door. "Enter," cried Enzo, not bothering to rise. It could only be Montifloro.

Other than the lights, there was nothing electrical or mechanical in the entire room. It was a sterile, lifeless environment—a cement tomb—which perfectly suited Enzo. Tonight, though the weather outside was hot and humid, the room was icy cold. In the far corner of the room, a dark mist seethed just beyond the glow of the dim yellow lights. Enzo wondered if a bulb might be out, then dismissed the blackness as unimportant as his cousin came through the doorway.

"Sorry for my lateness," said Montifloro, hurrying toward the throne. "Your lovely assistant was showing me the algae growth tanks on the third floor and I lost track of time."

"No matter," said Enzo, waving Montifloro to one of the black leather chairs. "How goes your investigation? Is everything in order? Is Ms. Hope cooperating fully? If not, I can find you someone who has been with the company longer, who knows more about the operations of the firm."

"No, no," said Montifloro, shaking his head. He appeared distressed at the thought. "That won't be necessary. Hope's assistance has proven to be quite satisfactory. She is extremely intelligent. An amazing woman, Enzo. Truly amazing."

"Quite the beauty, hey Montifloro?" said Enzo, chuckling. "You always had an eye for the ladies. That long dark hair, those exotic features, that lush figure. Looking at her, I sometimes wish I were still mortal."

"She has her charms," said Montifloro, speaking slowly. "I have never encountered a woman like her before. She is temptation personified."

"Too bad Pietro refuses the Embrace to any but members of the clan," said Enzo, casually. "Think of Ms. Hope as one of the Kindred. As one of the Damned, her beauty would last forever. Immortal. Undying. Instead, she is doomed to grow old and wrinkled. Her beauty will fade with age, while her mind grows feeble. Death is a terrible price, my cousin."

"Pietro only follows the dictates of the clan elders," said Montifloro. "I am sure he has little say in such matters."

"Nonsense," said Enzo. "Pietro is the master of the Mausoleum. The clan elders no longer trouble themselves with earthly matters. Despite Pietro's protests to the contrary, he, in truth, runs Clan Giovanni. As chairman of the board of directors, he controls the family wealth. And in this world, both the living and the undead are slaves to the power of the dollar."

Enzo paused, gathering his will. He didn't need to change Montifloro's beliefs, just bend his opinions in a different direction. "Consider the evidence, my dear cousin. Was he not the one who forced our clan into the long, bitter feud with the Mafia? What about our alliance with the French in World War Two? Again, the result of Pietro's maneuvering. And in an act without precedent in Giovanni affairs, did he not send you here to investigate my actions?"

"But Pietro claims he acts in the best interests of our family," said Montifloro.

"Does he?" replied Enzo. "Or does he act in the best interest of Pietro Giovanni?"

"Pietro is the chairman of the Mausoleum, Enzo," said Montifloro. "He is dedicated to the aims and goals of the clan. Your recent intrigues have you dancing with shadows."

"Perhaps," said Enzo, knowing it was time to stop pushing. A few more days with Ms. Hope would change Montifloro's mind more than any argument. "Continue your investigations, my cousin. At least I know I can trust you to submit a truthful report. Go, now. I am sure the charming Ms. Hope waits."

"Honor over death," said Montifloro, rising to his feet.

"Honor over death," repeated Enzo as his cousin turned and left the chamber. Once, the clan motto had meant something to him. Now he found it ridiculous.

"Honor over death?" echoed a deep, gravelly voice from a spot a few feet behind the black leather chair Montifloro had occupied only a few moments before. The invisible speaker laughed. "What a noble sentiment."

"Ezra," said Enzo, peering with narrowed eyes at the chair, "how long have you been here?"

"I arrived a few moments after your cousin," said the short, gray-haired man materializing out of nothingness. His thick hair hung in tangles, while his dark eyes sparkled with strange light. "It seemed best not to reveal myself until he departed. So I eavesdropped."

"A truly astonishing power, this ability of yours to pass from place to place," said Enzo. "Being able to vanish in an instant makes you invulnerable to attack."

"Unfortunately," said Ezra, "it is also a talent easily blocked by another willworker. In a battle between two mages, flight is usually impossible. The only retreat is death."

"A shame," declared Enzo, thinking the exact opposite. He preferred knowing his ally's weaknesses. Though he and Ezra plotted together, Enzo did not trust his partner. The gray-haired wizard controlled incredible powers, but he was demented. Working with him was like walking on a tightrope over a pool of hungry sharks. One wrong step could prove fatal.

"So," he said to Ezra, a touch of sarcasm in his voice, "Were you satisfied with my performance?"

Ezra smiled, giving his features a satanic cast. "I thought you sounded quite sincere. The honor of the clan and all that nonsense. Poor Montifloro is too devious for his own good. He sees plots everywhere. You've raised serious doubts in his mind about Pietro's behavior. Especially since his wishes run in the opposite direction. All that remains is for Hope to continue to press him on the Embrace. He soon shall be ours."

"There still remains Madeleine," said Enzo.

"The Dagger of the Giovanni," said Ezra, chuckling. "As I told you, she has her own reasons to want Pietro destroyed. Like most Kindred, she is loyal to herself above all others. Pull the right strings and Madeleine will dance to our tune. She will have no choice."

"Do not make the mistake of underestimating Pietro's granddaughter," cautioned Enzo. "Don Caravelli thought he could break the Dagger of the Giovanni. Dust marks his passing."

Moving without a sound, Ezra walked across the room to the door. He yanked it open. No one was on the other side. The antechamber was empty.

"Your secretary," he said, returning to the black leather chair, "the woman called Ms. Hargroves. Is she working tonight?"

"No," said Enzo. "She requested the evening off. She has a friend visiting the city and wants to show him around."

"Strange," said Enzo. "I have the distinct feeling of being watched." The madman shook his head. "Do you sense the presence as well?"

"It's merely the weight of thousands of tons of rock surrounding us," said Enzo. "Nothing more."

Privately, he thought it yet another example of his ally's encroaching insanity. Week by week, Ezra sank further and further into paranoia. Trafficking with the darkness exacted a terrible price. Enzo considered himself fortunate that as a vampire he was immune to such mental aberrations. His actions were motivated entirely by greed and the lust for power.

"How proceeds the rest of our plan?" he asked Ezra, intent on interrupting the mage's latest suspicion. If Ezra somehow concluded that Ms. Hargroves couldn't be trusted, her life was over. Enzo preferred not to lose his most efficient employee to his ally's delusions.

"Good," said the gray-haired man, his mood changing instantly. "Very, very good. Still, there are numerous complications that must be dealt with. Do you remember the debacle at the Casey cabal?"

"Of course," said Enzo. "I sent Mattias and the Knights of Pain to eliminate the prisoner who escaped from the Gray Collective. The fool blamed supernatural intervention for that miserable disaster."

"The fugitive still lives," said Enzo. "He calls himself Prisoner Seventeen, but his real name is Ethan Phillips. It is fortunate for us that he does not know the full extent of his powers as a willworker. Still, he is a formidable opponent, due to the experiments performed on him by the fools of the Gray Collective. The man must be destroyed. Utterly and completely destroyed."

"Why?" asked Enzo. "What possible threat could a single mortal present to our ambitions?"

Ezra didn't answer. Instead, his lips pressed tightly together, he leaned on the edge of the massive mahogany table in front of Enzo's throne. The wood shivered as if pressed by an immense weight. Enzo's eyes widened and he opened his mouth in protest. But he acted too late. With a crash that rang through the cement chamber, the huge table collapsed in a ruin of splintered wood.

"Termites?" asked Ezra, and he laughed. "Or perhaps the stress on the table legs suddenly proved to be too much. I guess we will never know the reason. It's a mystery."

The madman glared at Enzo. His eyes blazed like furnaces. "Do I make myself clear, Enzo? I want no misunderstanding. You are to obliterate this man, Ethan Phillips, and all those who travel with him. I don't care how you do it, or whom you use to do it. All that matters to me—and to our patron, Lord Steel—is that the task is done."

"Don't worry, my friend," said Enzo hurriedly. "You know I always follow your orders to the letter. All my efforts, and all the efforts of those I command, will focus on this nuisance. Do you know if he is still in the area?"

"At present, he is not on this plane of existence," Ezra replied. "But he will return shortly."

"When he does, I will be ready," Enzo muttered. "He shall not escape me."

"Good," said Ezra. "Now I must depart. My work for Lord Steel is never done."

"Good hunting," said Enzo.

With a nod, the mad mage was gone.

Enzo shook his head, but refrained from saying another word. Even a thousand miles away, Ezra possessed the power to hear remarks made about him. Enzo grimaced. He was becoming as paranoid as his insane ally. Cautiously, he looked around the room. It was empty. Even the dark shadow in the far corner had disappeared.

He rose from his throne and headed for the door. All of this talking had made him thirsty. Time to summon the Grim Brothers and take a drive to the beach.

Chapter Thirteen

They arrived at the Council Chamber shortly after a spectacular sunset. Seventeen wasn't sure how the illusion of a sun and two moons was achieved, but he accepted it as part of the magick of the Realm.

The meeting room was huge, capable of seating hundreds. The chamber was visually stunning, with mosaic floors, marble sculptures and spectacular carvings. Many hundreds of feet above the room rose the gigantic dome. A soft glow of light, magickal in origin, filled the entire chamber.

In the center of the room the Table Cenacle rested, constructed from the same blue bodhi wood used in building the Songgwang-sa Meditation Temple. Above the table floated a massive crystal sphere that Sam Haine called the Saxum Oculorum.

The table was surrounded by ten Seats of Power. Each chair was carved entirely from a huge gemstone that symbolized one of the Spheres of magick. Inlaid in a raised extension of the seats a symbol of that

Sphere glowed. Nine of the seats were reserved for the Nine Traditions. The tenth chair was carved from onyx and was reserved for outside envoys.

"Chair never had a symbol," said Sam Haine, whispering to Seventeen as they took seats in the vast gallery that surrounded the Table Cenacle. "Then just recently, without explanation, that strange sigil you can see appeared on it. All the Traditions tried to claim it was their doing, but nobody really knows how it happened. And lately, when nobody's around, the ten chairs have been rearranging themselves. Damned weird foolishness." The white-haired man's eyes twinkled. "But interesting."

"Lots of people here tonight," said Seventeen, looking around at the gallery. There were at least five hundred people present. "Is it usually so crowded?"

"Rarely," said Albert, his dry tone making it clear he did not approve. "Marianna packed the house by spreading rumors of a dramatic revelation this evening. Many of the Council meetings are not open to the general populace. But others can be attended by anyone interested. Few usually are."

"Most mages feel they got better things to do with their time," said Sam. "Remember, son, willworkers are real people. No different in many ways than the usual suspects. For all of their power, all of their vision, they're still a pretty self-centered bunch. Oftentimes, they lose sight of the big picture, get involved in petty political squabbling. Form little cabals devoted to a specific idea or attitude. Act like a bunch of headstrong teenagers. That's why I avoid doin' much joining. Can't stand the games. If you ever wonder why the Nine Traditions can't defeat the Technocracy, Seventeen, politics is the answer. Plain and simple. Ben Franklin had it right about hanging."

Seventeen had no idea what Sam meant but decided pursuing the matter would be unwise. Instead, he studied the small group of willworkers standing in a group talking beside the Table Cenacle.

"Six outta nine," said Sam Haine. "That ain't bad. Marianna really did old Kallikos proud. Though I still suspect it's a waste of time."

"Do you know who they are?" asked Seventeen. Sam Haine at times seemed an inexhaustible source of information. The Changing Man had been around, seen most everything, done it all. He was quite amazing.

"The short, thin Korean man with the shaved head, dressed in a purple robe, is Hymeny~ong S~unim," said Sam Haine. "He's the voice of the Akashic Brotherhood on the Council. Pleasant sort of character, though he has a fondness for jokes that don't make much sense."

"I met him once," said Shadow of the Dawn—her first words since entering the Council Chamber. "He is very wise."

"Can say the same for most everyone on the current Council," said Sam Haine, "except of course for that snake, Vargas São Cristavao."

He gestured at the withered, bony man with a hunched back and scarred features. Dressed in a fancy robe, São Cristavao sat in the Seat of Forces. He appeared impatient, anxious for the meeting to begin.

"He's an obnoxious old bird," said Sam. "Had a tough life, no question about that, but he's no charmer. Insults anyone he considers below his rank on the social ladder, and that's just about everybody. There was talk of replacing him with a young upstart, Gillan, but at present, that whole situation's being debated by the Masters of the Order of Hermes. So São Cristavao's still here. Of all the Council members, he's the most political. And you know what I think of politicians."

"You already know Marianna," said Albert. Their hostess from the afternoon wore slightly more than before, but not much. "The woman she is speaking with is Najjda Bantu, a close friend of mine. Like me, she was born in Africa. Though she appears only sixty or seventy, she is over three centuries old. Najjda represents the Celestial Chorus and fights hard for the poor people of all nations. She is a great inspiration to all who believe in the sanctity of the human spirit."

"The tall, tough-looking man in western clothes is Tom 'Laughing Eagle' Smithson," said Sam. "I'm not sure about the laughing part, as I never thought of him as having much of a sense of humor. Quiet and thoughtful, and he looks like he'd be tough man in a fight. An Indian shaman, he represents the Dreamspeakers on the Council."

"When we first entered, you spoke for a few minutes to the woman next to him," said Seventeen. "I assume she represents the Verbena."

Sam nodded. "Lady Charlotte Quay," he said. "I've known her ever since she was a teenager. Charlotte's gone through some difficult times, but she's a survivor. I like her. We're two of a kind."

"They may not be the most powerful willworkers in the Tellurian, Seventeen," said Albert, "but these are six of the most important. Kallikos has his audience. It will be interesting to see if they listen to his warning."

"Speaking of Kallikos," said Seventeen, "where is he?"

"Waitin' to make a big entrance, I'm sure," said Sam. "Our friend has a sense of the dramatic. Soon as Porthos arrives, things should start sizzling."

"Porthos?" said Seventeen. "You mentioned him this morning. Who is he and why is he so important?"

Blue lightning flashed at the far end of the hall. A black funnel cloud ten feet wide, a hundred feet high, appeared out of nothingness. From its center walked a gaunt man of indeterminate age. He wore a gray topcoat, black trousers and a white shirt. His long black hair hung in unkempt strings to his shoulders. A pair of thick glasses sat on the bridge of his nose. To Seventeen, the stranger looked like an absent-minded school teacher. Except for the fact that he emerged unscathed from a cyclone which swiftly disappeared after his exit. And he bristled with energy.

"Speak of the devil," murmured Sam Haine. "Porthos might not be the most powerful Tradition mage alive. I ain't sure. But the old boy's in the running."

Robert Weinberg

"I am here," announced Porthos, waving a hand at the Council members. "I assume you're ready to begin? Hurry, hurry up. I don't have all night, you know. What is this emergency meeting all about? Why did you need me tonight? My life is busy enough without these foolish interruptions." He stared at São Cristavao. "I thought I smelled rotting fish in the chamber. My mistake. Now I must make amends to the fish."

A pile of rotting fish suddenly appeared on the the table in front of Porthos. He bowed, spoke an eloquent apology, and waved his hand. The fish disappeared. The smell did not.

"He's a feisty old bird," whispered Sam, "and I kinda suspect he's not all there. So be careful dealing with him. Porthos means well, but then, so did Jack the Ripper."

"Please, Master Porthos," said Marianna, stifling a smile and motioning to the chairs. "No quarrels tonight. Everyone, be seated. Porthos, do me the honor and sit by me. We must begin. An important matter needs to be presented to the Council. Every moment is precious."

Porthos, taking the chair next to Marianna, muttered something to Tom Smithson. The shaman nodded and his lips crinkled in the slightest of smiles. São Cristavao glared at Porthos. *If looks could kill*, Seventeen decided, *Porthos would be lying dead on the floor.*

"And what is so important as to require the attention of the Council of Nine?" asked Porthos, seemingly oblivious to São Cristavao's anger. "Another attempt...."

"I asked Marianna to summon the Council." It was Kallikos, standing at the head of the stairs leading into the chamber. The Time Master wore a long blue silk robe decorated with elaborate stitching in gold and silver. On his head sat a turban of the same color. Several bright gems decorated Kallikos's right ear, shifting color from gold to emerald to ruby red. His long hair was neatly combed and tied back in a long ponytail hanging down his back. The tattoos on his fingers, always present, somehow seemed tonight to be more intense, almost alive. His golden skin burned with inner light. Kallikos was a commanding, dynamic figure. He radiated power as he slowly descended the steps to the Table Cenacle.

Porthos was on his feet. "My eyes deceive me," he declared, sounding bewildered, shocked. "This vision cannot be. You are dead. You have been dead for two hundred years."

Kallikos laughed. "You speak as though time meant something to me. Reports of my death, as a famous author once remarked, are greatly exaggerated."

"Who is this overdressed mystery man?" asked Vargas São Cristavao, his tone snide, almost insulting. "He looks familiar, but I don't ever remember meeting him before. Who is he and what does he want with the Council of Nine Mystick Traditions?"

"He looks familiar, my dear São Cristavao," said Marianna, sweetness and sarcasm mixing in her voice, "because paintings of him decorate chambers throughout this building and this Realm. He is part of our history. Though for the past century he has called himself Kallikos, he once used another name. You never met him, oh learned scholar, because his greatest work was done before your birth. This is the Time Master Akrites Salonikas. As to why he has returned to Horizon after five hundred years, I will let him tell you that himself."

"Akrites?" repeated São Cristavao, his face twisted in a sneer of disbelief. "Nonsense! You claim this impostor is the great seer, one of the original Nine, a member of the First Cabal?" He snorted in disgust. "A silk-clad, long-haired refugee from one of your tasteless orgies? I believe no such thing."

"Told you," whispered Sam Haine to Seventeen. "Damned insolent. And incredibly stupid."

Kallikos froze on the steps, his face turning slowly till he stared directly at his accuser. "Even in my self-imposed exile in the most barren, desolate lands," he said, his voice calm, deliberate, "...your fame snaked its path to my ears. I see now that your bile was not understated. You are a bitter, petty man, filled with your self-importance. The years have not been kind to you, little man. If you had not caused so much trouble amongst your fellow magicians, I would perhaps feel some sympathy for you. Instead, my heart is filled with contempt."

São Cristavao licked his lips, suddenly appearing unsure of himself. "If what I..." he began, but Kallikos gave him no chance to continue.

"You doubt my identity? You question that I am

Akrites Salonikas, a member of the First Cabal? Porthos, who knew me then, can tell you differently. Or Marianna, whom I have advised for nearly two centuries, will bear me witness. No matter. I see in your eyes you would dismiss their claims as part of some conspiracy aimed against you and those who stand behind you in the shadows."

Kallikos paused, his voice gaining in power. As before, though he did not speak loudly, the entire chamber resonated with the force of his words.

"My appearance this night, in this chamber, I foresaw in a vision nearly five hundred years ago. Some of the details have changed, as the future is not stable but in a constant state of flux. Still, most details remain the same. What my horrified eyes viewed centuries before has finally come to pass." Kallikos's voice turned cold and grim. "A great war for the control of reality itself is about to begin. There will be many casualties. My death is fast approaching. And so, Vargas São Cristavao, is yours."

São Cristavao's face turned ash-white. "I refuse to believe such foolishness," he replied, but his tone belied the words.

"Prophecy is a double-edged sword," said Kallikos. "It cuts deeply two ways. The ability to view the future is a blessing. As it is a terrible curse. Again and again, my dreams have been haunted by my own death. All of my efforts, all of my plans, could not halt the relentless march of destiny. There is nothing more I can do other than watch events unfold, knowing each one brings me closer and closer to the end."

"It's one thing to wonder when you're gonna die," muttered Sam Haine. "Quite another to know exactly when it's gonna happen. And how, and where. Enough to drive a man crazy."

"A war, Master Akrites?" said Hymeny~ong S~unim, his tone polite and respectful. "I assume you refer to the ongoing struggle with the Technocracy? We are about to enter a new phase of battle?"

"I wish it were so simple," said Kallikos—Seventeen could not think of him by any other name—as he walked over to the seated archmagi. Instead of taking a chair, he remained standing, addressing the Council from between Marianna and Porthos. "The Ascension War has spawned a greater threat than the Order of Reason. In their haste to create a new weapon to destroy us, the Technocrats have given life to a being that may plunge all humanity into eternal darkness."

"Impossible," declared São Cristavao, the color slowly returning to his cheeks. "We are not schoolchildren afraid of the dark. Has this menace a name? Or in all of your long years alone, was that forgotten?"

"The designers of this being called it the Ascension Warrior," said Kallikos. "But they were unaware of their creation's true identity. Our enemy has a name. A name that lives in infamy. Its name is…"

"Heylel Teomim, bani Solificati," came a voice from the top of the stairs.

Seventeen's eyes swung around, as did those of every other person in the Council chamber. There, standing on the first step, was a slender young blond woman. Jenni Smith. She looked around the room as if searching for someone. Her gaze met Seventeen's and held it. Smiling, she nodded, almost as if in triumph. Then, moving without the least evidence of concern, she descended the stairs to the Table Cenacle.

Chapter Fourteen

"Another member of the First Cabal?" said São Cristavao, sarcasm dripping from his voice. "Will such miracles never cease? I feel like I am in the midst of a children's puppet show, filled with deception and sleight of hand…"

"Quiet, young mackerel," said Porthos. He appeared puzzled. "This woman is a stranger to me. But she does not come alone. Lines of force stretch from her to a place far past Horizon."

"Damned straight," said Sam Haine to Seventeen. "Look at her features, son. Notice how they're flickering, starting to change. That girl's linked with someone not here. I have a bad, *bad* feeling about all this. Appears to me that our pattern-clone's about to make a statement. Just like Kallikos warned."

A cold chill passed through Seventeen. A vision of rivers of black blood swept through his mind. Unseen forces were stirring. The darkness was rising.

Reaching the bottom of the stairs, Jenni Smith walked straight to the Council table. Without invitation, she pulled back the mysterious tenth chair and sat down.

"Such arrogance," snapped São Cristavao, his white features twisted in anger. "How dare you?"

Jenni said nothing. Instead, she leaned back in the chair and folded her hands over her chest. Slowly, her features began to change. Her face seemed to melt into putty, flowing into itself, reforming into a new visage. At the same time, her body lengthened, grew, transformed. A soft murmur of astonishment ran through the crowd. Not about the shapechanging— a talent practiced by many on Horizon, including Marianna—but by the new face revealed. A hush fell across the assembly. Even São Cristavao seemed struck dumb in amazement.

The features were exactly as Seventeen remembered. But now they were overflowing with life. Powerful, intense, filled with great emotion. The face of a demigod. Or a demon. The inhuman, imperious face of the pattern-clone.

Jenni Smith transformed, spoke. But it was no longer her voice, but the smooth, musical tones of the creation of the Gray Collective.

"Our name is Heylel Teomim, renunciate of the Solificati, and, as some have called us, *barabbi*. Five hundred and twenty-seven years ago, we last spoke to the Council of Nine Traditions. Tonight, after half a millennium, we speak once again."

Heylel Teomim. The name rang in Seventeen's mind. From deep within his subconscious mind rose the title, *Thoabath.* Abomination. Heylel Teomim, the leader of the First Cabal. And their Betrayer to the Order of Reason, those willworkers who became known centuries later as the Technocracy. Heylel, the most despised traitor in the history of the Nine Traditions, reborn as the pattern-clone.

"Damned if it ain't possible," whispered Sam Haine. "That face is sexless, neutral. Could be male or female or even a combination. According to the tales, Heylel was an incredible being with the minds of both a man and a woman sharing the same body. 'We,' not 'I.'"

"Five hundred years ago, we were accused of being a traitor to the Nine Traditions," continued the pattern-clone, the voice claiming to be that of Heylel Teomim. "In our last statement to the Council, we refuted those charges and proved them false. If you doubt us, read our words as transcribed by those present. We know that they have been preserved, have been printed, have been debated for centuries. Read them and know we acted not out of anger, not out of jealousy or rage, not out of hatred. We acted from our deep concern that the Nine Traditions were doomed to fall beneath the united strength of the Order of Reason."

The being addressing the Council blazed with raw energy. "We warned you that the Order of Reason was growing at a frightening pace, and that though they were many, they worked as one. Their vision was quickly changing the world. And we foresaw that if the Nine Traditions did not put aside their differences, their hatreds, their squabbling, that magick would disappear before heartless logic. We went to our destruction gladly, hoping that our act of betrayal had succeeded in uniting the feuding Traditions so that they would merge together, act as brothers and sisters and fight a common foe. We sacrificed ourselves, and the lives of our dearest friends, the members of the First Cabal, in hopes of accomplishing this goal. Read, and remember."

"That is exactly what Heylel claimed in his final address to the Council," murmured Albert. "The truth behind those sentiments, of course, is subject to a fair amount of skepticism."

"The original Heylel probably believed exactly what he said," whispered Sam Haine. "Always found that people are willing to commit the most heinous crimes in the name of doing a good deed. Like I've said before, the road to Hell is paved with good intentions. Big question ain't if Heylel meant what he said, but if the clone is actually him reborn. Or someone just pretending. The real Heylel got himself Gilguled—wiped out and scattered by the greatest mages in the Council. I doubt that's the real Great Betrayer down there."

"Although," Albert countered, "anything is possible."

"When you destroyed us," Heylel continued, "we welcomed death, for the guilt of our crimes against those in the First Cabal weighed heavily on our hearts. We believed in no god, nor in any devil. Remaining alive, we faced a lifetime of self-torment, knowing that we had brought death to those we held most dear. With our warning to the Council, we embraced the destruction of our souls and our body with gladness. But all was not as it seemed."

Kallikos's features were pale. He remained silent, his eyes fixed on the pattern-clone's features. To Seventeen, the seer appeared to be...searching.

"Though we did not possess the gift of prophecy like my dearest friend, Akrites," said Heylel, "we could already see that the brief moment of unity brought about by the so-called Great Betrayal was already fading. That what we had hoped to accomplish was doomed to failure. That our efforts had been entirely in vain. That we would be blamed for the ills that plagued the Traditions, but nothing would be done to correct those flaws. So, though we welcomed death, we made secret plans for our eventual resurrection. We knew that someday the moment would come when only our leadership could save humanity. That time is now."

"Stories said Heylel had an ego the size of Horizon," declared Sam Haine softly. "Seems those tales were true enough."

"What rubbish," said São Cristavao, pushing back his chair from the table and making as if to rise. "I have heard enough of this gibberish. No one returns from Gilgul. The two souls of Heylel the Abomination were ripped from his body and destroyed. His body was ravaged by fire and ice, and the ashes scattered to the winds of Horizon. Your story is filled with lies."

"*SIT!*" thundered the voice of Heylel, and the fury of that voice dropped São Cristavao back into his throne, his face blank with fright. "Enough of your doubts and petty dislikes. We did not give you permission to leave this meeting. You may depart when and if we allow it. Not before."

Porthos cackled, a shrill, tittering laugh, not entirely sane. "You're either Heylel or his ghost," said the disheveled archmagus. "He also had little patience for fools."

Shaking back his unkempt mane of hair, Porthos seemed to gather energy to himself. The air in the council chamber suddenly crackled with static electricity. "I could destroy you right now, sitting there," he declared. "Burn you into ashes. Give me one reason I shouldn't."

"Because it would serve no purpose," answered Heylel. "Kill our servant and another will take her place. Our message will be heard. And beware what you say. Your powers have increased manyfold since last we spoke, Porthos, but they are still no match for ours."

"Enough threats," said Tom Smithson, speaking for the first time. "You say you have a message, One-Who-Calls-Himself-Heylel. Present it. The Council of Nine is listening."

"So be it," said the voice of the pattern-clone. "Listen to our words and prepare, for your answer will decide the fate of the Nine Traditions. Hear now the new testament of Heylel Teomim, whom you named *barabbi*."

Seventeen glanced at Shadow of the Dawn. Her eyes were clear, her features serene. The warrior maid could have been at a picnic for all of the emotion she displayed. A flicker of a smile passed across her lips as, sensing Seventeen's gaze, her eyes looked to his. Silently she reached out a hand and wrapped her fingers around his.

"In our final testament, we told you to unite, to join the Nine Traditions into an ordered, unified whole, for that was the only true Path to Ascension. Otherwise, we warned, the Order of Reason was fated to destroy you. Our words, we feared in that last speech, were spoken to those incapable of understanding the truth. We challenged you, five centuries ago, to prove us wrong. *You did not.*"

Heylel's voice was filled with contempt. "Instead of putting aside the differences that held you apart, you permitted them to grow, to divide you further. The Order of Reason grew until its beliefs defined reality, gained control of the Sleepers. The poor, the downtrodden, the helpless still remain. Their lot has not been changed, despite the passage of five hundred years. What of them? They remain ignored, forgotten. Who defends their interests, who helps raise them to Ascension?

"While you fought among yourselves, allowed ones such as this," and the speaker pointed at São Cristavao, "to gain control of the Traditions, the Cabal of Pure Thought evolved and advanced. The Technocracy, as they call themselves now, forced you back, put you on the defensive, won battle after battle in a war that continues to rage. Only their own internal strife has saved the Traditions from total annihilation. The fall of the First Cabal, the deaths that we caused in my hope of uniting the Traditions, meant nothing. We died in vain. That sacrifice must be righted."

"Utter…" began São Cristavao, then closed his mouth under the withering gaze of the pattern-clone.

"For five hundred years the Nine Traditions have fought the Order of Reason, the Technocracy, without victory. The dreams of the Primi have turned to dust. You have failed.

"The time to end this war has come. We have returned to do exactly that. The divisions that divide our ranks need to be broken down, dissolved. If this goal cannot be achieved from within, let it be done from without.

"We ask the Council of Nine to turn over their powers to us. We, Heylel Teomim, called *barabbi* and Abomination, possess the necessary will and the necessary strength to bring this senseless struggle to a close. Install us as your leader and we will lead you to Ascension."

"Never," said São Cristavao immediately. "Never, never, never. I would die before submitting to such utter nonsense."

"That choice," said Heylel, "is entirely yours."

"The world has gone through enormous changes in five hundred years," said Tom Smithson. "What once might have succeeded is no longer possible. Simple solutions do not exist in such a complex world. The Technocracy is an octopus, its tentacles enveloping every facet of the Sleepers' lives. Returning magick to the world is a struggle that requires patience."

"Five centuries of patience are enough," declared Heylel. "You have repeated excuses so often that you believe them true. Enough of them. Give us leadership of the Traditions and there will be no more delays, no more excuses. There will only be triumph."

"A noble dream," said Porthos. "Unattainable perhaps, but quite noble. Still, I feel confused. Exactly how do you expect to achieve what thousands of mages working for centuries could not, Heylel? Perhaps your powers are greater than mine. Perhaps not. But the combined might of those present at this table could press you flat. If all our efforts against the Technocracy have failed, how do you propose to defeat them? What miraculous plan do you offer?"

"We have our ways," replied Heylel. "Alliances to be forged, truces to be erected. Powers to be awakened. Forces who would come to our aid only if asked."

"Devils and demons, perhaps?" Porthos inquired. His eyes widened, his expression darkened. "At his trial, Heylel was accused of consorting with creatures from the Pit. I never believed such charges. Could I have been wrong?"

"Make no rash judgments," said Heylel. "No gods exist. Nor devils. We cannot join with those who have no basis in reality. We seek aid from those who have existed side by side with mankind for millennia. For the proper price, the Nine Traditions can become invincible."

"The right price?" spoke Kallikos. "Our souls? Or our blood?"

"The cost of victory requires sacrifice," said Heylel. "We once paid with our lives. If necessary, we will do the same again."

"Stirring words, but empty ones." It was Najjda Bantu, speaking for the first time. "My people have suffered for thousands, not hundreds, of years. We have heard promise after promise, seen savior after savior, and our lot remains the same. Now you come, a new messiah, with more words, more promises. The poor cry out for food, not Ascension. Show me how you will aid them, and I will be your most fervent disciple. But mere words are not enough. Show me, do not tell me."

"Najjda speaks wisely, as always," declared Lady Charlotte Quay. "No matter who leads, the poor stay always poor. Just as women have always been treated like shit for being born female. The world hasn't changed much since ancient times. Many of us are still denied our rights only because of our sex. Promises might sway the young and naïve. Not me. I've been fucked over too many barrels to keep believing in Santa Claus. I'm no longer naïve, and I've never been stupid. I know the taste of ashes. You come to us out of nowhere, making claims, spinning dreams, but giving us no proof." Lady Charlotte shook her head. "I'm ready to drop-kick the status quo, that's for damned sure, but I'm not hopping from one cold bed to another. Like my sister says, Heylel or whatever your name is, put up or shut up."

"It appears," said Porthos, "that sentiment at this table runs against your wishes, Heylel. What now? Shall we vote on your proposal?"

"We expected no less," replied Heylel. "What dictator ever gave up his throne willingly? We had hoped this Council possessed the wisdom to see beyond their own ambitions. But like your brethren of five hundred years ago, that is not the case. Nothing at all has changed. Nothing."

"Tell me, Heylel," said Kallikos suddenly, "what was the name of the hermit who perished by dire accident during our days together in the First Cabal?"

"Hermit?" said Heylel. "What hermit?"

"I thought you might ask that," Kallikos muttered.

"Your message has been presented, One-Who-Calls-Himself-Heylel," said Tom Smithson. "I believe I speak for the entire Council when I say that we reject...."

"Enough of this charade," interrupted São Cristavao angrily. "This abomination has made serious threats against me. The honor of the Council is at stake. Guards, seize the girl! We'll learn the truth about her mysterious benefactor quick enough."

Shadow of the Dawn no longer held Seventeen's hand. He caught a glimpse of the warrior maiden racing down the steps of the gallery.

"So much for the noble honor of the Council." Heylel scowled. A dozen guards, magicians all, rushed forward. As if in response, the overhead lights flickered. Then abruptly disappeared. Total blackness engulfed the Council chamber.

Blue lightning flashed. "I have her," shouted Porthos.

"Not her, *me*, you old fool!" exclaimed Lady Charlotte Quay.

"My apologies," said Porthos, with a laugh. Lightning flashed again. "So sorry."

"That wasn't me," cried Lady Charlotte. "Lights, lights!"

A heartbeat passed and then the illumination returned. Kallikos stood to one side of the tenth Council Chair. Shadow of the Dawn, gripping Whisper with both hands, was on the other. Not surprisingly, Jenni Smith, who had acted as the voice of Heylel, was not between them.

"Find the girl," snapped Lady Charlotte, her face flushed with anger. "She can't have gone far."

"Locate a shapechanger in a crowd?" said Tom Smithson. "Impossible."

"An entertaining diversion," said Porthos, running his long thin fingers through his black hair. "I found it all quite amusing. Perhaps now my warnings of changing times will be viewed by the Council with more respect. Even by such boorish individuals as São Cristavao."

"I don't think you need worry about any future disagreements with the representative of the Order of Hermes," said Kallikos. "Heylel was famed as the discoverer of the Philosopher's Stone. Some believed he possessed the golden touch. It may have been true."

São Cristavao sat in his chair, his face frozen in a mask of astonishment. Mouth open, eyes wide, he appeared ready to scream. But no sounds issued from the motionless figure. None could emerge from the throat of a statue.

During the instants that the lights were out, the Hermetic mage had undergone a frightening transformation. Flesh and blood, skin and bone had been changed from living tissue into solid gold. Vargas São Cristavao was gone. In his place sat an exact duplicate. A man of gold.

"How fitting," said Porthos, with a mad chuckle. He appeared delighted with São Cristavao's fate. "I always said the old buzzard was worth more dead than alive. Perhaps we could move his body to the front of this building. A reminder that politeness matters. Even among mages."

Chapter Fifteen

"Well, I guess we weren't the only ones who found out about Lauri Coup," said Ernest Nelson. He handed the morning paper to Sharon Reed. "Looks like we got here a little late."

Sharon stared at the headline. *Noted Cereal Chemist and Researcher Brutally Killed in Home Invasion* proclaimed the lead story. Below the bold print was a photo of a young woman's body sprawled out in the middle of a living room floor. The victim's head was bent at an unnatural angle, and her clothing was ripped to shreds. Though not apparent from the photo, the story made it clear that Dr. Coup had been terribly beaten by her assailants before her death. She had not, however, been raped, and there were no signs of torture. The apartment had been thoroughly ransacked. The newspaper quoted unnamed police sources as saying that the department suspected the killing was the work of a notorious girl gang located in the area. An arrest was promised shortly. Sharon knew that such remarks usually meant law enforcement officers had no clue to the attackers' identity. Lauri Coup's death would probably go down in the books as just another unsolved murder.

"I'm surprised she was allowed to live until now," said Sharon. "If the Nephandi are behind this plot, they usually don't leave loose ends dangling."

"No reason to kill her until someone started investigating," said Nelson. "Why draw attention to the woman by killing her? Might make the powers that be suspicious."

Their trip to Indianapolis had been as uneventful as it had been illegal. Every few hours, they pulled off the highway and stole a new vehicle, abandoning the previous one. Nelson insisted that they shouldn't keep any car too long. He was obsessive about being traced.

The cyborg, who had worked for years as a Technocratic assassin and special operative before his days at the Gray Collective, was equally adamant about not contacting any other Union members or Collectives for help. "No such thing as secure linkages any more," Nelson had declared while driving through Pennsylvania. "Soon as we surface, the sharks will be after us. Nephandi have infiltrated the Union and the Traditions. That's a fact of life. No real way of knowing who you can trust these days. Most of the time it doesn't matter. Only in situations where you're a target. Only way for us to stay alive is to stay hidden. When we need backup, I'll get us that. But until that situation arises, we maintain our cover. You and me. We can trust each other." He laughed. "At least, sort of. But nobody else."

Reluctantly, Sharon had been forced to agree. If the Reality Deviants had overrun an entire Technocrat station merely because John Doe had searched for information about the pattern-clone experiment, their mission was an obvious death trap. Nelson was right. The key to survival was not letting anyone know what they were doing.

"Well," she said. "What are we going to do now?"

"Maybe she left notes at work?" said Nelson. "Coup must have been part of a research team. Possible that she confided in one of the other members of her group. We could try to locate them."

Sharon nodded. "I never heard of her. And I was pretty well connected, knew most of the major players in the Convention. Coup wasn't a Research Director. Still, if she was the one who came up with the basic design work on the pattern-clone, she had to be pretty talented. Maybe she was a Research Associate. Could even have been a Primary Investigator."

"What's the difference?" asked Nelson.

"As an Associate, she would have worked for someone else. As an Investigator, she'd be in charge of her own laboratory." Sharon thought for a minute. "I should be able to access the Progenitor data bank without revealing my identity or location. There's a phone hookup that links me right to the central core computer. I can use Velma's code. After all," she added savagely, "she owes me."

Nelson shrugged. "Search'll probably send red flags flying all over the damned network. What the hell. We don't have any other leads. Still, if you learn anything important and we need to act, there's an old acquaintance I want to visit in the suburbs. Met him when I was stationed in Chicago for a few years."

"An old friend?" asked Sharon. "I didn't think you had any friends."

"Ha, ha," said Nelson. "I'm laughing. This old buzzard's everybody's buddy—if you got cash. His name is Tyrone Rhodes and he deals in weapons. High-powered stuff he sells to select clients. If we're going to investigate a murder, I want to be properly armed when we encounter the guilty parties. Somehow, I get the feeling they won't just surrender."

"Good point," said Sharon. "Wouldn't hurt to stop at a chemical supply store as well. They won't carry the poisons I use, but I can buy the proper supplies to mix my own."

Nelson laughed, this time for real. "Say what you want, Reed, but we're damned sure more alike than you think."

Two hours later, after side trips to replenish their weapon supplies, the Technocrats were on their way to the May Sinclair Laboratory in the northeast section of the city. According to Sharon's new computer readout, Sinclair Labs was a small independent genetic think-tank working on developing new and exciting food products for the Masses. More importantly, it was part of EcoR, a Progenitor Horizon Realm. Lauri Coup had been one of two Primary Investigators working at Sinclair. Her associate's name was Kurt Bylunt. There were also two students and a

Research Assistant assigned to the building. Sharon dismissed them as being unimportant.

"If Coup told anyone secrets, it was Bylunt," she asserted as Nelson navigated their automobile through downtown traffic. They were in a rental car now, as opposed to something stolen. In the city, the cyborg felt safer being strictly legal—though he had used one of John Doe's credit cards to secure the auto. Sharon didn't bother asking her companion how he had come by the plastic. Some mysteries were better just ignored. "I can't imagine she'd confide in anyone else there."

"Prejudice of command?" asked Nelson. "Research Directors only talk to Research Directors, Primary Investigators only socialize with their own, and so on and so on?"

"Not entirely," said Sharon. "Though there is a bit of minor social status associated with different levels in the Convention. More to do with age than skill, though. Except in the most unusual circumstances, it takes decades to rise to the level of Research Director. I was one of the youngest and I'm no teenager. Charles Reid, no relation and I'm pretty damned sure his real name isn't Reid, heads EcoR. Rumor has it that he's several hundred years old. Same is true for most of the RDs. Primary Investigators tend to be in their forties or fifties, though obviously in our Convention they might look a lot younger. Students are pretty much in their twenties. In the Progenitors, it's mostly how much you know and how long you've been with the Convention that determines your rank on the social ladder. Reid might fraternize with the PIs, but he's most comfortable with other Research Directors. Students can talk with their teachers, but the bonds are more business than social."

"Like you and Wade, huh?" asked Nelson, glancing at Sharon. He laughed coarsely. "I always figured the two of you were lovers. Screwing around in private."

Sharon grimaced. "Thanks for nothing. I prefer men, not other women. Velma was a dedicated assistant. She was loyal, intelligent, and when necessary, quite deadly."

"She had one other trait you're forgetting," said Nelson.

"What's that?" asked Sharon.

"She was an exceptional actress," said Nelson. A glance at his brutal, rugged features made it clear he was not joking. "Consider how well she fooled you for years. And pretty much the entire population of the Gray Collective, as well. Discover the truth about Velma Wade and we'll know the truth about the pattern-clone. The whole truth."

Sinclair Labs was a large modern two-story brick building in a quiet section of Indianapolis. After parking their rental car in the visitor parking lot, Sharon and Nelson entered the building and approached the reception desk.

"We'd like to see Dr. Bylunt," Sharon smiled at the petite blonde receptionist behind a glass window in the waiting room. "My name is Dr. Sharon Reed."

"Do you have an appointment?" the young woman asked. Her gaze was fixed suspiciously on Ernest

Nelson, waiting a few feet behind Reed. Dressed in a dark trenchcoat on a warm summer day, he exuded menace.

"No," said Sharon. "I don't, but...."

"I'm sorry," said the receptionist, her nasal voice indicating her complete lack of interest in Sharon's remarks, "but Dr. Bylunt is very busy at the moment. He can't see anyone without an appointment."

"Yes, I understand," said Sharon, feeling her temper starting to rise. The smile disappeared. A dangerous edge crept into her voice. "I'm sure Dr. Bylunt is very busy. *I don't care*. Get on that intercom *now* and tell him Research Director Sharon Reed wants to see him. I'm a close associate of his mentor, Dr. Reid of Virginia. The reason for my visit is quite important. And I do not like being kept waiting."

Gulping, the receptionist pushed a button and whispered into her headset. Listening to the inaudible response, the young woman's features turned white.

"Dr. Bylunt will be right down," she said, her voice trembling.

"Very good," said Sharon, turning away to conceal the satisfied smirk on her face.

"Sent them to Nepal, huh?" asked Nelson, grinning.

"Or Borneo," said Sharon. "I had a fondness for Borneo. There were head hunters in the jungles. Nepal just had yaks."

Dr. Bylunt was a short, heavyset man with jet-black beard, bushy black hair and astonishingly thick eyebrows. He wore a blue lab smock and thick horn-rim glasses.

"Sorry about the receptionist," he said with a strong Midwestern accent, sounding anxious as they walked through a sterile white hallway leading to his office in the rear of the building. "Give these pencil pushers a small amount of power and they become gods in their own minds. She's incapable of recognizing people of importance. Rarely get important visitors at Sinclair Labs."

He glanced apprehensively at Ernest Nelson, bulking huge beneath his dark coat. "And she's never encountered a machine-enhanced human before, either."

"No offense taken," said Sharon pleasantly. "Mr. Nelson is my bodyguard. We are engaged in a highly important mission for the Union. It's his job to keep me safe."

"Good, good." Bylunt's head bobbed up and down as he walked, reminding Sharon of a child's dunking bird, constantly in motion. "I must say, though we've never met, it's a great honor to have you visit my installation. Your work on genetically altered living spaces is a constant inspiration."

"Thank you," said Sharon, smiling again. "Always nice to hear good words about one's work. If I had more time, I'd fill you in on recent developments in the subject. Fascinating experiments with a living carpet."

Bylunt's eyes widened. "A living carpet? A brilliant development. I'd love to hear about it."

"I'll send you the information," said Sharon. "To-day, I must be quick."

"So sorry," said the dark-haired Investigator. He ushered them into his office, a small chamber with a steel desk and five steel chairs. The walls were lined with bookshelves covered with hundreds of volumes of medical and biological lore. In the rear of the room was a separate workstation holding a computer, monitor and printer. An orange light indicated the computer was on, but the monitor's screen was jet black.

"It's been like that for the past fifteen minutes," said Bylunt, waving them to seats. "Not sure what the problem could be. Some error with the main computer system. The X techs are working on it. I suspect they'll have it up again shortly."

He leaned back in his chair. "You mentioned a mission for the Union. How can I help? Things are somewhat in disarray here. My associate, a brilliant woman, Dr. Coup, was found murdered last night. Terrible tragedy, just terrible. Police are still investigating her death. Going to set back our work by months, that's for sure. Months at least."

"Your work?" said Nelson. "If you don't mind, what exactly were you and Dr. Coup doing lately?"

Bylunt glanced at Sharon as if seeking approval to speak. She nodded. "Mr. Nelson speaks with my voice," she declared. "You can speak freely in front of him."

"Lauri…er, Dr. Coup and I were developing a new type of breakfast cereal to appeal to the Masses," said

Bylunt. "We recently developed an additive that modified…."

"Thanks," interrupted Nelson, before Bylunt could say another word. "That's good enough. Doesn't sound like what we're looking for. Actually, we came to Indianapolis hoping to speak with Dr. Coup. It was quite a shock to discover she had been killed. You have any idea, any idea at all, who wanted your colleague dead?"

"Not a clue," said Bylunt. He tapped one finger on the steel desk, his features turning pale. When he spoke again, the words tumbled hurriedly out of his mouth. "She was a loyal member of the Union. Did whatever she was asked, never disobeyed a direct order."

"We're not here in regard to her loyalty," said Sharon, sensing the bearded man's discomfort. "I merely wanted to discuss a project she helped design last year. Nothing about her current work."

"I've already spoken with the local Syndicate representative," said Bylunt, naming the mysterious fifth branch of the Technocracy. "The agent in charge assured me that the murder exhibited no signs of being part of the ongoing troubles with the Tradition deviants."

"Forget them," said Nelson impatiently. "We're not concerned…."

The computer screen, black since they had entered the office, suddenly burst into dazzling color. A sea of reds, greens, blues and yellows twisted in a mind-numbing swirl with no apparent pattern or direction.

At the same time, a tumult of trumpets blared from the machine's speakers. Sharon glared at the monitor.

"What the hell?" said Nelson, but he could hardly be heard over the continued fanfare.

"Members of the Technocracy," came a woman's voice. "Heed the voice of reason. Listen to the Master of Harmony."

Sharon and Nelson exchanged sharp glances. There was no mistaking the speaker. It was Velma Wade.

The sea of brilliant colors swirled, rotated into a kaleidoscope pattern, then disappeared. A being's face filled the screen. Neither male nor female, it seemed to embody elements of both. Bright, almost hypnotic eyes stared out of the monitor, as if making personal contact with those who watched. It was the face of a god, or a devil. Again, Sharon recognized it immediately. Here was the pattern-clone, fully awake and functional.

"My friends," said the clone, slowly, its tones rich, deep, resonant, full of life. "The time for peace has come. Too many have died in the foolish effort known as the Ascension War. Humanity, the Masses, need guidance, not discord. We need to be leaders and teachers, not warriors. We are the Master of Harmony. Join with us to put an end to the strife. Together, we can raise mankind to Unity."

"How's he doing this?" Sharon whispered, as if afraid the pattern-clone might hear her. "He can't just be on this monitor. Damned monster must be all over."

"You bet," said Nelson. The cyborg grimaced. "Remember all the modifications Comptroller Klair put into the clone. Incredible micro-circuitry, nanobyte drivers, the works. All he needs do is touch a computer and he takes over the CPU. In this case, he's probably at some remote Union base. Seized control of the operating system there, then logged into the core computer linking all of the machines. Sooner or later, the engineers will pinpoint his location and destroy the link, but not before he gets the chance to say his piece."

"For five centuries," the clone continued, "the leaders of the Five Conventions have claimed that the Technocratic Union is winning the Ascension War. Your control over reality is strong, but it is not complete. The forces of the Nine Traditions survive. They continue to fight, while in the outermost darkness the creatures you call Nephandi grow more and more powerful. They gnaw at your insides, corrupting from within, threatening the very foundations of Reason. The world is being twisted by their warped desires, as foul becomes fair and fair becomes foul."

"Shakespeare," murmured Sharon. "Our clone is well educated for someone just reborn."

"Amazing what you can learn by merging your memory with that of a computer databank," replied Nelson.

"You—you are familiar with this being?" asked Dr. Bylunt. He was staring at the screen as if hypnotized by the pattern-clone. "Is *this* the reason you came to see me?"

"Five hundred years ago, we fought to end the war between the Order of Reason and the Nine Traditions. We sacrificed our lives, our essences, our all in that effort. We were destroyed, our ashes scattered to the winds. We hoped that our effort would prove not to be in vain. But power corrupts and absolute power corrupts all. In the centuries that followed, the Technocracy grew strong. The Five Conventions became bloated, lost sight of their original goals. We have returned to set things right. We have returned to bring Ascension to the masses, and unite all mankind in Unity. Even death and destruction cannot stop us."

"Notice how he keeps referring to himself as *we*. Delusions of grandeur? Or something more bizarre?" Nelson muttered.

The pattern-clone paused. Its eyes, expressive pools of darkness, seemed to stare directly at each one of them. "We are Heylel Teomim, once known as *barabbi*. Our words are not forgotten. Many of our teachings have become part of the Progenitors' creed. An equal number were adapted by Iteration X. We are part of your history. Our actions saved the Order of Reason from destruction by the Nine Traditions. We have returned from the Void to bring Unity to all. Today, we offer a small demonstration of our power. The future holds fire and ice. Follow us and reach the light. Stand with those who oppose us and be consumed by darkness."

The computer monitor went black. The technicians

Robert Weinberg

of Iteration X had finally regained control of the Technocracy mainframe. It didn't matter. The pattern-clone's message had been broadcast to Technocracy Collectives throughout the world.

"Hell," said Nelson. He stared at Sharon with a bleak expression. "When we screw up, we do it royally. He/she/it was pretty damn convincing. Nearly had me thinking about the joys of Unity for a second. I'll bet a lot of malcontents within the Union are pondering his offer. The Inner Council is going to want our heads."

"Not if we find the pattern-clone first and destroy it," said Sharon. "It's not Heylel. It can't be him. The Traditions destroyed his essence, burned his body, and scattered his ashes to the wind. No one returns from total annihilation. It's impossible. Absolutely not."

"Whatever you say," Nelson declared. "I'm not one to argue with an authority. But I suspect not everyone's going to be as sure as you. If the clone puts on some spectacular exhibit like he promised, then the situation is going to get messy very quickly."

The cyborg turned and looked at Dr. Bylunt. The bearded man sat immobile, his eyes still focused on the blank computer monitor. "Hey, Bylunt. What made you think we came to see you because of the pattern-clone? Something Dr. Coup said to you? Perhaps something you know about her clone-project from last year?"

Bylunt turned to them. "She never imagined anything like this happening," he declared, his voice shaking. "Never, never. It was merely an experiment in tissue regeneration. I swear it. That's all. That's all."

"Tissue regeneration?" said Sharon. "I don't like the sound of this. What are you talking about, Bylunt."

"No," said the Investigator, shaking his head. "I don't know the full story. Here." Pulling a sheet of paper from a desk drawer, he scribbled down an address. "Go to this location. The entrance is guarded, but you'll be able to get inside by yourselves. Beware of dogs. Inside are the answers. I swear."

Nelson studied the address. "Fifteen minutes from here," he said. He looked to Sharon. "You wanna take another ride?"

"Why not?" replied Sharon. Her eyes narrowed as she looked at Bylunt. "We'll see what answers we get. If they're not sufficient, we'll be back. I promise you that. And next time, we won't be so pleasant."

Chapter Sixteen

"Wake up, wake up, you sleepy head," the soft, sensual voice crooned in Ms. Hargroves's ear. "Wake up, wake, get out of bed."

Ms. Hargroves yawned, her eyes still pressed tightly shut. Then, as awareness flowed through her mind, she bolted straight up in bed. Her gaze darted wildly around the dark bedroom, searching the inky blackness for some sign of the owner of the voice.

The speaker wasn't difficult to locate. She sat perched on the large dresser directly across from the bed. A slender young woman, she wore a man's three-piece pinstripe suit, complete with bright purple necktie and matching handkerchief. Her short hair matched the color of her tie. Her eyes and lips did likewise. Thin eyebrows rose like two question marks above her near-sexless features. Though she had many names, many titles, the one she preferred was Empress Aliara. Members of the Technocracy thought of her as one of Those Beyond. The mages of the Nine Traditions called her a Dark Lord, a member of the

Maeljin Incarna. To Ms. Millicent Hargroves and Terrence Shade, she was their patron and mentor, the Queen of Desire.

Though Aliara, sitting on the edge of the dresser, giggling like a schoolgirl, appeared solid, she was nothing more than a shadow. The mirror behind her reflected empty space. The figure seen by Ms. Hargroves was a projection of the Dark Lord's will, given substance by the incredible force of her mind. Only in the Deep Universe and in the Horizon Realms which bordered that vast unexplored psychic jungle could Aliara maintain a physical presence.

"Mistress," said Ms. Hargroves. "I wasn't expecting you. My apologies for being asleep."

Ms. Hargroves worked the night shift at Everwell Chemicals and slept all day. She served as Enzo Giovanni's personal secretary. Though neither mage nor ghoul, she possessed incredibly sharp business sense, enough so that she knew more about the company and its CEO than nearly anyone else. Enzo considered her his most devoted and trusted servant. He had no idea that she reported to another.

"You were sleeping so peacefully," said Aliara, "so calm, so relaxed, that I almost hesitated to wake you. But I did anyway. You do not suffer from a guilty conscience for your activities."

Ms. Hargroves shrugged her shoulders. She disliked bantering with Aliara, but the Maeljin Incarna delighted in discussing her servants' lusts and desires. The Dark Lord possessed neither tact nor charm, but she was very, very powerful. And Ms. Hargroves thirsted for a small measure of that power.

"The world's a nasty place," said Ms. Hargroves, struggling to gain some measure of composure. "Why should I worry about someone else? Who worries about me? I sleep fine. Never felt guilty about anything I've done. Guilt is for fools."

Aliara giggled, a shrill inhuman sound. "Exactly the reason I recruited you," the Dark Lord declared. "Your attitude is refreshingly realistic. None of this altruistic foolishness spouted by the Traditions or the Technocracy. The lust for power gives you strength, not some misguided crap about helping others struggle to Ascension."

"I'm for myself," said Ms. Hargroves, not needing to exaggerate. "Me first. Everyone else is a distant second."

"What about Shade?" asked Aliara. "Has he proven useful?"

"The man's psychotic," answered Ms. Hargroves. "He's a homicidal maniac, and he laughs too damn much."

"Yes, I know," said Aliara, "but that doesn't answer my question. Has he been of any assistance to you in your work?"

"Shade does whatever I ask," said Ms. Hargroves. "He's the perfect assistant. He works very hard. Still, I find his presence disturbing. I prefer working alone."

"Your preferences are unimportant," said Aliara. "Summon him. Both of you need to hear the news I bring."

"Shade," called Ms. Hargroves, as she slipped out of the bed and pulled on a dressing gown. She turned on the overhead light, then sat down on the edge of the bed. "Come in here. At once."

The door to the bedroom opened and Shade bounced through. Dressed all in white, he was grinning like a fool. The smile vanished from his face when he spotted Aliara.

"My Lady," he croaked, his voice trembling. Shade appeared ready to swallow his tongue in fright. "I did not expect to see you here on Earth."

"I am filled with surprises, my dear Shade," said Aliara. Uncurling her legs, she slid off the dresser and walked across the room towards him. The red-faced man froze as she approached, only his eyes moving, following her every step. To Ms. Hargroves, he resembled a rabbit hypnotized by a cobra poised for the kill.

"Your skin has healed quite nicely," declared the Queen of Desire, a ghostly hand reaching out and caressing Shade's face with her slender fingers. "But I can still sense the marks beneath the flesh. Can you feel them, Shade? Are you aware of my mark upon you?"

"Yes, mistress," whispered Shade, his lips barely moving. "The memory remains."

"Good," said Aliara, a sultry smile on her lips, "very good. Serve me properly, Shade, and someday I will remove the pain and replace it with pleasure. Disappointment me, and you will discover that there are tortures that the human mind cannot even begin to imagine."

"I am your servant," said Shade, his red face chalk white. "I will not fail you."

"Sit," said Aliara, directing him next to Ms. Hargroves. "My time on Earth, even in this shadow form, is limited. I don't have minutes to waste on threats or promises. Listen, both of you, because I come with important information about the being known as the pattern-clone. And your new mission involving him."

"A new mission?" said Ms. Hargroves. "Then I'm free of Enzo and his brood?"

"Not yet," said Aliara. The slender young woman swung up onto the chest of drawers. Legs dangling off the side, she looked like a child playing dress-up in her father's clothing. Though only a demon child possessed such a diabolical smile. "You are to remain there until I say otherwise. Enzo and his mad friend Ezra are at the heart of this conspiracy. I am still not sure exactly how these plots tie together. But I know they must. There are no true coincidences in such matters."

"The pattern-clone is alive?" asked Shade. "The last you mentioned, it had disappeared from the Gray Collective."

"The clone has reappeared in grand fashion," said Aliara. "It claims to be the reincarnation of Heylel Teomim. As such, it has strong ties to the Nine Traditions and the Technocracy. In separate messages, the being states it has returned from beyond the veil to unite all mages under his banner, leading them all into a golden age of Unity and Ascension."

Shade giggled. "The purpose of creating the Ascension Warrior was to put an end to the war between the Traditions and the Technocracy. However, I doubt if Klair or Reed expected this sort of solution."

"I doubt that anyone need worry about a sudden outbreak of peace," said Aliara. "My spies report that the Council of Nine rejected Heylel's offer. And there is no question that the Inner Council of the Technocracy will do the same. Neither group is ready to give their command to a mysterious stranger who brags he is a messiah reborn."

"If my memory serves me correctly," said Shade, "Heylel was no hero. It's hard to believe either organization would trust any promises he makes."

"He claims that his betrayal was an act of sacrifice, not ambition," said Aliara. "Under Heylel's mantle, the clone condemns both the Traditions and the Technocracy for not progressing from their positions of five hundred years ago. Only under his benevolent rule can mankind finally achieve mass Ascension. I was told his lectures proved to be quite compelling." She sneered. "Almost believable."

"How do the clone's appeals affect us?" asked Ms. Hargroves. Always practical, she saw everything in the world in two camps: Matters of importance to her. And everything else. "Should we be concerned?"

"I'm not sure," said Aliara. "That is what I want to find out. Perhaps the pattern-clone is possessed by Heylel's dual spirits. It seems unlikely, but anything is possible. Still, it really doesn't matter. The identity of the clone is unimportant. Only its actions are of interest."

"Has the clone actually done anything other than state its purpose?" asked Shade.

"Not yet, but I suspect it will act soon," said Aliara. "The creature made veiled threats against the Technomancers and the Tradition mages. Nothing has occurred, but the words were spoken only a few hours ago. My spies in both societies reported to me within minutes after the twin diatribes. I feel certain that 'Heylel' means to back up its words with some sort of meaningful gesture. When that happens, we will be able to assess the true danger the being represents. And then we will act."

"For now?" asked Ms. Hargroves. This idle speculation bored her. All of her life, she had dealt with threats. She wasn't afraid of shadows. Let the pattern-clone prove its power. Then she would worry. Not before.

"Wait and watch," said Aliara. "Watch and wait. How does Enzo's plan progress?"

Ms. Hargroves shrugged. "He and Ezra seem well pleased. Montifloro acts like a fool over the slut, Hope. He wants to Embrace her, but he knows the leader of their clan, Pietro, would never permit him to do so. It is a bitter wedge Enzo has skillfully driven between Montifloro and Pietro. Exactly what he schemes to do next, I do not know."

"Find out," said Aliara. "But be very careful. His associate, Ezra, is a madman, but he is still an extremely powerful sorcerer. If he suspects you are tied to me, your death will be extremely painful."

Ms. Hargroves nodded. "I'm careful. That's my style. There won't be any mistakes. I don't make them."

"What of your other assignment, Shade?" asked Aliara, turning her head slightly to gaze at the fat man. "When will you deliver the Changing Man to my palace in Malfeas?"

"Shortly, Aliara," said Shade, blinking his red eyes nervously. "Very soon, I assure you. Sam Haine's not around. I've done some checking. No one is sure where he's gone or when he'll be back. But when he returns, my trap will be set and ready."

"Haine is in Horizon," said Aliara. "My spies reported him there in the company of his friends. He should not be there more than a few days."

"I've been leaving messages for him," said Shade. "Killing off one or two of his pupils each time I do so. The Changing Man's a proud old bird. He'll come hunting for me when he learns of the murders. And I'll be waiting, with a trap door to your dominion close by. One push and he'll be all yours."

Aliara laughed. A purple nimbus, like an electrical cloud, surrounded her head, showering eerie sparks across her violet hair. "His punishment will last a thousand lifetimes," she declared. "Ten thousand lifetimes, perhaps."

"What about his companions?" Shade inquired, a trifle nervously. "Chances are they won't let him come alone to answer my challenge. The tall African witch doctor, Albert, travels with him everywhere. You want him too? Or the girl with the swords? And how about Prisoner Seventeen? He's still alive, much to everyone's surprise."

"I only desire Sam Haine alive and sane in Malfeas," said Aliara. "Do with the others as you want. Kill them, as the act seems to please you. None of them matter to me. The escaped prisoner served as a diversion during the final development of the pattern-clone. Now that the being is alive, the prisoner is no longer of any importance."

"You're not the only one looking to kill them," said Ms. Hargroves. "Enzo passed the word that he wants this Prisoner Seventeen dead. I passed the word to our contacts among the cannibal bikers. When the fugitive returns to Rochester, he becomes a walking target."

"Curious," said Aliara. "This is the second time your vampire has tried to kill this man. Why does Enzo care about the escaped prisoner?"

"I gather the order comes from Ezra, not Enzo," said Ms. Hargroves. "Enzo dislikes being told what to do. But he knows not to disobey a direct command from his ally. This willworker, Ethan Phillips, is doomed."

"What?" said Aliara, her voice quivering. A look of absolute astonishment passed across her boyish features. Her body wavered; the image faded. With visible effort, she steadied the projection, returning to full substance. "What name did you speak?"

"Ethan Phillips," said Ms. Hargroves. "Enzo said it was the prisoner's true name."

Shade nodded in recognition. "Right. I remember him. Velma Wade caught him trying to infiltrate the Gray Collective. A spectacular specimen, we used him as a test case for a number of the most dangerous techniques involving the development of the pattern-clone. The experiments nearly destroyed him. Completely changed his features, reshaped his body."

"You witnessed this Ethan Phillips's capture?" asked Aliara. She had regained complete control of her body. But her hair was silver now, as were her eyes and lips. And her three-piece suit was a deep shade of scarlet.

"No, of course not," said Shade. "Collecting specimens for experimentation was not my job. Evidently, this Phillips tried to enter the Collective disguised as a minor lab technician. Wade recognized him from an encounter ten years earlier, when he'd wiped out half the staff of a research installation where she served. She rendered the spy unconscious, had a group of sauroids haul him to the detention center, then notified the Triumvirate of her capture."

"How convenient," said Aliara. "Wade knew him from an encounter several years earlier, you say. A chance meeting not witnessed by anyone of importance. And now Ezra wants Phillips destroyed at all costs. I am not surprised."

"I'm not sure I understand," said Ms. Hargroves. "Why is this Ethan Phillips so important?"

"*Fifty* years ago," said Aliara, "Ethan Phillips entered Malfeas, hunting for his lost love, a powerful willworker named Scarlett Dancer. She had disappeared in that Realm, searching for ultimate power. He didn't find her. Instead, he was captured by Lord Steel. For the past five decades, Phillips was held prisoner in the Duke of Hate's dungeons, suffering the tortures of the damned."

"So how did he end up in the Gray Collective?" asked Ms. Hargroves. She refrained from asking the other obvious question—how did Aliara know so much about Ethan Phillips?

"Solve that riddle," said Aliara, "and I suspect many questions will be answered. Including the mystery of the pattern-clone's true identity."

Chapter Seventeen

"Would you like a glass of wine?" asked Porthos, politely. "I can assure you it is a most astonishing vintage. Grown beyond the fields we know, it is unlike anything available on Earth. And no matter how much you drink, there are no unpleasant after-effects."

"Sounds fascinating," said Seventeen. "I'll try a glass."

"No thank you," said Shadow of the Dawn. "None for me."

Porthos chuckled. "Ever the vigilant warrior maid," he declared. He snapped his fingers. "Wine for me, and for Master Seventeen. Immediately."

As the last syllable died from Porthos's lips, the floor between him and his two guests mushroomed upward into a round cocktail table. In its center stood a tall green fluted wine bottle. Two pink glasses, elaborately shaped to resemble roses and filled with an amber liquid, rested in front of the archwizard and his astonished guest.

"In these quarters," said Porthos, raising his glass to his lips, "my every wish is a command. One of the benefits of living for nearly six hundred years."

They sat in a small octagonal chamber cluttered with plush pillows, magickal bric-a-brac, and hundreds of leather-bound grimoires. A spiral staircase led downward to the rest of Porthos's quarters. A steel ladder, decorated with strange and grotesque sigils, led upward to a trap door to the roof. According to Porthos, the mages now sat in the highest tower of the mystic castle, Doissetep, in the Shard Realm of Forces. Seventeen had no reason to doubt him.

"I'm still not sure why you brought us here," said Seventeen, sipping his wine. Porthos had not lied. The drink had a unique flavor, though Seventeen had few memories to serve as a comparison. "Something about a book?"

Porthos smiled and nodded. The dark-haired man appeared to be nothing more than a simple-minded doting uncle, not too bright and totally harmless. Seventeen knew that looks could be deceiving; Porthos controlled incredible magicks. Sam Haine and Kallikos had been quite clear in their warnings before Seventeen and Shadow had departed Horizon. The master mage was one of the most powerful willworkers alive. And he was quite mad.

"I am so sorry that you two are unable to see the wonders of Doissetep," said Porthos. "The castle is immense, one of the largest in all creation, and many are the marvels hidden within its walls. Its earthly manifestation was built before recorded history. For the last five hundred years, it has existed here in the Shade Realm of Forces. Five score archmagicians live in quarters only slightly less lavish than mine. There are many hundreds of servants, both human and otherwise, caring for our needs, satisfying our every request. Without the least bit of modesty, I can say without question that Doissetep is the greatest of all Tradition Chantries. Unfortunately, the rules here are quite strict. Visitors are discouraged within these walls, as they often stumble into arcane affairs. Though you are my guests, it is best that you remain here in my chambers, hidden from sight. Others in the castle might take exception to your presence."

"Even I, a young maid of humble origins and insignificant skill, have heard of the fabled fortress of Doissetep," said Shadow of the Dawn. "I am honored to be permitted entrance to its hallowed grounds."

"Bah," said Porthos, with a wave of a hand. "Doissetep is no church, no holy sanctuary. Too many within these walls think only of their own power and nothing of Ascension. There are more sinners than saints, and more madmen than either."

"You mentioned a book?" said Seventeen, anxious to keep Porthos focused. Though they had been in the archmage's quarters for nearly two hours, he had yet to explain his reasons for asking them to accompany him back to Doissetep. Seventeen suspected that Porthos might have already forgotten whatever they were.

"Look," said Porthos, pointing to one of the long, narrow windows that dotted the circular chamber. "A storm is gathering. In the Shade Realm of Forces, storms are quite impressive."

Intrigued despite his impatience, Seventeen stepped to the nearest aperture. Without a sound, Shadow of the Dawn joined him. Far in the distance, the reddish-purple sky crackled with immense bolts of yellow fire. Huge black clouds were approaching. The very air seemed alive with anger.

Looking down, Seventeen could see the vast holdings of Doissetep stretched across the top of the mountain like a gigantic spider. The black slate walls, grinning stone gargoyles and oblique spiraling towers gave the fortress a surrealistic look. Set on the tallest peak in an immense mountain range, the dark palace shouted its defiance to the rampaging elements. Hundreds of silver metal fingers dotted the ramparts—gigantic lightning rods to deflect the worst of the storms.

"Several years ago," Porthos interjected, as Seventeen and Shadow stared at the approaching tempest, "I decided to compile a book. It had become obvious to me that too few of our kind knew the history of the Great Betrayal, one of the most important events in our ongoing struggle. As one of the few survivors of the Foundation, I felt it was my duty to record the full story of those bitter days. Only by knowing the past can we understand the future."

Porthos gulped down the rest of his wine. Instantly the glass refilled. "Wanting to present the most accurate history possible, I consulted both the library of Doissetep and the archives of Horizon. Together, these two great collections provided me with the actual memoirs of several of the most important players in that drama. Transcribing their words in the most accurate translation I could manage, and adding a few notes of my own for clarification, I called the resulting volume *The Fragile Path: Testaments of the First Cabal.* Of all my writings, I consider the book my finest achievement."

The archmage stretched out his right hand, his bony fingers spread wide. In his palm, a slender volume with bright red covers and gold letters suddenly appeared. "Unfortunately," he continued, "this is the only copy."

Porthos's face twisted in an expression of annoyance. "A member of the Council of Nine claimed the book was inflammatory, sheer propaganda intent on slandering certain members of the Nine Traditions. Though he never actually read the testaments, the fool judged the contents by his own long-standing prejudices. He raised such a commotion that his colleagues finally agreed to review the manuscript carefully before allowing its publication. Though two whole years have passed, I still wait for their decision. I fear now that it no longer matters."

"I assume that Council member was São Cristavao?" said Seventeen.

"The insufferable old bastard," said Porthos, vehemently. "May he burn for all eternity in hell."

The archmage's face crinkled with thought. "Goodness," he said, grinning. "I had completely forgotten. The fires *have* engulfed the fool. He stepped on the

Robert Weinberg

wrong toes tonight. Normally, I do not speak harshly of the dead. But in São Cristavao's case, I make an exception. If I live not another day, I will die with a smile on my face, knowing that misbegotten toad of a man is no more."

"The book speaks of the one called Heylel?" asked Shadow of the Dawn.

"It does exactly that, sword maid," said Porthos. "It tells the tale of the First Cabal, their mission, their successes, and finally, of their Betrayal. Of particular interest are two sections: the final confession of Heylel Teomim, before his destruction. And perhaps of equal importance, the Revelation and Vision of Akrites the Seer."

"'An unending curtain of darkness covering the world,'" said Seventeen, as outside gouts of lightning lit the sky.

Porthos looked startled. Then he nodded. "A prediction of eternal night. When we destroyed Heylel, we thought that nightmare no longer existed. Now, five hundred years later, it creeps ever closer. I fear that if this being is truly Heylel returned, Akrites's prophecy may yet come to pass."

"Kallikos seems determined not to let that happen," said Seventeen. "He says the future is not fixed, that even the grimmest nightmares are only possibilities."

"He spoke truly," said Porthos, "but changing the future is not easy. A seer observes the most likely occurances. To rewrite his vision is not an easy task. That is why I asked the two of you to accompany me to Doissetep. The Council of Nine will deliberate weeks, perhaps months, before deciding on a course of action. By then, it will be too late. Heylel needs to be stopped immediately. Akrites alone, however, is no match for the Abomination. He needs assistance. And to defeat Heylel, you must first understand him."

Outside the tower, lightning flashed and thunder boomed. But no rain fell. Porthos frowned, tilting his head as if listening to noises only he could hear. "Strange," he muttered, "very strange."

He handed the book to Seventeen. "Something odd transpires in Doissetep. I need to investigate. In the meantime, feel free to begin reading. I shall return shortly."

Porthos snapped his fingers and vanished.

Seventeen stared at Shadow. "'Something odd'? I wonder what he meant by that?"

"As unwelcome and quite insignificant intruders," said Shadow of the Dawn, "I suspect such concerns are best left unexplored. Master Porthos wants us to read this text. I believe we should follow his wishes."

"Whatever you say," declared Seventeen, opening the red covers. "Though I'd still like to know what's happening in the castle. Can you read English?"

"I am fluent in seven different languages," said Shadow of the Dawn with the merest hint of a smile. "Let us start with the introductory chapter labeled *The Point of This Book* by Master Porthos."

They scanned the text in silence.

"Subtle the old boy is not," said Seventeen.

"I have no desire to be subtle," said Porthos, appearing out of nothingness next to them. "Subtle remarks

Robert Weinberg

are lost on the modern generation. My point is that some statements must be made boldly, leaving no question as to the meaning and reason for setting words to paper. Thus it is with this volume. The lessons to be learned are extremely important. People died for their beliefs. Others experienced terrible suffering. Their sacrifices must be remembered."

"Things settled in the castle?" asked Seventeen, unable to restrain his curiosity about more immediate affairs.

Porthos's frown deepened. "Doissetep houses wizards of incredible power. As in most Chantry Houses, these 'enlightened' souls have aligned themselves into cabals of like-minded individuals. Naturally, each group believes it possesses wisdom the others do not. They constantly scheme and plot against one another. As I mentioned earlier, most here are less concerned with aiding mankind than with furthering their own agenda. The balance of power is extremely delicate. Tonight, tempers seem to be more frayed than usual. The storm, I suspect, has people on edge. It will pass and cooler heads will prevail. They always do."

Casually, he reached out and plucked a piece of fruit from the air. "Would you care for an apple? A peach? Perhaps a pear? They are all quite delicious."

"No thanks," said Seventeen. He found Porthos's sudden switch in direction disconcerting. "I was just about to start reading the book."

"The book?" said Porthos. "Oh yes, of course, the book. *The Fragile Path*. My greatest achievement. Damned shame the material's been suppressed. Can't learn from history if you don't know what happened. Those who forget the past are doomed to repeat it, and all that."

"Exactly what I was thinking," said Seventeen. "That's why Shadow and I planned to read the book now. So we can discover the truth about the Great Betrayal."

"Splendid idea," said Porthos, chewing on his apple. "No need though for you to study the volume right away. Take up too much valuable time. I'll tell you the story. Quicker and easier that way. Leave out the unimportant stuff. You can fill in the details later."

With a heavy sigh, Seventeen closed the book. "Go ahead," he said. "Tell us."

"I will begin at the beginning," said Porthos, "for that is a very good place to start. In the year 1325, a group of philosophers and scientists calling themselves the Order of Reason decided that untamed and undisciplined magick was destroying the world and a single unified truth was needed to protect humanity. United by this common belief, the Order of Reason promoted science over magick, the 'ordinary' over the 'supernatural.'

"Working as a group, they succeeded, as science replaced mysticism throughout the world. Fear of the unknown helped them in their quest. Our kind found themselves powerless to fight the overwhelming tide of reason. Working with kings and princes of the time, the Order of Reason engaged in a militant crusade to wipe out all those who opposed their version of reality. Many magi perished in those dark days as those who refused to conform were condemned.

"Finally, several powerful willworkers concluded that unless mysticks of all practices and beliefs united to battle the Order of Reason, magick would disappear from the world. Slowly but surely these great mages, the original Primi, recruited others who shared their concerns. Working together, this alliance of willworkers created the magickal Realm known as Horizon.

"Once completed, this new sanctuary served as the site of the Grand Convocation. For nine years, hundreds of magi from all over the world journeyed to Horizon where they debated the best method to strike back against the Order of Reason. Finally, in 1466, the assembly formed the Council of Nine Mystick Traditions, dedicated to leading mankind to Ascension and the restoration of wonder to the world."

A crash, not thunder, drowned out Porthos's last words. The floor of the tower shook. Brows knitted with concern, the archmage vanished immediately.

"I'm starting to get worried," said Seventeen. "According to Sam Haine, Doissetep rivals Horizon as the most powerful Tradition stronghold in the Tellurian. What better place for Heylel to strike?"

Shadow of the Dawn touched her twin swords, as if seeking reassurance from the cold steel. "Master Porthos spoke of a delicate balance. Kallikos once told me that Heylel was a master of the subtle gesture. Besides being a great sorcerer, he understood how to achieve great results from small maneuvers."

"Disturbing," said Porthos, reappearing out of nothingness. "I cannot remember such outbursts of temper in the past century. Luckily, no one was killed in that last exchange. I spoke to Walter Thrun, head of Chantry security. He assured me that the problems were minor and under control. Hopefully, he is not mistaken."

"Shadow of the Dawn mentioned that Heylel was a master of intrigue," said Seventeen. "Could he be somehow involved in these quarrels?"

"None could match the traitor's cunning," said Porthos. "But the mages of Doissetep are not pawns to be moved about a human chessboard. We are not so easily influenced."

"When tempers grow short," said Shadow of the Dawn, "a small push is all that is needed to start a duel."

"Yes, yes," said Porthos, "the wisdom of the East. Pithy sayings and all that mumbo jumbo. The sound of one hand clapping. I appreciate your concern. But there is nothing to worry about."

The archmage reached out and pulled the half-eaten apple from nowhere. He took another bite. "Now, where was I? Ah yes, the founding of the Nine Traditions."

He sat down, the floor rising up and forming a chair beneath him. "At the conclusion of the Great Convocation, the newly formed Council of Nine appointed what became known as the First Cabal. This select ministry was a gathering of some of the finest mages in Horizon. Placed at the head of the group was Heylel

Teomim, a unique being with two Avatars, two personalities in one body. This dual nature, possessing both male and female attributes, gave him a unique view of the world. Heylel, famous for his creation of the Philosopher's Stone, was the greatest of the Solificati, the Alchemists. Considered one of the wisest mages of the age, he was the natural choice as leader of the First Cabal.

"Their mission was to travel across the earth, battling the Order of Reason while helping the helpless, fighting disease and famine, freeing the enslaved. It was a great cause, a mighty effort to battle reason with mercy. They traveled throughout Europe and the Middle East. For nearly four years, they spread a message of hope, of brotherhood, of enlightenment. And then came the Great Betrayal.

"In the summer of 1470, Heylel contacted the leaders of the Order of Reason and conspired to trap the First Cabal. An army of Inquisitors, led by Heylel and twelve Templars from the Cabal of Pure Thought, descended on the group in the province of Narbonne. In the ensuing battle, three of the eight were killed. Four were captured. One died a hero. Akrites escaped. Returning to Horizon, he organized a rescue party. Not only were they able to save three of the four prisoners, but the rescuers also succeeded in capturing Heylel. The traitor was tried and found guilty of betraying its comrades. In November of that year, its twin Avatars were destroyed and its body burned to ashes."

"But why?" asked Seventeen. "Does your book explain why Heylel betrayed the Traditions?"

"In the Abomination's final confession, the traitor claims, as you heard in the Council chambers last night, to have committed the crime to save the Council. That it saw that the Order of Reason would triumph if the Traditions did not unite with the same purpose and dedication displayed by our enemies. Heylel's words rang with strong emotion. Among others, he had betrayed the mother of his children, Eloine, *bani* Verbena, and his closest friend, Akrites Salonikas, the Seer. In his final statement to the Council of Nine, Heylel stated that he welcomed death, for the guilt he felt was too great to bear. I witnessed his destruction and attest to the fact that the traitor approached his end without remorse. Though his crimes were great, he believed they were necessary."

"Porthos! Porthos!" A woman's voice echoed through the chamber. "Come quickly."

Porthos vanished. The entire tower shook, as if engulfed by a sudden earthquake.

Seventeen was on his feet. Shadow of the Dawn remained seated, her face serene. "I think Porthos has underestimated the situation here," said Seventeen.

"Undoubtedly," said Shadow. "However, the archmage transported us to this Realm by his magick. Without his assistance, we are trapped here. Worry only about those things you can control. Do not concern yourself with events that are beyond attention."

The room shook, more violently than before. Seventeen rushed to the window. Staring at the fortress far below, he gasped in dismay. Huge gaps had appeared in the castle walls. In one spot, it appeared as if a gigantic hand had reached down and ripped out one entire section of the building.

"I can hear screams," said Shadow of the Dawn. For all of the swordswoman's calm words about maintaining inner peace and tranquillity, she kept her hands close to her blades. "Doissetep trembles on the brink of open warfare between its cabals."

Purple lightning flashed in the heavens and was answered from below. A jagged bolt of pure energy ripped upward through the roof of a distant wing of the fortress, slashing into the black thunderclouds like a molten hammer. Shadow of the Dawn shuddered. "Many just died."

"We can climb up the ladder to the roof," said Seventeen. The room was rocking back and forth, as if buffeted by incredibly strong winds. "Or follow the stairs downward into the citadel."

"I recommend neither choice," said Porthos. The archmage dropped into his chair, an expression of anguish on his face. His glasses were gone and his greasy black hair appeared singed. Tears filled his eyes. "How could I have been so blind? Fights to the death have broken out in the main halls. Archmage battles archmage. The mightiest of all Realms, the oldest Chantry in existence, is ripping itself apart. The end approaches. Doissetep is dying. Destroyed not by magick, but by jealousy."

"What's happening?" asked Seventeen. "What's going on?"

Bricks fell from the roof, the walls shook, but Porthos seemed oblivious to the destruction. Raising his wine glass, the archmage drained it in a gulp.

"Cancer eats Doissetep alive," said Porthos. He sounded bitter, angry. "Long held in check, it broke out tonight in full force. You were correct in suspecting the hand of the Abomination in this disaster. Yet Heylel did nothing other than spread the word of his return. Suspicion and deceit did the rest."

"A delicate balance," said Shadow of the Dawn. "Each cabal mistrusted the others, but as long as none held an advantage, they felt safe. A balance of powers, once tilted, can never be restored."

"Exactly," said Porthos. He waved a hand and the room stopped shaking. But nothing could banish the sounds of battle outside their sanctuary. "Four strong cabals believe that they alone should control Doissetep. The Druai'shi, to which I belong; the Janissaries; the Order of Bonisagus; and the Followers of Tylalus. Other less powerful groups also desire a share of command. Doissetep is a battleground of hubris gone mad. For decades, each organization has plotted and schemed against the others, seeking an advantage in the eternal struggle. Never openly, always in secret. But always an uneasy truce held, for none wished open conflict with their fellow wizards. All understood that war between wizards was unpredictable and could be deadly to everyone involved.

"Until tonight."

Lightning flashed, thunder bellowed, most of it coming from below, so often that the windows glowed as brightly as beacons. "Word of Heylel's return spread like wildfire through the fortress," said Porthos, shaking his head in despair. "But somehow the details were twisted, changed. No doubt the whispered lies of Heylel's agents. There were tales of a bargain made by me with the Abomination. My rivalry with São Cristavao was well known by my enemies throughout the Chantry. Thus, in their eyes, his death took on an entirely different meaning. The fools saw it as partial payment for my support."

"That's insane," said Seventeen. "How could—"

He was suddenly unable to speak. Nor could he breathe. The air in the chamber had turned to water. Liquid filled his throat, his lungs. Not even Seventeen's unique survival traits could cope with total immersion. A curtain of blackness engulfed him. And then, it disappeared.

"Nicely done," muttered Porthos as Seventeen sucked down deep breaths of air. Normally unflappable, Shadow of the Dawn appeared startled and confused. "Water elemental submerged the chamber."

Five feet away, something huge, yellow and befanged materialized. Shadow of Dawn's swords were in her hands when Porthos sneered at the horror and commanded, "Begone, annoyance." The horror disappeared in a puff of red smoke.

"A unnameable from the Dimension of Nightmares," said the archmage. "No more time to discuss Heylel's treachery, I'm afraid. What you observe at present are the lesser attacks that inch through my defenses. Vast forces are pounding Doissetep to dust. The entire mountain top is getting ready to erupt. Great power is building beneath us. Rage held in check for centuries is about to be released. Soon, even my most gallant efforts will not be enough to hold back the fury. You two must be gone before that occurs."

"Us?" said Seventeen. "What about you?"

"For more than five hundred years, this mighty fortress has been my home," said Porthos. "I cannot desert it now. If Doissetep falls, Porthos Fitz-Empress falls with it."

"The Nine Traditions need your strength to combat the pattern-clone," said Shadow. "There is no dishonor in flight. Your death will only aid Heylel's plans."

"Be that as it may," said Porthos, his expression set in stone. "I cannot leave. Doissetep is a gigantic powder keg of magickal energy about to detonate. When it does, the force of the explosion will reverberate through the Tellurian. The universe will shake. If I do not remain to muffle the blast, many thousands, perhaps millions, will die. I will not permit this to happen."

"But…" said Seventeen.

"No arguments," said Porthos. "Allow an old man to make one final noble gesture. Farewell."

Porthos pointed one long finger at Seventeen and Shadow. Instinctively, they clasped hands. Incredible energies flared in the chamber. The world turned black.

<u>Chapter Eighteen</u>

In absolute and total darkness, Seventeen saw without eyes, heard without ears…

Doissetep screams in agony. The fortress, dark and brooding, vast beyond any citadel ever built on Earth, trembles atop a mighty peak, in the center of a chain of mountains only slightly less menacing. Red fires slash at its core, energy vortices swirl above it as men like gods engage in their final deadly games. In the distance, the land itself is torn apart by flame. Volcanoes erupt, spreading lava over the forests and fields of the Realm. Huge cracks open in the earth as wild forces attack the heart of the land. A dull throbbing grows louder and louder. A titanic wave of sound rises up from the black stone fortress as the voices of thousands cry out in dread anticipation.

For an instant, the entire universe seems to stop as matter and energy flow from one state to the other. Time pauses as magickal energies beyond mortal comprehension collide with enough force to alter the very nature of reality. Less than a blink of an eye, the beat of a heart, the moment lasts. And then, with a roar that shrieks through all creation, Doissetep explodes.

In Manchester, England, the huge old wooden mansion was called the Haunted Palace. Built hundreds of years ago, the place had a grisly reputation. No one knew its original builder, but local historians were quick to point out that the place had been the site of more than a dozen murders, thirty-seven suicides, and at least one reported act of cannibalism. Those rascals foolish enough to accept the Psychic Society's challenge to spend a night in the mansion invariably ended up in the city asylum, babbling of ghostly hands reaching from the walls, voices whispering inside their minds, and sights so gruesome they could not be set to paper.

Willworkers of the Nine Traditions found the old mansion disturbing, and few dared spend more than a night or two in its twisted corridors and ancient halls. Over the centuries, countless ghosts had been exorcised from the building. Yet it still remained haunted by certain grim spirits who could not be named.

When it burst into flames that night, burning to the ground in only minutes, scientists from the city blamed an underground gas leak for the inferno. Most townspeople had other explanations, mostly dealing with sulfur and brimstone.

In a lake in the northern regions of Minnesota, a group of fishermen were startled when several huge red blots, bearing a striking resemblance to blood, rose up from the depths of the supposedly Bottomless Lake. They received a greater shock when, seconds later, a gigantic shape surfaced from the water beneath their boat. Their astonishment turned to cries of horror as they discovered themselves staring at what could only be a pleiosaur, a long-necked aquatic dinosaur from many millions of years ago. The creature roared in mortal agony, sending the small craft tumbling off its back. With memories of *King Kong* terribly clear in their minds, the frightened vacationers swam desperately for land, expecting any moment to be picked up in the mouth of the monstrous beast and gobbled down as a snack.

No one died, though the hair of one of the four, an unimaginative young man named Tom Alden, turned bleach white. Huffing and puffing on the shore of the lake, the quartet turned to discover the long-extinct monster had come to the surface to die. It floated lifelessly on the water not far from the smashed timbers of their vessel. Within an hour, the body had somehow melted into the lake.

The fishermen, after much deliberation, decided that any recitation of their adventure would land them in an institution. They swore a vow of silence, washed down by two six-packs from their nearby camp site. The only one who ever broke his word was Tom Alden, later nicknamed Whitey, who in a drunken stupor described in great detail the events to his wife. Fortunately, Mrs. Alden, who possessed even less imagination than her husband, assumed he was

Robert Weinberg

merely covering up a weekend of drunkenness and debauchery, and filed for divorce.

In an ancient burial site near Tain, Scotland, a half-dozen Black Spiral Dancers, evil werewolves in the service of the Wyrm, were engaged in a savage attack on the crypt. The guardian of the tomb, a powerful spirit named Old Enoch, was hard-pressed to combat the raiders. Dozens of bane-spirits swarmed beside the wolf-things. Though armed with a massive two-handed runeblade, Old Enoch was only one and his enemies were many. For the first time in an age, it seemed possible that the forces of dementia would overwhelm the tomb and capture its wellspring of Quintessence.

Neither Enoch nor his enemies were prepared for the titanic blast of psychic energy that suddenly sheared through the tunnels of the crypt, sweeping all magickal beings before it in a tidal wave of undiminished ferocity. The Black Spiral Dancers, mighty warriors all, were slammed into the walls of the tomb with such force that their bones were crushed. The same wave ripped the Bane spirits to vapors, scattering their shreds across half of Scotland. In instants, the burial site disappeared as if it had never existed. Only Old Enoch survived the cataclysm, and he ended up in Loch Lomond, his senses befuddled, his rune sword buried in the muck.

In New York City, twelve hundred automobile windshields shattered at the same moment. Half of these belonged to cars parked on city streets, and the damage was attributed to a major street gang initiation. Much more difficult to explain were the six hundred other windshields that exploded and imploded in cars that were in motion at the time. Faulty glass, a freak atmospheric weather condition, a secret CIA experiment using giant tuning forks, a meteor shower of ice shards, and several other equally unlikely explanations bombarded the city's talk shows for the next week. More real were the four hundred people who suffered cuts, ranging from minor nicks to serious wounds. Three people died—two suffering heart attacks from the shock, the third impaled by a six-inch glass shard in her right eye. Civil suits filed from the disaster totaled eight billion dollars, proving to lawyers throughout the metropolitan area that nothing happens without a good reason.

Located in a remote region of Slovenia, the Arms of Var stood as one of the most intriguing mysteries of the region. No one knew who had built the monuments or for what reason. Three huge monoliths, they were made out of gray slate, mottled with strange patterns of deep green and dark crimson.

The Arms of Var, which bore a name whose origin was lost in the tides of time, resembled immense stone forearms reaching out of the mountainous soil of the region. The hands of each arm, however, possessed seven fingers, stretched skyward as if reaching for something unseen. The superstitious peasants of the area whispered that anyone sitting in those hands disappeared from the Earth. Though scientists scoffed at the tale, none of the university professors who came from time to time to examine the unusual formations actually climbed between those clutching fingers.

Though barely known to the outside world, (no photograph of the Arms seemed to develop properly), the monuments were considered a Slovenian national treasure. Worries about their destruction caused the government to station a small army contingent close by. Not too close, though, since guards who spent too much time near the outstretched hands often disappeared or went insane.

A peal of demonic laughter, booming so loud that it caused several small avalanches in the surrounding mountains, announced an astonishing transformation. Nearly a hundred peasants, led by Father Radju of the local church, hurried to the monuments. None of the six soldiers stationed at the site could be found. Nor were they ever seen again.

More frightening than the soldiers' disappearance or the laughter was the change that had taken place in the Arms of Var. The twenty-one long fingers no longer reached for the sun. Instead, the digits had curled into fists. The three massive hands appeared raised in defiance to the heavens.

Calmly, Father Radju shepherded the terrified villagers back to their homes, reassuring them that God still watched over them. There was a natural explanation for the bizarre transformation. The professors from the university, he promised, would explain it all. Then, when all were settled and an uneasy peace hung over the village, Father Radju returned to his home and, for the first time in forty years, downed a shot of brandy.

Three thousand light bulbs burst in Singapore. The local authorities, not knowing whom to blame, rounded up all of the workers at the local power plant. After several hours of useless questions, the police finally concluded that the destruction was caused by persons or parties unknown. The weary employees were released, with a stern warning not to let the incident happen again.

In the secret Horizon Realm of Vali Shallar, the two suns high in the sky dimmed, as if a cloud passed across their faces. In his sanctum in the great Tower, Alvin Reynolds rushed to his computer. Messages from Virtual Adepts from across the Tellurian flooded the net. No one knew for sure what had just occurred. But many could guess.

The water in the cascades outside of the town of Acajutla, El Salvador, turned blood red. The natural crystal basins near the bottom of the falls snapped with an audible crack, as if suddenly slammed by a hammer. Across the swamp, more than a dozen gigantic alligators splashed into the water. Werebeasts known as the Mokolé, they considered the waterfall part of their domain. Foes of the mages who sucked magickal energy from the water, they reveled in the destruction the crimson implied.

Robert Weinberg

For a brief, horrific moment, the Digital Web flickers and goes blank.

When it comes back online three seconds later, dozens of mages are dead. Hundreds of other are dazed or catatonic with shock. Formatted Sectors have been erased. Mundane web sites have crashed. Whole networks have been scrambled or wiped clean. It will take years to reboot the system.

Soon, the Virtual Adepts will call this day White Monday, after the huge Whiteout that occurred. Others will refer to the Great Crash of '97. The Technocrats have no need for such drivel. With the tireless determination that has always marked the existence of the Union, the Technocrats set their jaws firmly and get back to work...

In the mountains of Tennessee, an earthquake shakes a grass-covered knoll on which stands a grouping of large granite blocks. From high overhead, the rocks form a pattern resembling two intersecting arrows. After the ground calms, the design is no longer evident. A pack of Red Talon werewolves, blaming the disaster on a small group of Technomancers stationed in a nearby town, raid the village, ripping the bioengineered humans to pieces.

In Kuwait, sixteen oil wells catch fire. The resulting explosions kills thirty-seven men and women. The sites are capped and the blazes extinguished. The reason for the holocaust remains undetermined.

On Horizon, tongues of energy dart from a dozen hidden entrances to the Realm. A blazing light flashes for a microsecond, then goes dark. Such links to other Horizon Realms are strictly forbidden, but enforcing such a rule is impossible. There is little question that all of the routes lead to Doissetep. No one attempts to enter the doorway to the Shade Realm of Forces.

Attending a strategy meeting with the five members of the Council of Nine, Kallikos, once known as Akrites, breathes a heavy sigh of despair.

"Another step on the downward path," he declares. "One after another, the chains of the future grow tighter around our necks."

No one else says a word. There is nothing to say. Everyone is in shock. Along with Horizon, Doissetep served as an anchor for the Nine Traditions. Without it, they feel cast adrift.

In Malfeas, Aliara frowns. She does not like what the destruction implies.

Elsewhere, Lord Steel laughs.

An explosion rocks one of the wealthiest neighborhoods in Boston. A large, two-story mansion known as the Delono House disappears in a black cloud of wood and steel. The huge ten-car garage is engulfed by the blast, warping the autos into twisted piles of scrap metal. When the dust settles, many hours later, all that remains is a huge crater, much deeper than a normal basement. Numerous bodies are found, all of them burned and mangled beyond identification.

A similar detonation destroys Fulroony Manor in England. Casualties are many, and several smaller homes on the estate are consumed by a fire so intense that it melts steel. A series of sharp explosions punctures the blaze. Along with more than a dozen cars, a helicopter is also destroyed. There appear to be no survivors, but since no one in the area was ever sure exactly how many people lived at the Manor, or who they were, a precise list of the dead and missing is impossible.

In Toledo, Spain, an old three-story building, large and stately, in the center of the downtown business section collapses with a roar. Tons and tons of brick crash to the street, killing dozens of customers in the surrounding shops. There is no logical explanation for the disaster.

...the fall of Doissetep and the death of Porthos Fitz-Empress.

Overwhelmed by what he had just seen, Seventeen took a few minutes to realize he was no longer wrapped in darkness. The sky above him was black, but filled with stars. The ground beneath him was firm. In the distance, there were sounds of life.

Gingerly, he pushed himself up off the dirt to a sitting position. A few feet away, he saw Shadow of the Dawn rise smoothly to her bare feet with the fluid grace of her namesake. She was as elemental as the night. Her gaze searched the area until she found him.

Seventeen wearily raised a hand in greeting. Shadow smiled.

"You saw?" he asked. "You witnessed the end?"

She nodded, the smile vanishing from her face. "He died," she declared, "protecting others. It was a noble end, a true warrior's death."

"Any idea where we are?" he asked, trying to make out details of their location in the darkness. "Looks like flat prairie."

"There are many huge stones nearby," said Shadow. She pointed at massive shapes in the night. "They appear to have fallen."

Seventeen turned slowly in a circle, surveying their arrival point. No question about it. They had arrived in the exact center of a vast ring of stone lintels. The monoliths, however, were no longer standing. The force of Doissetep's destruction had knocked the ancient temple flat.

"Stonehenge," said Seventeen, the name springing from his subconscious. "One of the most ancient places of worship on Earth, and a Node of incredible potency."

Anxiously, he grabbed Shadow of the Dawn's hand. "We better move. When the locals discover this place has been destroyed, they're not going to be happy. Better if we're not around to be blamed."

"I sense several Chantry Houses nearby," said Shadow. "We can take shelter in one of them."

"Good idea," said Seventeen. "Hey, what's this?"

A solitary stone remained standing among the tumbled ruins. A rough-hewn altar. Resting on it was a slender red book that glowed with a magickal light. Reaching out, Seventeen lifted the volume off the rock. He knew without any doubt that here was Porthos's final gift. In his hands, he held the archmage's sole copy of *The Fragile Path*.

<u>Chapter Nineteen</u>

There were loud, angry voices up ahead in the parking lot. Madeleine, always cautious, faded behind an interstate tanker as she sought the cause of the disturbance. She'd thought the speakers sounded familiar. They were.

The Riley brothers were back. So was Willy Smith. As usual, they had decided to entertain themselves at other peoples' expense. The "other people," in this case, were the Rat Pack.

Brian lay crumpled on the asphalt. His Metallica T-shirt was wet with blood. Willy Smith stood over him, grinning, a baseball bat in his hands. Lucy, furious, thrashed and kicked in Cain's grip. The big man had wrapped the girl in her own chain, binding her arms to her sides. Pete held one hand over his face, staggering. The knife in his hand glittered impotently in the parking lot glare. Allyson dodged in and out of arm's reach, cutting at Abel's callused hands with her bayonet. From the looks of the things, she had scored a few small hits, but the biker's leather jacket protected his body from the blade. He laughed, clearly playing with the girl. As Madeleine watched, Sybil heaved a bottle at Cain. It hit him solid, bounced off and shattered behind him. Sarah was crouched over to one side, sobbing. Spots of blood marked her progress there.

It was, in short, a massacre. And Madeleine had seen enough of it. The apes who called themselves "Hellblazers" were about to discover the true heat of hell's flames.

The monster looked around. No one was watching. Considering the noise, this wasn't surprising. No one listened to screams at Sleazy Sams', unless they wanted to lend encouragement. Good. Madeleine had several secrets she wished to keep. The children were going to learn the nature of their benefactor soon enough. And the Hellblazers weren't going to be telling anyone what they'd seen.

Cain heaved Lucy over his shoulder. "Come on, kid. Let's go have some fun. It's not like you're a virgin or nothin', and I'm as good as any trucker."

Lucy's response was a flood of profanity that would have deafened a marine. Her feet flew through empty air, her knees thudding against the big man's chest and face. He laughed, a bit unsteady but far stronger than she. The blows seemed to make him more excited.

Soundlessly, Madeleine sank into the asphalt parking lot. Many vampires possessed a power known as the "earth meld"; with it, they could pass into solid ground and hide within the soil. Madeleine was one of the very few who had discovered the secret of moving *through* the ground—a special talent that made her one of the most dangerous assassins in the world.

"You a big man?" Willy roared to the pile at his feet. "You wanna learn to fight, ya little shithead? Fighting *hurts*, boy. See?" The baseball bat thudded into Brian's chest. Something cracked. The boy screamed. "*Hurts*, don't it?" Willy bellowed, his voice sounding eerily like his father's once had.

Abel grabbed Allyson's wrist and hauled her off-balance. She swung at him and missed. His open hand slapped her hard enough to knock the girl off her feet. "*Bastard!!*" Sybil wailed, leaping on the big man's back. In her corner, Sarah tried to stand. Her legs collapsed. So did she.

Pete lunged at his brother's tormentor. The boy's lead pipe thumped off the back of Willy's head, knocking him sprawling. The Hellblazer grunted frantically, clawing at the back of his head, dazed and furious. Pete dragged Brian to his feet. "Ooo, you little bastard! *Ooo*, you little *bastard!*" Willy was practically *channeling* his father now, moaning with the same drunken whine his old man had perfected. "I'm gonna skin you alive and hang you on my wall!"

Blood was on the wind.

Abel slammed Sybil into the side of a car. She hung on. He swung around and slammed her into another car. "Ya bald little nigger freak," he cried, "*get offa me!*"

He never got a chance to slam her again.

Like a shadow, Madeleine sprang from the asphalt.

All her cool composure was gone. In its place raged the blood-drinking monster called the Dagger of the Giovanni.

Her hand took him in the crotch, then ripped. Abel shrieked like a boiled child. Two, three, four, five times she ripped into his body. Each time she took a handful. By the sixth time, there was nothing left to grasp. Abel still screamed, silent now with shredded lungs. Sybil stared, her own mouth open wide. The attack had taken five seconds. Abel fell, taking Sybil with him.

Next.

Willy was still trying to stand when Madeleine made that impossible. Her fingers arced for his eyes. The last thing he saw was the ghost of his father, swinging his fist.

The pain lasted longer than his vision did.

Seven cars suffered the impact of his body. The dents it made were quite impressive, and the colors of viscera mingled darkly with the paint.

Next.

Cain gaped as the other men turned into crimson fountains. Madeleine moved faster than the eye could follow. Everything was a blur and a spray. Then she came for him.

Lucy slipped free as Madeleine lunged. She hit the pavement hard, but not as hard as Cain. He hit it several times. In pieces.

Silence.

Then the sound of mumbled praying, and someone's helpless retching.

Sarah stared at their benefactor with a combination of awe, horror and love. Mama had always said that angels were terrible in their anger, and if Sarah had ever doubted the woman in black's divinity, that doubt was erased forever.

Even when Madeleine Giovanni licked the blood from her fingers and fed on Abel's corpse.

"Uh." That was all Allyson could say as she backed away from their terrifying benefactor, poised to run like hell.

Lucy was slightly more eloquent: "Mother-*fucker*!" She repeated it like a mantra, clutching herself tightly, till the words lost every bit of sense.

Brian and Pete said nothing, although their eyes darted about fearfully. They were used to silence. Dad had made sure of that.

"Now *that*," said Sybil finally, recovering herself and wiping her mouth shakily, "is one bad-ass bitch."

The red haze receded as the blood fever cooled. Madeleine looked up, straightening her skirt, to meet the eyes of six thunderstruck young people. "Perhaps," she said as if nothing had happened, "we should talk."

Hypnotized by the suddenness of the violence and by Madeleine's matter-of-fact tone, the Rat Pack slowly followed after her.

They dumped the corpses off the side of the road. The Hellblazers' bikes went in after them, crunching in the underbrush. The cannibals would be blamed for one more atrocity, but it was doubtful anyone would mourn the deaths for long.

"So what happened?" asked the Dagger of the

Giovanni as she bathed in a cold stream nearby. Sarah had nervoulsy averted her gaze from Madeleine's nakedness and Brian was in too much pain to care. Sybil washed blood from the monster's clothes as Lucy hugged her moaning friend and stared at Madeleine. Pete just stood watch, his arms folded across his thin chest, flannel shirt rippling in the night breeze. His face was as unreadable as the stone he stood upon.

Allyson answered. As the leader, it was sort of her duty to report to the woman who had clearly been their savior. "Normally, we stay far away from outlaws, especially those three fuckers. Why ask for trouble, right? But tonight some drunk dropped his wallet near the bikes. Lucy was picking it up when the fat dude showed up."

"Lucy discovers many 'fallen wallets,'" Madeleine remarked, rinsing her hair in the icy creek. "She must be very lucky."

Allyson laughed nervously. "Yeah, well, I don't know if 'lucky' is the right word for Luce, but she definitely finds a lot of dropped shit."

"She must be more careful." The words were simple, but filled with meaning.

Allyson drew her knees up to her chin, hunching herself smaller. "She will be. I promise."

Lucy nodded. The thin moonlight still shone on her bloody face. The normally vocal girl had not spoken since they left the scene. Silence kept her from screaming.

"Leo has been feeding you well?" asked Madeleine.

Allyson nodded vigorously. "Leo's cool. He's been really good to us lately."

"Good," Madeleine remarked. "And the woman with the two swords? Have you encountered her again?"

"Not a sign of her or her boyfriend, the guy in the fancy shirt," said Allyson. "We've been searching, but no luck so far. Maybe she's left the neighborhood."

"Perhaps for the moment," said Madeleine. "A conversation I overheard recently suggests that she is with several companions elsewhere. But the speaker sounded certain she would return shortly. When she does, I want to know where she is. And with whom."

"You got it," said Allyson, quietly. "The Rat Pack does its job."

Madeleine smiled. "Continue with your fine efforts." She paused as Sybil handed her the damp garments, frowning as she squeezed water from the fabric.

Sybil tensed at Madeleine's displeasure. "Um, I can try to dry them out some more. They're not still bloody, are they?"

The monster smiled. "No, Sybil, they are fine. Thank you. I can see that you work well in a crisis…" she moved her gaze across the Rat Pack, meeting every eye in turn… "and tonight was indeed a crisis. I do not make excuses for what I am, nor do I expect you to discuss it with strangers. Understood?"

The teenagers nodded, with a mixture of fear and fascination.

"Um, Madeleine," whispered Lucy. "Thank you. I

mean, *really* thank you, for everything and stuff, not just for tonight, but for tonight, too, y'know—"

Madeleine cut off the sudden torrent of words. "You needed me. I was there. When I need you, I expect you will be there as well."

"You bet. Totally."

"Whatever you need," Pete said suddenly, "we'll do it if we can."

"Yeah." Brian's voice was weak and strained.

"I will walk in glory with the Lord and His hosts," said Sarah.

"Will you knock that off?" snapped Sybil. "You're creepin' me out."

"That'd be a 'yes,'" Allyson said at last.

"Good." Madeleine slid her hose up and pulled the damp dress over her head, wrinkling her nose slightly at the feel of cold, wet fabric. "I have an important meeting to attend, and I am already late. I trust we will not repeat tonight's escapade?"

"Not with *them*, anyway," Sybil muttered.

"Nope," Lucy assured her. "We're gonna be a lot more careful."

The scent of blood still carried on the breeze. Madeleine tried to ignore it, but she couldn't deny that the biker's vitae had been foul and tainted. These children, on the other hand, were thin but....

She pushed the thought away.

Madeleine recovered quickly. "If any of you find yourselves threatened again, or if you need to contact me for some deeply important emergency, think my name—Madeleine Giovanni—as hard as you can. If it is after sundown, and if I consider it important enough, I will come to you. Do *not*," she stated, scanning the group, "abuse this gift. It is a special dispensation for my loyal friends, and must not be misused. Understood?"

The Rat Pack clearly understood the importance of its benefactor's good graces.

Madeleine straightened her dress and slipped her shoes on. "Good. I believe that the Rat Pack has had enough excitement for one night."

"Got that right," muttered Sybil.

"Take care," said the Dagger of the Giovanni, "and begone. Clean yourselves, nurse each other as you have before. I will have Leo arrange for special care if you need it. I have a meeting to attend to. Farewell!" So saying, she melted into the earth and was gone.

Sleazy Sam's had not changed. Madeleine nodded to Leo but didn't approach the bar. A booth in the rear stood empty. She slipped onto the bench away from the door. Though no one entering the tavern would see her, Madeleine wasn't worried about being missed.

"Hey, babe!" This typical specimen of barroom trash spoke in a slurred, affected Southern accent. Its artificiality was as painful as the sight of his flabby gut, which he, shirtless, had on proud display. The Grand Belly hung over the edge of his tight blue jeans, cinched at the waist by a braided leather belt. The man wore a biker's vest (clearly for show only—it lacked the flaws of real streetware) and cowboy boots with authentic scuffs. His scruffy face looked like the bottom of a beer glass on a Friday night. "C'mon down here," he drawled, "and gimme some sugar."

"No thank you," said Madeleine. First Willy Smith, now this pest. She had no patience for this tonight. Abel's beer-sodden blood had left her a bit dizzy and she needed all her wits now. The scent of vitae still hung about her. Her "date" would surely notice.

"Hey, c'mon, ma'am, don't be like that," the pig insisted. He goggled up at her with drunken wonder. "A woman as beautiful as you shouldn't be alone in a place like this. It ain't safe."

"Thank you for your concern," she said, setting steel fingers on his shoulder just tightly enough to hurt. "But I am quite safe. And I will not be alone. I have come to meet someone, and he can be quite jealous." Her eyes glowed just the faintest tinge of red. "Violently so, sometimes. I would not want anything *untoward* to happen to a fine man like yourself."

"Uh, sure," the swine replied. He caught sight of a nightmare and leaned back to his beer. "Just trying to be friendly."

"Madeleine, you are the mistress of the understated threat," said Montifloro. As expected, he had slipped into the booth without notice. While Madeleine possessed unique powers of deception, Montifloro was the master of blending in with his surroundings. He went where he wanted, did what was necessary, without ever being noticed. It was not just an exercise of his vampiric powers. It was a subtlety that formed an essential part of his character. "And that perfume you wear. So…intoxicating."

Short and frail, Montifloro appeared to be an ordinary businessman in his late thirties. He had thick black hair and dark eyes. As always, he was impeccably dressed in an Armani suit and Tuscany shoes. Only his pale white features hinted that he might be something more than he seemed.

"It is good to see you again, cousin," said Madeleine. "I was concerned you might miss our meeting."

"Afraid I would be spending my time with the lovely Ms. Hope?" asked Montifloro, a whisper of laughter in his tone. "Or worried I might be plotting to overthrow Pietro so that I could make that lovely young lady mine for all eternity?"

Madeleine smiled. "I should have known you would sense my presence in that concrete tomb, cousin. While I felt certain you were merely acting, your performance was quite convincing. It fooled both Enzo and Ezra. They think they have you teetering on the brink of open revolt against my grandfather."

"Ezra?" said Montifloro. "He was present as well? Invisible, I assume? If I had realized before entering I was going to play before a full house, I would have been much more melodramatic. A few tears of black blood for effect."

He waved a hand at a slovenly waitress walking past their table. "A bottle of your best red wine, dear lady," he commanded.

"Yeah, dream on, Romeo," the waitress sneered.

He chuckled as the woman headed for the bar. "Not

that the quality matters in our present state, but old habits die hard. I always order the best, though I can never drink."

"You were quite convincing the other night," said Madeleine. "This girl, Hope? Enzo seems to think she is a beauty. Are you tempted by her at all?"

"Tempted?" replied Montifloro, with a laugh. "Repelled is a better word. If you think I gave a masterly performance for our cousin, you should see me fawn over his puppet. The woman is a cheap whore, given a superficial polish by Enzo and his lackey, a very strange woman named Ms. Hargroves. Though I have no evidence, I suspect that gaunt specter is more than a mere secretary."

"Ezra does not trust her either," said Madeleine. "Though Enzo expressed his complete confidence in her abilities."

"Thank you, my dear," said Montifloro, to the waitress as she set down a bottle of Mad Dog and two glasses. He handed her a fifty-dollar bill. "Please, keep the change. A small tribute to your charm."

"You are too easy with your money, Montifloro," said Madeleine, as the astonished waitress departed.

"I have earned our clan many millions, dear cousin," said Montifloro, pouring each of them a full glass of the red. "My expenses are minimal compared to the return I generate. Besides, I spend freely now, for tomorrow may never come."

"You fear for your existence?" asked Madeleine.

"Of course," said Montifloro. "As should you. We play a very dangerous game. There is much to learn before my work is complete. Pietro wants a full report about Enzo's activities and I intend to deliver it to him. In the meantime, I am dealing with two power-hungry, paranoid lunatics. One hint that I am not the fool they suppose, and my body will be dust. I walk a tightrope over the infernal pit, and the flames of hell are licking at both ends."

"You have courage, Montifloro," said Madeleine. "Of the two tasks given us by Pietro, yours is by far the more perilous."

Montifloro shrugged. "You are the Dagger of the Giovanni," he said with a smile. "I am the poison."

"I must admit," said Madeleine, "that I was astonished Enzo was so confident of your seduction. Though he and I were never close, from the way you described him in the past, I always thought our clansman was quite astute. He displayed little intelligence during the course of the evening while I watched him. Ezra clearly dominated their exchanges. And as mentioned, he thinks that you—the most cunning and duplicitous member of our clan—have been seduced by a mere mortal. These are not the thoughts of a master plotter."

"I agree totally with you, Madeleine," Montifloro declared. "It is a sad commentary on the state of our cousin's wits that he thinks we are so easily fooled. His scheme to turn me against Pietro is painfully obvious. That he has similar hopes for you as well are equally transparent. Once, he was a master tactician, who could spin a web with subtle grace. No longer. Enzo's mind is slipping badly if he truly thinks we can be manipulated in such a manner."

"He dines with the devil," said Madeleine. "Ezra is completely insane, warped beyond imagining. This Ms. Hargroves has ties with the unnameable. Their influence has corrupted Enzo, turned him into a fool."

"There is more than that," said Montifloro. "Enzo has always been ambitious. That he wants to replace Pietro as head of our clan is no surprise. Such rivalries are the true lifeblood of the Kindred. Still, from small snips of conversation with him, I deduce he dreams even greater dreams. Enzo desires to rule everything. Kine and Kindred, human and vampire. Greed has overwhelmed his good sense. Vast shadows stir in the darkness behind him."

"Pietro spoke of Endron International, the energy conglomerate," said Madeleine. "Enzo is a member of their Board of Directors."

"But who controls Endron?" asked Montifloro. "That is the real question. I sense an even greater power, one that seeks to twist and reshape all of creation. Perhaps I grasp at phantoms, Madeleine, but the past few days I have been carefully studying the books of Enzo's corporation. The financial structure of Everwell, of Endron, suggests a vast mega-organization siphoning funds from those companies—and many others, too. Everything points to one huge, monolithic organization dedicated to the absolute domination of the Earth."

"Very similar in scope to the ultimate plans of Clan Giovanni," said Madeleine, no longer smiling.

"Exactly," said Montifloro. "Needless to say, between two such competing powers, there can never be peace. Only war, until one or the other is completely destroyed."

"And have you discovered a name for this secret empire?" asked Madeleine. "Our possible rivals?"

"I have," said Montifloro. "*Pentex.*"

Chapter Twenty

Charles Klair's footsteps echoed like a drumbeat, a sharp, staccato cadence pounding through the quiet streets of the slums. Long after midnight, the cobblestone byways in this rundown section of Albany were deserted. No one stirred as he walked in measured, even steps in the inky darkness. Somehow the street people, the homeless, the solitary gangbangers, even the stray dogs that normally inhabited the back alleys and tenement doorways sensed that this was a man to avoid. Half-opened windows slammed closed as his footfalls approached. Doors were pushed shut. Conversations inside apartments muted, then ceased. It was as if the Angel of Death moved across the cobblestones. Which was not far from the truth.

The Comptroller, as he still thought of himself, had arrived in Albany earlier that evening. His original destination had been the headquarters of Dynamic Security. He soon discovered that the building no longer existed. A major gas explosion the day before had leveled the entire structure, killing more than a hundred employees. Firefighters were still sorting the wreckage, hunting for survivors, but there was little hope that anyone would be found alive. Already certain rabble-rousing radio talk show hosts were hinting of a possible terrorist connection. No group had come forth to claim credit for the incredible destruction, but most felt it was only a matter of time. Eco-terrorists, a favorite whipping boy of the right, were the prime suspects. Or left-wing lunatics of the pro-choice movement. Neither had any dealings with Dynamic Security, but when explosions occurred, common sense was always the first casualty.

Well-educated in the methods of the Syndicate and the New World Order, Klair recognized defensive fallback maneuvers immediately. Listening to all the details of the explosion, it soon became clear to him that the NWO headquarters had been overrun by a horde of Reality Deviants. The explosion had come much later, after the attackers had left. The bomb was a Syndicate operation, done to erase all traces of the raid. The Union understood that the existence of Reality Deviants needed to be kept hidden from the Masses. The truth might be out there, but it was not for the unenlightened. Gas main explosions and terrorists made convenient scapegoats.

A phone call to an outlying Iteration X station made it possible for him to tap into the Construct computer network without even leaving the telephone kiosk. His internal modem, linked directly to his memory, ran a hundred times faster than an ordinary machine and downloaded all the information he required in a few seconds.

Sharon Reed and X344, now using his original name, Ernest Nelson, had been at Dynamic Security when the attack had taken place. This, he could confirm. However, as best as could be determined by the identification teams sent into the wreckage, neither the cyborg nor the Progenitor leader's bodies had been among the victims discovered in the building. Either they had been captured by the raiders, or they had escaped. Klair meant to determine which. Tonight.

A dim throbbing filled the street. Lights flickered as if in time with the music. The noise came from a large brick building a hundred feet ahead. Above it, a bright red neon sign proclaimed "The Club of Lost Souls." The words were wrapped around a glowing picture of Charles Laughton and Bela Lugosi, taken from the 1930s' movie, *Isle of Lost Souls*.

The film, and the book upon which it had been based, *The Island of Dr. Moreau* by H.G. Wells, had always been a major annoyance to the Progenitors. They considered Wells' attack on genetic manipulation a personal affront, just as Iteration X had felt *The Time Machine*, with its subhuman morlocks, was been a thinly veiled diatribe against its goals. Klair, who had grown up on a steady diet of science fiction films, liked both movies but also knew better than to contradict Technocracy policy.

According to the NWO computer data banks, the dance club was a notorious hangout for the worst elements of the state capital. It served as a gathering place for members of the vampire cult known as the Sabbat. And if rumors could be believed, it was also a secret rendezvous point for Fallen mages—*Nephandi*.

Klair reasoned that if anyone knew the fate of Reed and Nelson, he would find that person at this Club of Lost Souls. He knew that extracting information from them might prove difficult. Most likely, it would mean engaging in extreme violence. Police interference in this section of town was unlikely. He was totally on his own. Klair smiled. Once he would have avoided such situations. Now, he was looking forward to it.

There were a few junked cars parked in front of the club. A drunken loser sat in a heap, his head resting against one of the walls. Bleary bloodshot eyes stared up at Klair. The man licked his lips, then gathered his legs beneath him and scurried off into the night. Laughing softly, the Comptroller took the last few steps to the club's front entrance.

A heavy steel door barred the way. Above it was a compact video camera. A buzzer waited on the right side of the entrance, and a heavy metallic mesh welcome mat with the words *Moreau was a real cut-up* draped across the ground.

Klair glanced up at the camera. A simple machine. He reached up and touched it, taking command of the computer-driven imagery. Instead of showing a tall, gangly, hairless man dressed in loose-fitting black pants and baggy black shirt, he was now short and thin, with ashen features, shaven head and a nose ring. Nodding in approval, Klair pressed the buzzer.

"What's the word?" asked a lifeless voice from a hidden speaker on the opposite wall.

"'Are we not men?'" quoted Klair. He found such gimmickry foolish. He could have easily smashed in the door, but that would have warned the patrons. Better they were unprepared for his entrance.

"Open sesame," said the unseen voice. The heavy metal door swung open. "Enter, brother."

Candles dotted the black expanse of the inner chamber. Bright lights exploded, swept and faded across the room. The Electric Hellfire Club bellowed *"God is dead! Satan lives!"* from a deafening sound array. Four black-wrapped figures writhed on the dance floor, simulating sex, death and damnation at once. A pack of brooding misfits lined the bar, watching the dancers with a mixture of lust and scorn. On the walls, crude murals celebrated torture, mutilation and hard-core bondage.

How trite. How predictable. Klair had expected something grander from the hosts of the Fallen.

Klair scanned the room with electric eyes, noting each important feature before moving on. Twelve figures, apparently human, occupied the chamber. Klair's analysis pinpointed nine humans and three vampires. Quintessence scans revealed glowing auras around three of the living ones. Magi, most likely Nephandi. None of them seemed especially powerful. This was a minor relaxation zone, then. A playground for the faction's lesser members.

Perhaps they knew what Klair wanted to know. Perhaps not. Either way, it was going to be a pleasure to find out. Not that Klair needed pleasure. Such trivia was for the Masses and the Deviants, not for him.

The bartender, a huge mountain of a man, well over six feet tall with immensely broad shoulders, a barrel chest, and short-clipped red hair, looked at Klair with a puzzled expression. "You looked different on a TV monitor," he said, his voice loud and surly.

Klair nodded. Though the barkeep appeared mortal, he was not breathing. His eyelids did not blink. And the thin red line on one cheek was dried human blood. "I don't photograph well," said Klair, stepping closer to the bar.

With a mental shrug, Klair activated the gunnery sequence. Five fingers on his left hand clicked together, snapped, slid into a fist and dropped on a hinge. A small but lethal chain-gun emerged from the stump of his wrist and fired.

A hail of exploding anti-personnel shells ripped the bar patrons into bloody confetti. They would find out the truth about God and Satan soon enough. Another burst jerked the dancers around like firecracker marionettes. The strobe lights slowed every detail of the carnage.

With a curse, the bartender spun. Klair grasped the vampire's throat with his right hand and squeezed.

Fingers that could bend steel bars without effort crushed the vampire's neck. Yanking hard, Klair hauled him over the top of the bar and threw him to the floor. Pinning him to the wood, the Comptroller slapped the huge man three times across the face.

Robert Weinberg

Each blow smashed bones to fragments. The monster roared. Though nearly unkillable, he could still feel pain.

The bartender tried to wrench himself free, but Klair's grip was solid. For an instant the Comptroller looked up, placing his enemies. Stunned by the hail of bullets and his sudden attack on the bartender, they were just starting to move. The two other vampires, a short, slender woman with blade-like nails and a swarthy-looking man with wide shoulders and face like a gorilla, seemed unsure what to do. The three Nephandi appeared satisfied to watch with twisted glee. They had no idea that Klair was after them, not the Kindred.

It was no effort at all to transform his free hand from chain-gun into cutting edge. Microns thick, made of a metal not of earthly origin, the blade could slice through flesh and bone and nearly anything else. Moving with speed only made possible by the most advanced computer systems, Klair slashed downward at the bartender's neck. The creature didn't have time to scream. Resistance was minimal. Klair's hand chunked inches into the wooden floor, and the vampire's head rolled beneath a nearby table. In seconds, the decapitated monster started to dissolve. There were three sure methods of killing a member of the Kindred. Decapitation was the most practical.

"Get him!" screamed the woman with the claw-like nails, pushing her swarthy companion at Klair. "Rip the bastard's heart out!"

Growling like an animal, the male vampire hurtled

forward at the Comptroller. Klair, his reflexes powered by microcircuits working at near light-speed, barely moved. Instead, he turned and faced his new attacker, both his hands now changed into Primium steel cutting blades. He let the Kindred's forward momentum do much of his work. Flashing through the air like a Japanese steak-house chef, Klair sliced the startled vampire into a half-dozen pieces. By the time the second monster dropped in sections to the floor, he was already beginning to dissolve.

"Get away from me!" shrieked the third and final vampire. With her gaze fixed on Klair, she was trying desperately to circle him and reach the door. Her eyes grew wide as she tried to exert the power of her will against him. Klair laughed. His mind was not so easy controlled.

Transforming his hands back to normal, he grabbed a wooden chair and tore it to pieces. Sensing his purpose, the woman screamed and sprinted for the exit. She moved with inhuman speed, but Klair was just as fast. With three quick flicks, his finger honed the edge of one chair leg to a dull point. It wasn't much of a stake, but it was enough.

The power behind Klair's thrust would have driven the makeshift spear through a brick wall. Flesh and bone offered little resistance. The vampire dropped to the floor, not dead but paralyzed. As long as the stake remained in place in her heart, she was harmless, unable to move. For now, for Klair, that was enough. Later, he would drag her outside to melt in the sunrise.

Robert Weinberg

The three Nephandi applauded as he turned. Their faces were alight with a insane glow. "Neat stuff," said a tall, heavyset man wearing black leather pants and a black vest. His skin was covered everywhere with tattoos. "Goin' on a murder binge?"

"They weren't obeying the motto," said Klair, taking a slow step closer to the three Nephandi.

"The motto?" This came from a girl—short, slender, with blood red hair, red eyebrows, and bright blue eyes. She wore a black bra and white shorts. By Klair's count, she was pierced in seven parts of her body that showed. He suspected there were more rings as well in places that did not. "What motto?"

"Yeah," said the third of the trio. He was tall, very thin, with dark skin, short hair and a ragged fringe beard. His cheeks were marked with mystic symbols, as was his bare chest. Wrapped around his waist, instead of a belt, was a sleeping serpent. "What the fuck are you talkin' about?"

"The password for the bar," said Klair, taking another step closer. He was near enough to touch the man with the snake. "Are we not men?"

"Hey, brother," said the man with all the tattoos. He made "brother" sound like a curse. "What's your deal?"

Klair shrugged. "Don't you think it's an important question?" he asked. The switch from normal hand to chain-gun was instant and effortless. Raising his arm, he pushed the weapon into the half-opened mouth of the man with the snake. Klair felt a powerful will try to jam the bullets, but his mind was much more focused. The gun jumped as a dozen shells blew the top of his victim's head off.

"Romeo!" The girl with the piercings screamed. She was the one Klair planned to question. Women were weak. They bent under pressure. "You killed Romeo!"

"Men are those beings who think logically," said Klair, thrusting the girl to the side and grabbing the tattooed man with his normal hand. "Those who support Unity are true men. Those who oppose it are Reality Deviants and do not deserve to live."

"You're fuckin' crazy," roared the tattooed man, trying to wrench free from Klair. But the Comptroller's fingers were like a vise. He swung the gun up to finish the job.

Snarling with rage, the girl with the rings leapt onto Klair's back, her fingers gouging for his eyes. Despite his new reflexes and near-invulnerable form, Klair was not an experienced fighter. Caught by surprise, he flinched, squeezing his eyes shut, momentarily loosening his grip on the tattooed man.

"Try this for logical," spat the man in black leather. The girl leapt back and fell away, and a wave of fire roared to life, engulfing Klair. Wreathed in flame, the Comptroller laughed. He felt nothing. Opening his eyes, he stared at the tattooed man. The bizarre inked figures were crawling about the Nephandi willworker's body. They were part of his magick.

"Enough," said Klair and the fires puffed out. His lips twisted in a grimace of pure hate, the tattooed man stumbled back among the tables. Slowly, methodically, relentlessly, Klair followed. He wondered what had happened to the girl. She had not left—the door to the bar hadn't been touched. She was around somewhere, and up to no good.

The answer was quick coming. From behind the bar, a gun boomed. The shell struck Klair in the side of the head. A soft-nosed, crossed titanium steel shell designed for maximum damage, the bullet was of the type fondly known among terrorists as "the mangler." It shredded targets like a steel grater. Still, the shell was meant for ordinary targets, like everyday shoppers. Or schoolchildren. It was not designed to stop advanced cybernetic life forms like Comptroller Klair.

Pausing for a moment, Klair turned and searched the room for the girl's exact position. She was crouched behind the wood-and-pipe bar, both hands on the counter holding the pistol steady. Her body jerked as she squeezed the trigger a second time. Another shell splattered harmlessly across Klair's chest. The woman was distracting him from finishing her tattooed companion. Klair could not permit either of them to escape.

The gun would be too lethal for this purpose. Instead, Klair snapped his fingers. The vibration, magnified to disrupter pitch, jammed the gun's firing mechanism. *Click. Click.* A curse. The girl tossed the pistol to the side, reached under the bar, and pulled out a sawed-off shotgun. She was just raising the weapon when the laser hidden by Klair's left eye burned her fingers, charring the flesh black. With a screech of pain, the girl dropped the shotgun and collapsed behind the bar. She would only be down for a minute or two, but Klair felt certain that would be enough to finish off her companion.

Something large and green with a hundred tentacles and a circle of eyes atop its huge head faced Klair as he turned back to locate his original quarry. The Comptroller waved a hand in dismissal. The illusion was a minor one, not even affecting his sense of smell. It vanished, revealing the tattooed man directly in Klair's path. In his hands he held a long black leather whip. A typical Nephandi weapon, its touch burned flesh. Screaming obscenities, the tattooed man lashed out at the Comptroller's head.

The leather thong wrapped around Klair's neck like a serpent. The whip had a strange half-life of its own. Howling madly, the tattooed man yanked it forward, trying to pull the Comptroller off his feet. Against a normal man, it would have worked. The Comptroller was not even remotely normal. The leather stretched, but Klair didn't move.

"An illogical attack," said Klair, grabbing hold of the whip with one hand and tearing it from his attacker's grip. Two steps, and the Comptroller wrapped the leather coils around the man's neck. The tattooed man managed to scream once before the tightening noose cut off his breath. He died instants later, when Klair pulled the whip so tight that it nearly severed the Nephandi's head from his shoulders. "Never match strength with an unknown enemy."

Now only the girl remained. She was running

wildly for the door when Klair grabbed her. Carefully gauging his strength, he flung her against the nearest wall. Not too hard. He wanted her alive and able to speak.

Stunned, she slumped to the floor and looked up at him with bleary, bitter eyes. Her fingers were burnt, her body badly bruised. But there was no surrender in her face. "Kill me, you bastard," she declared. "I'm not afraid of you."

"Then you are extremely stupid," said Klair. "I want to ask you a few questions. Answer them and I will give you your freedom. Refuse and you will join your companions in hell."

"Fuck you! Better hell than betray Al!" sneered the girl.

"The poison within your cheek and beneath your tongue no longer has any potency," said Klair, kneeling beside the girl. "Nor will the needle beneath your left breast puncture your heart if you make the correct motion. I neutralized those options several micro-seconds ago. You cannot cheat me that easily."

"Fuck off, metalhead," the girl snarled. "I got nothing to say to you."

"On the contrary," said Klair, "I believe you do."

He held up his right hand, extended his first finger. The metallic skin flowed like quicksilver, re-forming the digit into a corkscrew-shaped sliver of steel four inches long. "I noticed you have a number of piercings," said Klair. "I thought I would provide you with several more. In spots determined, by computer analysis, to cause maximum pain. Continual and never ending. Shall we start with your kneecaps? Then move on to the small of your back?"

The girl broke out in a sweat. Her eyes grew wide as she saw that Klair's finger was somehow rotating like a drill attached to his palm.

"I remember, as a child, listening to dentists who said 'this won't hurt a bit,'" said Klair, taking hold of the girl's right knee with his left hand. Though she struggled, it was impossible for her to move. He brought the tip of his drill finger in contact with her white flesh. "In contrast, let me say that this will hurt quite badly."

The steel had barely broken her skin, sending a trickle of warm blood down her leg, when the girl gasped, "Stop, I'll talk. Who the hell cares. What do you want to know?"

"I appreciate your cooperation," said Klair. He raised his hand so the drill was right before the girl's eyes. "Last night, a group of Nephandi raided Dynamic Security. You were with that war party?"

"Of course," said the girl. "Everybody went to play." She laughed. "We had a fun time, ripping the guts out of Technobabies. They died screaming. Friends and relatives of yours, I hope."

"The destruction appeared extensive," said Klair, his voice calm, unaffected by her words. "Did you achieve your objectives? Were you given specific orders about certain people you were to find?"

The girl paused. A wave of the drill got her talking: "Three targets. Some computer programmer. Wailer got him, smashed him flat. Two others, a woman and a cyborg. Tough mothers. They somehow fought their way free. Won't be safe for long, though. Wailer's tracking 'em down."

"The Wailer," repeated Klair, dredging up information pulled from the NWO computer databanks. "The name given to a major Nephandi lord in this region. He was the one who ordered the attack?"

"Who the fuck knows?" said the girl. "I ain't no mastermind. He's the one who gives the orders."

"Implying that perhaps someone else was actually in charge of the operation," said Klair. "How interesting. Please tell me who that might be, or I will be forced to operate. An eyeball would make a good target."

"There's rumors," said the girl hurriedly. "That's all. Just rumors. Everyone hears them. Talk of someone important who runs the whole show, stays behind the scenes. Crazy old guy who's really in charge."

"And his name?"

"Ezra," said the girl. "No last name. Just Ezra."

"Thank you," said Klair. His finger no longer resembled a drill. "One more question and we will be done. Do you have any idea where the two fugitives from your raid went? The ones this Wailer is chasing?"

"Not a clue," said the girl. "Won't matter anyway. When the Wailer finds 'em, that's it. He's walking death."

"A well-turned phrase," said Klair. "Here is your freedom."

He smashed a balled fist into the girl's face. Death was instantaneous. Nephandi, even ones with minor powers, were Reality Deviants of the worst kind. They could not be allowed to live.

Klair rose smoothly to his feet. A fire would cleanse this place and burn any evidence of his visit, as well as finish the vampire he had staked. After that was completed, he would plan his next move. Either he followed the Wailer and his targets, Nelson and Reed, or he located this mysterious figure, Ezra. No matter which path he chose, Klair felt certain in the end the results would be the same.

Chapter Twenty-One

The grounds of the estate were huge, with the main building set back twenty yards from the street. A stone wall eight feet high surrounded the entire area. Barbed wire covered the top. A single gate of woven steel bars was the only entrance. Next to the bell was a large sign: *Beware of Dogs. Trespassers will be Devoured.*

"Not very friendly," said Sharon Reed, pressing the buzzer.

"Earth's not a friendly place," said Nelson. "In another few hours, when the city's dark, the streets around here turn into a jungle. Not safe for a woman like you to walk alone once night descends. Not unless she enjoys rape, possibly torture. Gangs rule the big cities, except for the high-rent districts. Cops don't have the manpower or the armament to fight back."

"So much for a brave new world," said Sharon, pressing the buzzer again. This time she held her finger down for a minute. "It appears that Burgess was more of a prophet than Huxley."

"Whatever you say," declared Nelson. "I always thought Huxley was an optimist. Never read Burgess. My favorite book is *Android Avenger*."

"I'm not familiar with that," said Sharon. She pressed the buzzer a third time. "Though I can guess why you like it. Do you get the feeling we are being ignored?"

"You expected otherwise?" asked Nelson. "Two hidden video cameras were scanning us until I shut them down a few seconds ago. Might be more in the mansion that I can't detect. Lots of electronic gadgetry in the place. Fifteen animals roaming the grounds. Sound pretty large for dogs. My hearing's sharp, but I can't tell one beast from another. You figure we should forget about an invitation and walk in uninvited?"

"Nelson," said Sharon, "I feel almost depressed to admit that I find your lack of manners much to my own taste. I want answers and I want them now. Dogs or no dogs, I say we crash the party."

Grinning, the cyborg gripped the steel gate and pulled. Bars twisted like taffy. In seconds, he had made an opening wide enough for them to squeeze through. "Me first," he said. "Just in case the hounds come running. I'll signal if it seems safe."

After waiting a minute, he waved Sharon through. Then the cyborg twisted the bars back into place. "No reason to alert anyone that there's intruders around."

The estate grounds were covered with thick, lush grass along with a scattering of bushes and a few small trees. A cement path cut a straight line through the lawn to the front door of the mansion.

"No windows," said Nelson as they walked towards the entrance. "Brick and cement walls, with steel backing. Place is built like a fortress."

"Must have cost a small fortune to build," said Sharon.

"Probably…" began Nelson, then swung to the right, pushing Sharon to the ground. His arms swung up, chain-guns emerging from beneath his overcoat.

The dogs attacked in a pack. Five of them, three feet high at the shoulder—mutated bulldogs with mouths the size of a open furnace and eyes that blazed with red fire. Sharon, who had designed numerous bioengineered monsters, found the creatures only slightly interesting. They moved fairly quickly for their short legs, and made no sound. Sharon suspected they possessed no vocal cords.

An ordinary man would have fallen beneath the rush. But Ernest Nelson was different. A blend of man and machine, he moved with almost robotic precision. Years of fighting foes of the Technocracy had honed his combat skills to perfection. He was able to direct the lethal fire from his chain-guns in two directions at the same time. And he never missed.

Of the five killer dogs, only one made it close enough actually to threaten them. That last beast Nelson grabbed with hands that could bend steel bars, and tore to pieces. He tossed the shredded corpse a dozen feet away.

"Sorry," he apologized to Sharon for the blood

splashed on her garments. "Heard them coming, figured it would be safer for you lying on the ground than getting in my way."

"Minor inconvenience," said Sharon, stepping up to the front door of the house. It was locked. And a sign to one side warned again, *Beware of dog*. "We better get inside before the rest of them arrive. I don't want to spend the evening watching you kill guard dogs."

"Repetitious," said Nelson. He slammed a steel fist into the door. Nothing happened. Grimacing, the cyborg hit it again. With the same results.

"Primium," he said, sounding disgusted. "We'd need a tank to batter our way inside."

"Perhaps," said Sharon, motioning him out of the way. There was a keyhole in the door. She pressed her palm against it. Tumblers grated. Bolts clattered. The huge door swung open. "Perhaps not."

"How did you do that?" asked Nelson as they entered the building. The hall was a sheet-metal rectangle eight feet high, six feet wide, and extending twenty feet to a second door.

"Progenitor trade secret," said Sharon, with a laugh. Once they were three steps into the hallway, the light above them went out. And the door they had passed through closed with a click. "Wonder what's beyond the next door."

It was another dog. A much bigger dog, the size of a lion, that roared when Sharon pushed the door open. Jet black, it appeared to be a mutated Doberman.

Robert Weinberg

"My guns don't work," said Nelson. "Some sort of field in here neutralizing my firepower. Looks like I'll have to handle this baby the old-fashioned way. Stand back. Might get messy."

"No need to break into a sweat," said Sharon. She walked up to the monstrous beast and patted it on the nose. "Down, Stanley. Down, boy."

The dog whined, then folded its legs and lay down on the floor. Sharon rubbed it behind the ears. An immense tongue stretched out and licked her entire arm.

"Don't tell me," said Nelson. "You created this particular monster."

"This specific dog?" said Sharon. "No. That would be an unbelievable coincidence. But I was the Researcher who designed the entire line. Remember what I told John Doe about the friend we're trying to locate? Whenever I create any life form, I program in certain automatic response mechanisms. These mutated Dobermans recognize my scent. There's a kill code built into this breed as well. No reason for me to use it. Now, let's find the dog's owner. I'm getting tired of the run-around."

Sharon put her hands on the dog's head and stared deep into the beast's eyes. "Find your master, Stanley," she said. "Find your master."

The dog rose to its feet and turned around, facing yet another locked door. No need for Sharon to perform her trick. The mutated Doberman pushed through the panel as if it were cardboard and headed down a winding corridor.

"You built them strong," said Nelson, staring at the Primium-reinforced door. "Name all the dogs Stanley?"

"Of course," said Sharon, as they made after the beast. "In honor of a laboratory technician mauled to death by an early prototype. I thought it was only appropriate."

"Very touching," said Nelson. "This place is like a maze. Damned hallways leading everywhere. Looks like the dog is going down into the basement."

A trail of smashed doors guided them. From time to time the gigantic Doberman let out a howl, as if letting them know where it was. They encountered no other animals, and no other people.

Finally, they ended up in a large circular chamber, twenty feet in diameter, several levels beneath the ground. Sitting in a chair in front of a computer console, patting the huge Doberman on its head, was a woman Sharon and Nelson both immediately recognized.

"The real Lauri Coup, I presume," said Sharon.

The blonde nodded. "The killers took out a Type A clone," said Coup. Her voice was soft, pleasant. "She worked in my home as an aide, doing odd jobs, answering the phone, that sort of stuff. When the raiders attacked, she pretended to be me while I exited through a secret transport door in my bedroom. Thought it would be best to stay out of sight for several months, then resurface under another name. Only Bylunt knew the truth. We were so close I couldn't let him think I was dead."

"How do you know you can trust him?" said Nelson. "He could have been the one who betrayed you."

"Kurt?" said Dr. Coup. "Never."

She smiled, the confident smile of a woman who was convinced of her own good looks. "He worships me. Never would do a thing to harm me."

"He gave us your address," said Sharon.

"Like me, he recognized your name immediately, Research Director Reed," said Coup. "He must have felt you could be trusted."

"Dangerous to make assumptions like that," said Nelson, scouting around the huge chamber. "What is this place anyway?"

"Secondary research facility," said Lauri Coup. "Used for clone manufacture and genetic manipulation. Dr. Reid worked here for a while, then grew bored and moved most of the staff to EcoR. There's still some growth tanks another level down. That's where I grew those mutated bulldogs that roam the ground. Except for me, the place is deserted."

"Why the hell didn't you just let us in?" asked Nelson, seeing banks of video monitors across one entire section of the room. The three-dozen screens displayed every room in the mansion's upper level, as well as most of the grounds outside.

"I'm trusting but I'm not crazy," said Coup. "Nor did I know you came from Kurt. Any communication would immediately betray I was still alive. I recognized Dr. Reed from her photos, but until she tamed Stanley and set him off to locate me, I couldn't be sure she wasn't an impostor sent to track me down and finish the botched execution."

"Do you have any idea why you were attacked?" asked Sharon Reed. "The police labeled it a home invasion. According to your friend Bylunt, so did the Syndicate."

"No such luck," said Coup. "The killers were Nephandi. Normal mortals would never have been able to bypass the traps I kept around my residence. And my clone was quite capable of defending herself against ordinary thugs."

Coup paused. "As for the reason behind the attack, I can only assume it's the same thing that brought you here. The DNA cell research I performed last year that led to the Gray Collective clone project."

"Exactly," said Sharon. "An exceptional job of genetic engineering. Quite a score for a Primary Investigator. Incredible work, actually, to be able to design a cell of such complexity."

Coup's features hardened. "You know, don't you?"

"Of course," said Sharon. She smiled at the puzzled look on Nelson's face. The cyborg had no idea what they were discussing.

"Ms. Coup didn't design the cell we used to grow the pattern-clone. Bylunt gave that much away when we visited him. She took an already-developed sample and merely presented it as her own creation. Instead of growing an entirely new being, we merely rebuilt an old one, someone who had already lived. If that broadcast can be believed, Heylel Teomim."

"What?" said Coup. "What broadcast?"

"Being isolated, you miss all the fun stuff," said Nelson. "The pattern-clone appeared on Technocracy computers all over Creation. It claims to be the infamous Reality Deviant from five hundred years ago. Damned thing claims it wants to end the Ascension War, merge the Union with the Traditions. Stupid stuff, but sure to cause a stir."

"I had no idea," said Coup. She appeared nervous, ill at ease. "She never told me anything about the sample."

"She?" repeated Sharon, icy fingers circling her throat. "Who are you talking about?"

"We studied together," said Lauri Coup, her voice trembling. "Her name was Resha Maise. The two of us served as Research Associates for Dr. Atkins on the East Coast. Worked there five years ago, helping him conduct experiments on sound wave generation. After that, we drifted apart, me coming to the Midwest, serving as Associate on EcoR. I don't know what Resha did. Didn't hear from her until just over a year ago."

"Atkins," said Sharon, looking at Ernest Nelson. "Tell me why that name rings a bell."

"Reality Deviant of the worst kind," said the cyborg. "One of ours who turned. Seduced by Those Beyond. Went berserk one night, killed all of his aides, burned down his lab, destroyed all of his research documents, then disappeared."

"Curiouser and curiouser," said Sharon, her mind whirling with point and counterpoint. "Was this friend of yours, this Resha, close with Dr. Atkins?"

"Definitely," said Coup. "Lots of talk in the labs that the two of them were secretly lovers. I never asked Resha. Figured it was none of my business."

Sharon frowned. She considered everything her business. Blackmail always paid wonderful benefits if used properly. "Continue what you were saying."

"I'm ambitious," said Coup. "Made no secret about it. Wanted to run my own lab, have complete control over my experiments. But being raised to Research Director takes years of service. It requires lots of patience. I'm not the patient type. That's why I did it. Wanted to make a big splash, figured a major score would push me up to Investigator level."

"Did what?" said Sharon, though she was sure she knew.

"Resha came to me in my lab late one night, around twelve months ago. Said she knew of my ambitions, wanted to help. She had a tissue culture with her. Told me that it possessed a near-perfect genetic pattern. Handled correctly, the clone could be modified by both our Convention and Iteration X. It could become the superhuman specimen researchers had been trying to develop for hundreds of years. Resha gave it to me, said I should present it as my discovery, take all the credit."

"But she never told you where the sample came from? And you didn't bother to ask?"

"I told you I was ambitious," said Coup. "Resha was offering me fame, success, with no strings attached. No way I could turn her down."

Nelson laughed. "No strings."

"I believed her," said Coup. "No reason for me not to. When I presented the sample to the Symposium, it was hailed as a major breakthrough. They put you," and she looked at Sharon, "in charge of the growth project. But I got my own lab. And was elevated to Investigator. Seemed like a good deal to me."

"What did this Resha look like?" asked Nelson.

"She was a shapeshifter," said Coup. "Changed her appearance every few weeks."

"Why am I not surprised?" Nelson muttered. "How'd you know she was who she claimed she was?"

"DNA scan," Coup replied.

Sharon nodded. "Everything is starting to tie together in very unpleasant fashion. Resha, a shapechanger, works for Dr. Atkins. Dr. Atkins becomes one of the Nephandi and disappears. Did she convert him, or did he convert her? Resha approaches you and offers a perfect cell specimen to develop into a clone, keeping her identity secret. I'm placed in charge of the operation, with Velma Wade as my assistant. The clone turns out to be a Reality Deviant, possibly Heylel Teomim. When we attempt to investigate the background to the experiment, our base is attacked by a horde of Nephandi. In the meantime, others try to eliminate you."

"It sure sounds to me like the Technocratic Union's been manipulated by Velma, Resha and their friends," said Nelson. "And that they're all Nephandi."

"Not necessarily," said Sharon. "The women could be playing a double…"

Alarm bells rang throughout the chamber. The noise was deafening. Lauri Coup swung her chair around and stared at the video monitors. "More intruders," she declared, pointing to the viewscreens that displayed the front entrance. "An entire gang, from the looks of it."

"Nephandi war party," said Nelson.

A dozen or more figures were crowded into the front yard. Big, powerfully built men, they all wore black. Each of them carried a high-powered automatic weapon.

"Notice their cheeks," said Nelson. "The tattoos? The markings signal that they're killer elite. These lunatics either complete their mission or die. No compromise. They're cult members, not willworkers. Just heavily into death and destruction. Cannon fodder for the Nephandi. Probably led by one powerful Shaytan or Administrati."

"Here come the dogs," Sharon said.

Guns roared. Animals died. None of them got within yards of the gang. The cultists continued to fire at the bodies long after the last dog was still. They laughed insanely as the bullets ripped the bodies to bloody pulp. Even in the underground control chamber, the gunfire was deafening.

"There go the dogs," Nelson replied.

A barrel-shaped man, wearing a black overcoat and slouch hat, raised one hand. Instantly the noise stopped. "There's your leader," said Nelson. "If all that gunplay doesn't bring the police, I think it's fair to assume that the cops have been paid off."

The man in the slouch hat pointed at the front door. For an instant, his face was revealed by the video camera above the entrance. Lauri Coup gasped. A shrill, piercing whistle rounded the control chamber. Instantly, the outside monitors went black. The sound vanished.

"Why do I feel like we're the three little pigs?" said Nelson, with a harsh, humorless laugh, "And the big bad wolf just knocked on the front door of our house of twigs?"

"Dr. Atkins," said Lauri Coup, her features white. "That was Dr. Atkins."

"The expert on sound waves," said Sharon.

"The Wailer," said Ernest Nelson.

Chapter Twenty-Two

It took Seventeen and Shadow of the Dawn three days to return to the Casey cabal. The trip—by car, then plane, then car again—proceeded entirely without incident. Everywhere, Tradition mages they encountered seemed to be walking about in stunned disbelief. Doissetep, the mighty fortress, the oldest and most famous of all Chantries, was no more.

In England, the impact was doubled by the toppling of Stonehenge. To willworkers throughout Britain, it was as if someone had slipped into the palace and murdered the Queen. It was a time of mourning, of somber reflection. And most of all, of fear. If Heylel had been able to destroy Doissetep, and no one doubted that in some manner the Abomination was behind the castle's destruction, then what would the rebel do next? Was even Horizon safe?

In America, the reaction was more of rage than fright. For decades, the Technocracy had dominated American culture and thought. The New World Order and the Syndicate were firmly entrenched in the seats of power. The Traditions had deep roots in Europe and England. In the United States, on the other hand, mysticks were dangerously outnumbered by members of the Technocratic Union. Though they had no hard evidence, willworkers throughout America blamed the Technocracy for the destruction of Doissetep. To them, it was merely another battle in the unending Ascension War. And they wanted revenge.

Already lovers, Seventeen and Shadow drew very close in those three days. Their shared memories of the destruction of the castle and its repercussions seemed to bind them more strongly even than emotion. That they loved each other, they had no doubt. That their spirits were linked as well was equally obvious to them. Few words passed between them about the subject. There was no need.

Late at night, during those three days, Seventeen rarely slept. His near-perfect body needed little rest. The nanobyte drivers in his bloodstream cleared it of all waste, and his energy level remained at a constant high, requiring only massive amounts of food from time to time to keep him running in perfect condition. A few hours of idle time for his brain, letting the tension of the day's events drain out of his system, was all he needed.

While Shadow rested at his side, Seventeen thought about Ethan Phillips and Scarlett Dancer. They had been lovers, he knew, but that had been a half-century ago. That their passion had been incred-

ibly strong, Seventeen had no doubts. He knew it was
true. That Phillips went searching for her in Malfeas,
the faraway lair of the Maeljin Incarna, he knew without question was also true. What he had found there,
how he had lost fifty years of his life and all of his
memories, was the mystery. Seventeen wasn't sure
that he wanted to know the answers. Especially now
that he had found Shadow of the Dawn. For, despite
his lack of memory, he was sure of certain facts. He
had found Scarlett Dancer in Malfeas. She had still
been alive. And though he had absolutely no idea
how he knew, Seventeen felt certain that, five decades later, she was not dead.

They reached the forests around Rochester as
evening was falling, riding in a old Chevy convert-
ible borrowed from a friendly mage in the New York
City area. While nothing fancy, it ran smoothly
thanks in part to several minor spells. It was safer to
use than a rented vehicle, which would immediately
list them in NWO data banks. While Seventeen suspected that Heylel threatened both the Traditions
and the Technocracy, he had no illusions about the
Union. Ever since his escape, the leaders of the Gray
Collective had wanted him dead. Just because the
pattern-clone was alive and causing trouble, there was
no reason to suspect the orders about his execution
had been reversed.

Driving through the winding roads leading to the
Casey Cabal Chantry House brought back memories
of his escape from the Gray Collective. Though it
seemed like an eternity had passed since that night,

Seventeen realized it had only been a few weeks earlier.

"I fought a squad of Hit Marks on this same highway," he said to Shadow of the Dawn, who was handling the driving. For all of his physical skills, Seventeen had little confidence in his ability to deal with an automobile. "Dropped into a gorge to convince them I was dead. Sam Haine and Albert stumbled across me when I pulled myself out."

The warrior maid smiled. "I suspect that there was little coincidence involved in that meeting," she said. "The Changing Man strikes me as someone who never stumbles across anyone. He always knows exactly what he is doing, despite his protests otherwise."

Seventeen chuckled. "Sam works hard to maintain that folksy image, but it only goes so far. He's awfully sharp. No question that he's as smart as they come."

"He is a wise man," said Shadow. "As such, he keeps his own council."

She pointed to a shallow dip in the road just ahead. "Over there," she said, "Kallikos and I fought a group of motorcycle cannibals. We had heard tales of outlaws roaming the highways, feeding off their human prey. But neither of us expected that those words were meant literally."

"Cannibals?" said Seventeen, with a grimace of disgust. "What did you do with them?"

"Killed them, of course," said Shadow. "There were five men. I offered them their lives if they chose to depart in peace, but they refused. Having made the gesture, I felt no hesitation about eliminating them all. Only the girl survived, though she was as guilty as her friends. She acted as bait for the unwary. Still, Kallikos insisted we let her go free after impressing a strong warning upon her thoughts. He claimed we would meet her again."

"Cannibals roaming the highways," said Seventeen. "Amazing how low modern civilization has sunk."

Shadow shrugged. "Do not despair overmuch. My teachers at the Fukuoka Chantry House, where I learned the wisdom of *Do*, taught me that the world changes little from incarnation to incarnation. The Wheel turns, that is all. Drahma continues. A thousand years ago, at the turn of the Millennium, tens of thousands prepared for the end of the world as religious leaders preached that apocalypse approached. Five hundred years ago, it was the same. The cycle repeats now. Death and destruction are always with us. Mankind needs no special anniversary to celebrate madness. There are plenty of excuses available."

"But the mindless, senseless violence in the cities, in the towns…" began Seventeen.

"…is no worse than it was in the past," said Shadow of the Dawn. "History is a series of atrocities and murders justified by the winners who write ill of their opponents. The Crusaders fought to free the Holy Land. Yet they killed more innocents during their passage through Europe than Moslems did in all the time spent in the Middle East. The Inquisition, a group of religious fanatics who still exist in secret in this modern age, persecuted men and women they suspected of being witches and warlocks, burning

Robert Weinberg

many of them at the stake, crushing others to death with huge stones, all in the name of their god's will. While many mages died, in numbers they were just a fraction of the many thousands who were killed by these zealots, all in the effort to save the souls of those they feared."

Shadow paused, but only to gather her breath. "What of Pharaoh, who ordered all the first-born male children of the Hebrew slaves to be killed so that none would arise to free the captives? Or Genghis Khan, who had a pyramid constructed of the heads of those who opposed him in battle? Or the Native Americans who were slaughtered at Wounded Knee? Or...."

"Enough," said Seventeen. "You've made your point. People have always been bloodthirsty barbarians. Life's no different than it was throughout history. Only the constraints are a little stronger."

"Civilization now has more rules," said Shadow. "Modern man is two steps away from the darkness instead of one. Those who abandon themselves to their savage lusts must deal with more levels of authority. But the instincts remain the same. As I said, the Wheel turns, but mankind does not change."

"Not a pleasant thought," said Seventeen, feeling the weight of modern civilization on his shoulders. "And unless we find some way to defeat the pattern-clone, modern civilization will collapse into eternal darkness. Do you have any idea what Kallikos plans to do to stop Heylel?"

"No," said Shadow. "He never confided his plans to

me. Evidently his visions of the future are much more detailed than he reveals to anyone. The seer seems to know in general terms each step his enemy plans. Yet Kallikos is unable to prevent the events from occurring."

"I've noticed the same thing," said Seventeen. "It's like he's following an expressway road map, guiding us from rest stop to rest stop, but not sure exactly what each location holds? Yet hoping that at one of the locations, we'll locate an exit and be able to leave the highway instead of taking it all the way to the end."

"The end being Armageddon," said Shadow.

"Perhaps," said Seventeen. "Only Kallikos knows. If even he does."

They rode in silence for the last few minutes of their journey, finally turning down the short dirt road leading to the Casey Cabal. It was past ten-thirty at night. "It'll be good to see Sam Haine and Albert again," said Seventeen. "I must admit I've missed them both."

"They are fine companions," said Shadow. "Loyal and true. And in Sam Haine's case, irreverent. His voice is one of good sense amongst those bound by narrow thinking."

"Odd," said Seventeen as Shadow drove the car up to the big old farmhouse that served as the main headquarters for the cabal. Two mages, both armed with shotguns, stood guard on the porch. No one else was in sight. "Wonder where everyone is?"

"Down at the sacred spring," said one of the pair, a young man named Sean Rohwiller whom Seventeen had met briefly a week before. "Holding a big council meeting. Grim stuff's been happening since you've been gone. They'll tell you all the details."

"Grim stuff," repeated Seventeen as he and Shadow hurried along the path leading to the grove of trees surrounding the mystic pond. "That doesn't sound good."

"There is death in the air tonight," said Shadow of the Dawn, touching her two swords. "The land smells of blood."

There were approximately a dozen people sitting on the grass by the spring. Several sentry fires burned, casting a dim glow over the participants. Seventeen spotted Albert but did not see Sam Haine. Several familiar faces, friends he had made during his visit, were also missing. Claudia Johnson, an attractive, middle-aged black woman who helped lead the Chantry, was standing, evidently addressing the others. She stopped speaking as Seventeen and Shadow arrived.

"Thank the Goddess," said Claudia. "You still might be in time."

"In time?" repeated Seventeen. "In time for what?"

"Sam's gone," said Albert, rising to his full height. The giant's features looked worried. "He insisted on leaving alone."

"Gone?" said Seventeen. "What are you talking about?"

"Please," said Shadow of the Dawn, "explain what has happened as quickly as possible. I see that surely every moment counts."

"The incidents began right after you disappeared,"

said Claudia. "A maniac, an extremely powerful willworker who calls himself Terrence Shade, started killing members of the cabal. Not everyone in a group. One, sometimes two, at most. Always mentioning his name, making sure that he was seen committing the act, so that there was no doubt of his guilt. In all cases, he told the others present to give his regards to Sam Haine. That Empress Aliara, Countess of Desire, repaid her debts ten-fold. Despite all our efforts, all of our magick, the killer remained at large."

"We returned several days ago from Horizon," said Albert. "Sam was pretty shaken when he heard the news. He assumed full responsibility for the murders, knew that this Shade was killing members of the Casey cabal because they were his friends. It hurt him to think that others were dying for something he had done."

"Aliara is evil," said Shadow of the Dawn. "The Changing Man should feel no shame for what he did to her. That she strikes back at him through others is another demonstration of her poison."

"Terrence Shade," said Seventeen, his brow wrinkled in thought. "He was at the Gray Collective. I'm not sure exactly what he did, or what Convention he served. But I remember him coming to the lab several times, being addressed respectfully by technicians working there. He must have been Aliara's spy even then."

"Where is Sam now?" asked Shadow. "That is what matters."

"Early this evening, someone called by phone and asked for him," said Albert. "No one thought to monitor the call. Sam muttered a few vague words to me about having a meeting later tonight and needing to make a few arrangements before it took place. Then, without informing me of any other details, he left. Alone. No one has seen him since. Only after a few hours, when he did not return, I began to worry. By then, it was much too late to trace his movements."

"The call was from Shade," said Seventeen.

"So we think," said Claudia. "Using a time-dilation spell, we tried to reconstruct the message. But whoever spoke to Sam used a powerful blocking magick throughout the call. We could hear nothing of their conversation."

"We must therefore assume the worst," said Shadow. "How long has he been gone? And what do you plan to do?"

"Sam left about three hours ago," said Albert. "Normally, I'd say leave him alone. He is a proud man, fights his own fights, dislikes outside interference. But this time, the situation is different. Shade is obviously working for Aliara. Sam is walking into a trap. Who knows what powers he faces, or how many enemies await?"

"Besides," said Claudia, a determined look on her face, "this Shade has been killing members of our cabal. Sam might be our friend, close to us all, but we're not kids who need to be protected. The Casey cabal stands together." Other members of the cabal nodded in agreement. "We appreciate Sam's help, but we fight our own battles."

"If Shade arranged a meeting," said Shadow, "he most likely told Sam to come alone or not at all. Still, what you say is true. This battle is one Sam Haine should not fight without allies. We must do all that we can to aid him."

"Exactly what we decided," said Claudia. "Only problem is how. You have any suggestions?"

"My teachers taught me that to locate a hidden enemy, you must think like him," said Shadow. "Sam Haine is a powerful mage. Shade knows this. Destroying the Changing Man will not be easy, no matter what powers Shade possesses. Since the madman could dictate the time and place of their meeting, it seems most likely that it would be at a location and hour that gives him the greatest advantage."

"The Maeljin Incarna derive their powers from suffering, hatred and despair," said Claudia. "Thus, the Dark Lords are strongest in places that generate such emotions. As would be their agents. Shade probably told Sam to come to the asylum for the criminally insane on the south side of the city. Or the Everwell Chemical Plant. Or," and the woman paused, as if realizing she had the right answer, "the toxic waste dump on the shore of Lake Ontario."

"A toxic waste site," said Shadow of the Dawn, her fingers touching the steel of her two blades. "That must be where the meeting is. Not yet, for the Dark Lords become more powerful as the night grows blacker. We still have time. I suspect the meeting between the two is not scheduled for at least another hour."

"Midnight," said Seventeen. "When the forces of evil are at their peak."

"We can make it if we rush," said Claudia. "It's on the other side of the city, and there's no direct route."

"Two cars," said Shadow of the Dawn. "Seventeen and I in one, with two of your best. Albert and you with another two in the other. Enough to provide Sam with support, yet few enough to act quietly."

"We'll rendezvous at the site," said Claudia. "May the Goddess be with us."

Shadow of the Dawn, her features solemn, nodded. Seventeen noticed, however, she kept one hand on the hilt of Whisper. The warrior maid was a diplomat and respected the beliefs of others. Still, she put her faith not in gods or goddesses but in cold steel.

Chapter Twenty-Three

The taste of blood was fresh on Enzo's lips when he pushed open the door to his inner sanctum far beneath the city streets. Hunting was always best in the summer. He could pick and chose his victims from the thousands who flocked to the beaches and stayed late to enjoy the cool night breezes. Selecting the perfect specimen and draining her dry was an excellent way to start the evening.

His mood dissolved the instant he walked into the room. Enzo's eyes narrowed when he saw a figure lounging on his throne, one leg hooked casually across an arm of the elaborate chair. "Ezra, my friend," he said, forcing his temper into line, "you surprise me as always with your presence."

"I am full of surprises," said the gray-haired mage. A deep cut, only partly healed, ran across his forehead. One of his eyes was badly bruised, and the tips of three of his fingers were blackened and bloody. His outfit was ripped and torn, and he appeared more ragged and bedraggled than usual. Enzo knew better than to ask questions. In time, Ezra would reveal all.

"The seduction continues well," said the vampire, resting his bulk on the chair facing the throne. Ezra made no show of rising and Enzo was wise enough not to press the point. "Montifloro again complained to me about Pietro's stubbornness. The woman, Hope, inflames his lusts. A few more days, and he will be willing to do whatever we require."

"Fine, fine," said Ezra, nodding, as if not even hearing what Enzo was saying. "Any sign of that bitch, Madeleine? She should have appeared by now. I left her enough clues, gave her an easy trail to follow. Even let that idiot photographer take my picture. She should be in the city. What do your spies report?"

"A woman dressed in black and fitting my cousin's description was spotted one night at that roadside bar controlled by Clan Giovanni," said Ezra. "My two informants thought it might be Madeleine, but were not able to say for sure. She was talking to the photographer when they first approached her. Stupid fools, they pressed too hard and were almost killed by an outsider who took offense at their actions. I expect to receive another report from them shortly. It should clarify matters."

"Two spies?" said Enzo. "Why a pair?"

"Cain and Abel Riley," said Enzo. "Not as smart as the Grim brothers, but they are ruthless enough. And with few wits, they are easily controlled."

"Montifloro makes an effective spokesperson," said Ezra. "With him championing your cause, the elders would undoubtedly select you as the one to take Pietro's place as ruler of the Mausoleum. But only Madeleine has the skills necessary to destroy her sire. Unless we convince her to cooperate with our scheme, it is doomed to failure."

"Do not worry," said Enzo. "Everyone has a price, be it blood, power or prestige. No Kindred is untouchable. Not even the Dagger of the Giovanni. Madeleine can be bought. We merely need to make her an offer that she finds irresistible."

"A life for a life," said Ezra, with a smile. "That is what we will tell her. She has one weakness and I know who it is. But we cannot delay long. Our master grows impatient. And I am experiencing problems of my own."

"Surely nothing you cannot handle," said Enzo, keeping his tone neutral.

"My sister," said Ezra. "I knew that Rambam would not interfere with my plans. He is too sentimental, too soft. But Judith is made of blood and iron. She attacked me last night. I was lucky to escape with only minor wounds. If she finds me again, all of Lord Steel's power might not be enough to save me. She is a devil."

Enzo restrained himself from remarking that she took after her brother. He had never met Judith but Ezra had talked about her before. A powerful willworker, she possessed none of her brother's ambition or drive. She was content merely to aid their father, Rambam, and pursue her own studies of esoteric lore. That she was hunting Ezra was not good news. If Ezra hurt his sister, their father might be drawn into the conflict. And though Ezra claimed to be the most powerful mage of his family, Enzo suspected that the gray-haired man's madness had twisted his vision.

"You are certain she cannot track you here?" he asked.

"I hid my tracks carefully," said Ezra. "Judith will not find me as long as I remain quiet. Still, we need to proceed with our schemes quickly. Once we gain control over Clan Giovanni and the Nine Traditions, we will be in a position of tremendous power. Neither my sister nor my father will threaten me after that takes place. They will not dare."

"A few days, a few weeks," said Enzo. "Then, the world will be ours."

"Masters of the world," said Ezra, rising quietly from the throne. He walked on cat's feet to the door of the sanctum. "Lords of creation. I like the sound of it."

Savagely, he yanked open the door. Standing there, her features serene, untroubled, was Ms. Hargroves. She stepped into the room. "Thank you," she said to Ezra, sarcasm thick in her voice. "Amazing senses you must have, to realize I was coming down the hall."

Ezra glared at the gaunt woman. "How long were you outside the door? How much did you hear?"

"Hear?" said Ms. Hargroves, smiling. "Why, I heard nothing. I'm not paid to hear, Mr. Ezra. I only do what is required by Mr. Giovanni, and nothing else."

"Leave her alone, Ezra," said Enzo, settling into his throne. He found the madman's paranoia tiresome.

Let him worry about real problems, like his sister and father. Threatening his secretary was lunacy.

"Why are you here, Ms. Hargroves?" he asked. "What news?"

"Remember you asked me to keep close watch on comings and goings at that farmhouse outside of town?" she said. "Well, evidently two of the troublemakers you described have returned to the place. The one named Sam Haine and his friend, Albert, are back."

"Excellent," said Enzo. He grinned, his eyes blazing. "This time, though, we need to attack in force. Employ every gang in the area. Raise the bounty to a million dollars a head. Two million if necessary. No matter what the cost, I want those troublemakers killed."

"Wait," said Ms. Hargroves, her face sliding into an expression that Enzo found disturbing. "There's more. Sam Haine left the farmhouse late this afternoon— alone—evidently on a mission of vengeance. A madman has been killing members of the Casey cabal for the past few days. Tonight, he arranged a meeting with Haine. I know where and when."

"I told you, Ezra," said Enzo, grinning wolfishly. "Ms. Hargroves is worth her weight in gold. Where is this encounter to take place?"

"The toxic waste dump outside of the city," said Ms. Hargroves. "At midnight."

Enzo howled with delight. "Summon them all!" he cried. "Mattias and his crew of maniacs. The cannibal gangs who roam the roads outside the city. The scum of the streets. Anyone. All of them. Five million for the head of my enemy! Let them tear his body to pieces and devour it, I don't care. All I want is his head."

"Why not lead them yourself?" asked Ezra, staring at Enzo with an insane expression on his face.

"Madeleine would like that," Enzo replied. "Leave the safety of my citadel and put myself at her mercy? Never. Since these deaths are so vital to Lord Steel, I put the same proposition to you, my friend. *You* lead the men."

"Never," Ezra growled. "Not with my sister on the prowl. I need to stay hidden. But this mission is too important to leave to amateurs." The madman stared at Ms. Hargroves, pure venom in his eyes. "Why not have your so, so efficient secretary lead the crew? Let her prove her worth."

"Ezra, enough foolishness," Enzo snapped, straining to control his temper. "Killers in this city are cheap and easy to find. Good help is not. A hundred cannibals are not worth one Ms. Hargroves."

"As you wish," said Ezra, with a shrug. "But if the attack is a failure, the blame rests on your shoulders."

"I will send the brothers Grim in her place," said Enzo. "As my ghouls, they possess more than human strength, and are not easily swayed by magick. They will kill the wizard or die trying."

Ezra squeezed his eyes shut, as if suddenly overcome with emotion. "A good offer," he declared, opening his eyes wide. "But trying is not enough. We require success, or both of us will suffer the consequences. Are your favorite lunatics in the building?"

Enzo glanced as Ms. Hargroves. She nodded. "They're upstairs, teaching Hope how to skin a rabbit. While it's still alive, of course."

"Bring them to the laboratory," said Ezra. "Immediately."

Ms. Hargroves looked to Enzo. He nodded. "Do what Ezra says," he commanded. "We shall be waiting there."

It took the wizard five minutes to locate the chemicals he required and another fifteen minutes to brew them together in the proper fashion, reciting spells under his breath as he stirred the mix. When he was finished, the glass bowl was half-filled with a clear mixture that smelled faintly of roses. The Grim brothers stared at it suspiciously.

"We supposed to drink that crap?" asked Mark, the brother who did most of the talking.

"Not unless you want your insides to melt," said Ezra, chuckling. "This liquid is lycosis, an ancient poison recently rediscovered and refined through modern chemical analysis. It is the most potent poison in the world. One drop can kill a hundred men. Hold out your hands. I want to examine your fingers."

Staring at Ezra as if he was crazy, the Grim brothers did as they were told. The sorcerer looked closely at the men's fingers, rubbing his gnarled digits across their flesh.

"Very good," he said, when finished. "Dip your hands into the solution."

"Are you fuckin' crazy?" said Mark, stepping back from the liquid. "Not on your life."

"Not on mine," said Ezra. "On yours. Do as I command or die. Stop worrying, you fool. I sealed your flesh closed. The poison cannot harm you now."

Taking a deep breath, Mark Grim dipped his fingertips into the clear liquid. Nothing happened. Raising his hands from the bowl, he grinned with pleasure. "Feels fine."

"The poison remains potent for several hours," Ezra said, as Jason Grim placed his fingers into the bowl. "After that, it loses its effectiveness quickly. One scratch is all you need to kill an enemy. Lycosis attacks the blood and all the healing magick of Nine Traditions is helpless against it."

"Go to the toxic waste dump," Enzo commanded. "My enemies are there. I want their heads. Summon your friends, your allies, any who wish to serve me. As many as necessary to finish the job. Kill until there are no more to be killed. Do not return until my foes are dead."

"We'll rip out their eyes, boss." Mark Grim smiled, flexing his fingers. His long yellow fingernails glowed like claws. "And we'll bring you their fuckin' heads on a platter."

Enzo smiled. "Do so, and your rewards will be greater than your wildest dreams." Then the smile was gone, replaced by an expression of absolute malevolence. "Fail, and your punishment will be more frightening than your worst nightmares."

Chapter Twenty-Four

Shortly after rising each night, Madeleine sent her sire Pietro an e-mail bringing him up to date on her activities so far. Knowing full well the lack of security on the internet, she worded her messages vaguely, letting Pietro fill in the blanks with knowledge only the two of them shared. Her letters read almost like travel brochures, referring to distant lands and cities, and to historical events taking place throughout the past century. In this fashion, Madeleine remained confident that the Master of the Mausoleum knew exactly what the situation was regarding Enzo. If she were somehow to fail, the next agent sent after the rebel would have her notes to follow. Dangerous and lethal, Madeleine Giovanni was also extremely efficient.

Her computer was battery-powered and her phone was cellular. Using them together, she could send her sire messages from anywhere, at any time. Her base was a specially designed and reinforced mini-van she had picked up at clan headquarters in Manhattan. On an earlier visit to the States, she'd used a full-sized truck for her headquarters, but the vehicle had proven too easy for her enemies to locate. The mini-van suited her needs perfectly. During the day, she parked it in a twenty-four hour underground lot in the Rochester suburbs. At night, she used it to explore the streets of the city, gathering information about Enzo and his activities, and traveling to the countryside when needed.

The red light on her server had just turned green, indicating her latest e-mail had been transmitted onto the net, when Madeleine heard a ghostly voice calling her name.

"Madeleine! Madeleine!" The words rang in her mind. "C'mon, Madeleine, we need you!"

It was either Lucy or Allyson. Certainly one of the two. Something was wrong. She needed to reach the children as soon as possible.

Exiting the rear of the van, Madeleine carefully locked the vehicle and set the alarms. She wasn't worried about it being stolen. The skull and crossbones on the window and the words *Property of Giovanni Co.* beneath the symbol were a warning that even the dumbest car-thief understood. Those foolish enough to rob Giovanni property usually were found a few hours later, dumped in front of a police station with their hands, feet, and other vital parts cut off and stuffed in their pockets and their eyes, ears and tongue missing. Worst of all, the thieves deposited were always still alive.

This close to midnight, the city streets were empty.

Madeleine walked quickly into the shadows. Anyone observing her would have noted that she appeared more and more insubstantial with each step. In seconds, the attractive young woman had transformed into a dark cloud of mist. Moving with the swiftness of the wind, she flew down the byway in the general direction of Sleazy Sam's.

The Rat Pack was waiting for her, clustered in a dark corner of Sleazy Sam's parking lot, when she arrived less than five minutes later. Eyes opened wide as Madeleine materialized seemingly out of thin air.

"Jesus," whispered Sarah. The word might have been a prayer, an invocation or a curse.

"You summoned me," said Madeleine. She looked around the lot. It was empty. Very strange. "I assume this is important."

"You got that right," Allyson replied.

"Let me tell her!" Lucy interrupted. Her bright eyes shone with excitement and a bit of fear.

"Fine." Allyson shrugged. "Go on."

"First of all," the blonde girl exclaimed in a loud whisper, "the chick with the swords came back." She leaned in close to Madeleine. "Me an' Pete were checking out the farm you told us about. Y'know, the witch house. Anyway, a bunch of new guys showed up there the other day. This fat old dude with white hair and beard, and this *gigantic* fuckin' black dude. I mean, like, really thin, but tall as shit and really cool-looking. We didn't think much about them—I mean, they were important and everything, I guess, but we didn't want to call you down here just 'caus'a that."

"The swordswoman was here." Madeleine stated.

"Yeah." Lucy nodded. "Anyway, the white-haired guy drove off tonight by himself, right around sunset, and he looked really pissed. Miss *Supercop* showed up soon after that, with this massive babe…I mean, this guy who's so damn muscular he looks like rock. I mean, fuckin' *rock*, and he's not wearing a shirt or anything, so you can see every detail…."

"Except the one that matters to Lucy," Sybil interjected. Brian looked annoyed.

"According to my researches," said Madeleine, "the muscular man is known as Prisoner Seventeen. He is supposedly quite dangerous."

"He looked like he could bench-press Arnold Schwarzenegger," Brian admitted resentfully. He sounded jealous.

"Go on," said Madeleine. "This news is interesting but not urgent."

"The big news," said Allyson, "was here. Tonight."

"*Big* news," Lucy added, not to be denied her place in Madeleine's good graces. "Shit's really gone down bad around here. This place was just fuckin' crawling with the evillest bastards in the goddamned state. I mean hundreds of killers. *Hundreds*! Truckers, bikers, gang dudes in fancy cars, skins, rednecks, the whole fuckin' crew. They were fightin' with each other in the parking lot, and a couple of people got wasted before they called a truce and left. Bodies all over the fucking place and not a cop in sight."

"A rumble, perhaps," Madeleine shrugged.

"Much bigger than that," said Allyson. "I've never

seen anything like this. Lucy's not exaggerating when she says hundreds. Cars, trucks, bikes everywhere. It was like an outlaw convention, and we weren't going anywhere near it."

"They're heading off to a meet," Sybil added. "Someone's going to get his ass kicked."

"What about Leo?" Madeleine inquired. "Is he working tonight?"

"He's always there," said Pete. The quiet boy spoke hesitantly, as if afraid of the sound of his own voice. "And he's all right, I guess. At least, I think he is...."

"There was some shooting in there a few minutes ago," Lucy blurted. "That's why we called you. Lots of yelling from inside. We saw Sister Cannibal Susie go in there with a couple of shotguns. Then BOOM! BOOM! BOOM! Windows get smashed, guns go off, people start runnin' out the door. Finally Susie gets out and walks away. Why they didn't waste her, I don't know, but she got in her truck and drove off. Most of the other dudes were on their way by then, too...."

"The Devil's caravan," Sarah added in her sepulchral voice.

"Something's happening, Madeleine," Allyson finished. "Something huge. That's why Susie's on the warpath. Lots of traffic tonight. Gangs on the move. All heading west. Figured you better know."

"I think it is time I asked Leo a few questions," said Madeleine. She nodded to her retainers. "A job well done by the Rat Pack. You continue to justify my faith in your abilities."

"Yeah," said Lucy, a bit disconcerted. "We're the fuckin' best."

The bar was deserted. Leo sat on a barstool, drinking a bottle of beer. His face was bloodstained, and a crude bandage was wrapped around his upper arm. He nodded at Madeleine when she approached. "Thought you'd arrive sooner or later," he said, draining the bottle and reaching for another. "Didn't know how to make contact. Figured the kids would do it for me."

"They did," said Madeleine. She scanned the room. Stacked up against the back wall, already attracting flies, were the bodies of three men in black leather. Each had been nailed by a shotgun at close range. "What happened?"

"Word's out on the street," said Leo. "Nothing overt, but whispers all night, passing from one screwball to another. Your cousin Enzo wants someone dead really bad. He's offered a bounty of five million bucks for the head of an old guy named Sam Haine. No questions asked how it was obtained. The fee's paid in cash, and Enzo offers the same price for anybody else found with the dead guy. In these parts, not much money floating around, five million dollars makes you rich. All sorts of wonderful shit you can do with that kind of reward. So the hunt is on.

"Gangs have been stopping in all night, getting tanked on the way to the killin'. Cannibals, road hogs, even some crooked cops. They all want that money. Well, evidently Sister Susie heard about the bounty too. She busted in here, carrying two shotguns, screaming her usual stuff about sinners repenting.

Those boys weren't very smart. Thought they could take her out." He spat on the floor. "They thought wrong. One of 'em squeezed a shot off. Fucked up my arm. Susie didn't even stick around to apologize. She's off to the rendezvous, I'll bet. Crazy lady aims to convert the heathen. Suspect she's making a big mistake this time. Girl's going to be outgunned a couple of hundred to one. Nobody's going to be in the mood to listen to her raving."

Leo chugged down another beer. "End of story. Honest cops are snug in their cocoons tonight. They're staying off the roads. My regular customers decided sticking around could be dangerous. Can't say I blame them. All hell's about to break loose, Madeleine. Moon's blood-crimson. Lots of people are gonna die. You can bet on it."

"The enemy of my enemy is my ally," said Madeleine. "Enzo and Ezra fear Sam Haine and his friends. Therefore, I feel obligated to warn them of their peril. Beyond that, I will save them if I can."

"Or get wasted trying," Leo replied.

"Dying," said Madeleine Giovanni, "is the one fate I do not fear."

Chapter Twenty-Six

Sitting at the center of the toxic waste site, Terrence Shade waited patiently for midnight to arrive. That was the hour he had told Sam Haine to meet him at dump. He had no doubt that the Reality Deviant would be on time. No doubt at all.

Like most of his foolish breed, Sam Haine believed in such concepts as loyalty and honor. Shade recognized those beliefs as unimportant in themselves. But he appreciated their worth in setting his trap. *Always capitalize on your enemy's weaknesses* was one of the first things he had learned in his training days with the New World Order. This entire escapade had been based on that principle.

Sam Haine believed in paying his debts. He assumed obligations without being asked. The old man thought that justice meant something. He loved his friends with a fierce, unyielding loyalty. Shade considered all of these beliefs ridiculous—still, they had served him well in setting his trap.

Shade looked down at his watch. It was twenty minutes to the hour. Any time now, Haine would be arriving at the dump's front gate. He would read the warning signs, *Caution! Hazardous Waste Materials Within! Proceed at Your Own Risk*, perhaps hesitate for a moment, then enter. Ten minutes' walking would bring him here, to the large open area at the center of the site. Where Shade waited, alone, exactly as he had promised.

Tonight, in honor of the occasion, Shade wore all white. White pants, white shirt, white belt, white socks, white shoes. He wore a white hat, but no sunglasses. His red eyes glowed in the fires that surrounded him.

"'Double, double, toil and trouble,'" crooned Shade, "'Fire burn and cauldron bubble.'"

The words were maddeningly appropriate. Everywhere, huge fires flickered. The ground bubbled like an insane cauldron. The waste dump was immense, nearly a mile long by a mile wide, surrounded only by a barbed wire fence on three sides, the polluted waters of Lake Ontario on the other. The site served as a primary dumping ground for major industries and government agencies from all over New York State. It was perhaps the most notorious pollution site on the East Coast. Up close, it resembled Hell on Earth. Many preachers had made the obvious analogy, giving form to the worst nightmares of their congregations. Shade loved it here. In many ways, the site reminded him of Malfeas. Except that it was much brighter. And much less noisy.

Huge stacks of human refuse and garbage burned

with pale blue-green flame, day and night, all year round. Clouds of black soot rose into the sky, blotting out the moon and stars at night, the sun during the day. Eternal red chemical fires, feeding on pits of industrial sludge and raw sewage, dotted the landscape like volcanic craters, crackling and spitting poisonous clouds out over the waters. Buoys offshore warned that swimming in the area could be dangerous. The bones of those foolish enough to try littered the sands for a mile in either direction. Nothing lived in the lake. Nothing natural, that is.

Huge steel drums of deadly poisons stood in long straight lines, forming a maze of metal corridors that covered much of the site. Immense piles of rotting asbestos panels pulled from the interior of school buildings rose hundreds of feet in the air, like the pale white altars of some blind, idiot god. The ground of the site was barren, harsh and desolate as a desert, baked clean of all life. Huge cracks ran in jagged lines from one refuse pile to another. It appeared as if the land itself had been turned into glass, then shattered by some gigantic hammer. The air was foul, choked with fumes rising from the rents in the earth.

Few people dared enter the dump without wearing protective gear. The atmosphere was deadly to the lungs; the ever-present corrosive chemical mist caused horrible damage to exposed skin and eyes. For years, the place had served a favorite execution spot for the mob. Instead of wasting bullets, crime lords tossed their enemies into the glowing chemical pits. Not even their bones survived.

"Come to me, my pretty," said Shade, rubbing his hands together, anticipating Haine's arrival. The man in white sat on top of a huge thirty-gallon oil drum filled with hydrochloric acid. The ground around him was clear for ten yards in every direction. It was the perfect spot for a confrontation. Not that Shade intended to fight. His only purpose in luring Sam Haine to the dump was to push him into the invisible doorway a few steps to the right.

The passage was a temporary one, a wyrmhole created by the blood sacrifices of several hundred of Aliara's faithful servitors. The tunnel connected Earth to the Near Umbra, the Near Umbra to a Far Calumn, and the Far Calumn to Malfeas. Anyone falling through the doorway would eventually end up in the Queen of Desire's palace. An extremely fragile construct, the hole between dimensions could only be used twice before collapsing. Once, it had served as the gateway into the real world for Shade. He intended to use the passage for the second and final time as the instrument of Aliara's vengeance.

"'By the prickings of my thumbs,'" he chanted, feeling a tingling run through his body, "'something wicked this way comes.'"

A figure stepped out from behind a huge pile of bloodstained hospital bandages and surgical dressings. Shade swallowed, suddenly feeling very uneasy. Though she was fifty feet away, concealed by drifting yellow clouds of noxious gas, there was no mistaking his patron, the Countess of Desire, Empress Aliara.

Walking slowly, she approached Shade, skirting the small pools of chemical waste dotting the ground. Though merely an image projected from Malfeas, "Aliara" enjoyed acting as if she was real. Why she was visiting the waste site, Shade did not know. He was definitely *not* pleased to see her.

A few inches over five feet tall, Aliara was nearly sexless with her man's clothing and her androgynous features. Her face glowed with an inhuman vitality, and a faint smile curled across her cruel lips. The Dark Lord wore a charcoal gray pin-striped suit with a bright green tie, matching socks, and a handkerchief stuffed in the top pocket. Her short hair, almost shaved, was exactly the same color, as were her blazing eyes. Even her lips and cheeks were tinted the same brilliant green. It was the exact same garb and color she had assumed when she had entered the Gray Collective. And taken command of Shade's psyche.

Nervously Shade looked around for some sign of Sam Haine. If his victim caught a glimpse of Aliara, he'd know immediately that Shade's phone call had been a trap. The Dark Lord was actually jeopardizing Shade's chances of fulfilling her own wishes. It was an uncomfortable position, fraught with peril, and Shade did not know what to do. Or say. Aliara did not accept criticism well. Dark Lords disliked admitting they made mistakes.

"Well, Shade," said Aliara, speaking barely loud enough for him to hear her words. "What news? I thought it best to check on your progress."

"My scheme proceeds exactly as planned, mistress," said Shade, hurrying his words. "I killed six of Haine's pupils, making sure that he would know who had done it. Then I called him, challenged the old man to a duel in your name, and swore that if he did not come alone, many more of his friends would die. He is scheduled to arrive any moment." Shade hesitated for a moment, then plunged on. "If he sees you, mistress, he will instantly flee and the trap will fail."

"Do not worry, Shade," said Aliara. She seemed much more solid and substantial here at the waste dump. Not surprisingly, as much of her nurturing energy was generated at sites like these across the globe. "Only you can see me. If Sam Haine arrives, he will see only you, speaking to the empty air."

"Even that might scare him away," said Shade, still feeling nervous.

"You underestimate the old fool," said Aliara, waving a delicate hand in dismissal of Shade's words. The man in white quivered, remembering how the Dark Lord's touch had seared his skin like acid. "Sam Haine already knows that this meeting is a trap. How could it be anything else? The old man is not stupid, merely over-confident. He obviously has such incredible faith in his own abilities that he is willing to gamble he can out-think you even in the midst of corruption and decay."

Shade snickered. "What a fool. What an absolute fool. In this setting, the Nephandi hold sway. My strength is greater than that of any Tradition mage or Technomancer. If Sam Haine tries to strike me from afar, the backlash will destroy him. Only face to face, hand to hand, can he defeat me. And that won't happen. Not with the door to Malfeas close at hand."

"The door," said Aliara, her smile widening. "A fitting end to the willworker. You push him through the tunnel and he falls into Malfeas. Proper repayment for his treatment of me. Delicious irony."

The Countess of Desire frowned. Her green eyes stared at Shade. His discomfort increased. "Are you certain," she said, her voice seductively smooth, "that the passage works? That when Sam Haine falls into the trap, he will end up in my palace on Malfeas?"

"Of course," said Shade. "Of course it will work. I used the tunnel to travel here. It is a convoluted route, but it will hold together for a second use. After that, it will collapse. But I am convinced it will work."

"Are you sure?" said Aliara. "Are you absolutely sure?"

The Dark Lord was very near now. Shade trembled with fear. Aliara's presence was so overpowering, it almost felt as if she stood next to him in the flesh. The toxic waste dump gave her much greater substance than Ms. Hargroves's apartment. "I have not returned here since the day I reappeared in this world," Shade whispered. "But it seems unlikely that anything could have happened to the tunnel since then."

"What if Sam Haine came here early?" Aliara's voice was just as quiet. "What if he discovered the tunnel and closed it? Wouldn't that be an unexpected surprise, Shade?"

"Close the tunnel?" Shade backed away from Aliara. "That's impossible. Isn't it?"

"You are naïve, Shade," she replied. "The passage is wide open. While Dark Lords cannot travel through such wyrmholes, any human can. If Sam Haine pushed through another body, someone else in his place, the tunnel would close up, disappear, and this entire trap would collapse."

"Another body?" Shade's voice rose. "He wouldn't dare!"

Anxiously, Shade rushed over to the invisible doorway. He dared not touch it, for fear of falling. Still, standing in front of it and reaching out with his mind, the passage appeared intact and unharmed. "It's fine," he said to Aliara as she walked up behind him. "Your fears are groundless."

"That depends entirely on your point of view." Aliara slammed both her fists into the small of Shade's back. The force of the blow sent him tumbling forward.

He shrieked, desperately trying to regain his balance. It was impossible, absolutely impossible, for the Dark Lord to touch anyone in the material world. Aliara couldn't do this, she *couldn't*. Shade flailed with both arms, trying to grab hold of something. Laughing loudly, Aliara hit him a second time, pushing him straight at the dimensional gate.

Robert Weinberg

With a scream of absolute terror, Shade fell across the invisible threshold. "You tell the Empress," Aliara called after him, "the Changing Man sends his regards."

Chapter Twenty-Seven

When the eight of them reached the center of the toxic waste dump a few minutes after midnight, they found Sam Haine alone, sitting on a metal drum, smoking one of his smokeless cigars and wearing a wide-brimmed white hat. He did not look happy. Considering the corruption all around him, that was not surprising. "About time," he muttered. "What took you so long?"

"Traffic," said Albert. "Bad traffic in this neighborhood late at night. Where did you get the hat?"

"Fat guy dressed all in white," said Sam, rising to his feet. He spun the hat around on one finger. "Name of Shade. Believe it not, the gentleman had red eyes. Me and him had some business to settle. Glad you folks thought enough of me to come to my rescue, but you shoulda known better. Be a cold, cold day in hell before a slime like Shade can out-think the Changing Man."

"We felt you might need assistance guarding…"

began Shadow of the Dawn, then whirled, her two swords already raised in fighting stance.

Ten feet away, the figure of a young woman coalesced out of an inky cloud. Seventeen blinked, then stared quickly at his companions. All of them appeared equally surprised. This power was new to them as well.

"Please, do not be alarmed," said the stranger. She spoke in precise, clipped terms, as if English was not her native tongue. Slender, of medium height, she had jet-black hair, bright red lips and skin like chalk. The newcomer wore a simple black tank dress, black stockings and low heels. Around her neck hung a silver necklace decorated with an elaborate G. Beautiful though she was, her attraction had a hard, sinister edge. Seventeen knew without asking that she was not human. This was one of the Damned. A vampire.

"What do you want?" asked Claudia Johnson. "We have no quarrel with your kind."

"Unfortunately, that is not true" said the young woman, staring curiously for a moment at Shadow of the Dawn. The warrior maid dipped her head as if acknowledging the other's presence, then in a surprising show of faith, sheathed her weapons. The vampire's gaze shifted to Seventeen. Her look was sharp, penetrating, yet he felt she meant them no harm. "There are those of the Kindred who wish you ill. You must flee this wretched hellhole immediately."

"Why the hurry?" said Sam Haine. "I just got rid of one pest. Are there more coming?"

"Many more," said the young woman. "My name is

Madeleine Giovanni, of Clan Giovanni. My clansman, a renegade named Enzo Giovanni, is the director of Everwell Chemicals. For reasons not entirely clear to me, he wants you four dead," and she pointed to Sam Haine, Albert, Shadow of the Dawn and Seventeen. "Tonight, he discovered you would be at this waste dump. Enzo posted a reward of five million dollars for each of your heads. Several hundred outlaws, gangbangers, cannibals and worse are on their way here."

"Sounds crazy to me," Claudia Johnson retorted. "Makes no sense. How do we know it's not some sort of Kindred trick?"

"There," said Madeleine Giovanni, turning and pointing in the direction of the gate to the site. "Here comes my proof. Stand your ground. No time left to flee."

They arrived in a wave, at least a hundred of them. Big and small, fat and lean, men and women, young and old. Unable to steer their motorcycles and pickups over the acid pits and torn earth, they had come on foot. A rag-tag army of killers, carrying rifles and pistols and baseball bats and carving knifes and chainsaws and worse. One huge man even held a scythe. Many of the outlaws wore black leather, but others wore jeans or skirts.

Seventeen spotted a young man in a suit and tie, armed with a pair of bowie knives. Next to him stood a redhead, perhaps sixteen or seventeen years old, in a white gossamer dress, steel gloves ending in incheslong spikes on her hands. A dozen steps back were

Robert Weinberg

three old men waving machetes. The crowd had nothing in common other than weapons and an insane desire to kill. Screaming obscenities, they rolled across the ground of the waste dump like a human *tsunami*, a tidal wave of death directed at the Awakened Ones. The companions could no longer doubt Madeleine Giovanni's claim. The living, breathing, hating proof was here in full force.

Shadow of the Dawn wrapped her arms around Seventeen's neck, pulled his face to hers, and seared his mouth with a passionate kiss. Then, with one smooth motion, she unsheathed both swords. The blades, Whisper and Scream, glowed with mystic energy. Though faced with an unbroken line of enemies, there was no hesitation in Shadow's step. Moving like the wind, she ran forward, bringing the attack to the attackers.

"Honor over death," said Madeleine Giovanni, a smile on her lips as she watched Shadow's assault. Without another word, the vampire followed, gliding across the ground with inhuman speed. Though she carried no weapons, she did not appear concerned by the overwhelming odds.

Bending down, Seventeen grabbed a seven-foot length of rusted steel pipe. Balancing on the balls of his feet, he awaited the onrushing horde. He fought best in a stationary position. Around him, his fellow mages assumed similar poses. Faced with incredible odds, they appeared unafraid. Sam Haine held a bowie knife seemingly drawn from nowhere. Though a pacifist by nature, Albert gripped his massive ironwood walking stick in both hands, murmuring apologies to nameless gods for the violence he was about to commit.

Claudia Johnson and her fellow Verbena stood a few steps back, hands linked, faces knotted in concentration. A glimmer of force shimmered in the air. Their polluted, unnatural surroundings diminished much of their magick, but the willworkers still commanded great powers. "Guns won't fire," said Claudia. "And most of the crowd, lesser minds, will be confused and off-balance. Coincidence will go against them. Still, it's going to be hand-to-hand combat. Beware of knives and swords, for we can do nothing against them. No mercy, for they have none in their hearts."

Then there was no more time to talk.

Ten faced a hundred or more. Overwhelming odds, except that numbered among those ten were an Akashic Brotherhood Dragon Claw, the Dagger of the Giovanni, and a reassembled man with nanobyte blood, all aided and protected by magick willworkers. It was part battle, part slaughter.

Shadow of the Dawn moved like her namesake, darting from one opponent to another, her swords flashing, weaving a net of steel, killing with quick, sure cuts. Tonight the warrior used no fancy maneuvers, no unusual techniques. Just strike and strike and strike. Surrounded by foes, she didn't need to watch out for allies. Shadow spun about, twirling in a ballet of carnage. In mere minutes, she was covered with blood. Never uttering a sound, the warrior maid let

Whisper and Scream speak for her. The two swords shrieked their defiance to the world.

Madeleine Giovanni used only her hands to kill. Those hands moved faster than the eye could follow. A man collapsed, his rib cage ripped from his body. A woman's neck spurted blood as claws slashed across her throat. Another biker dropped as his head collapsed. Madeleine also fought in silence. With her black clothes and dead white skin, she was a figure of absolute terror.

To Seventeen, catching glimpses of both women in action, Shadow was a merciless executioner. Madeleine Giovanni was the personification of death.

Those outlaws who escaped the two women fared no better when they reached Seventeen and his allies. Seventeen, his bioengineered body working in high gear, wielded the steel pipe like a baseball bat, slamming it back and forth among his attackers with deadly abandon. As in earlier fights, old reflexes came into play. The biotech giant found himself wielding his metal staff with unexpected but welcome skill.

Those few lucky enough to avoid his blows fell beneath Sam Haine's knife or Albert's stave. Three bikers actually made it past the three fighters to Claudia Johnson's group, only to wither and die, their skin shriveling to dust as they collapsed into a rotted pile of bones before the mages. The goddess was not forgiving.

Ten minutes passed in an instant. The human wave, torn apart by Shadow and Madeleine, parted, wavered against Seventeen and his friends, then broke. Bleeding and badly injured, the attackers retreated. They left behind a wasteland of corpses. More than half their number had died in the suicidal attack. The tortured earth of the waste dump was covered with blood. Dreams of wealth had been met by the harsh reality of annihilation.

The remaining bikers milled about in a disorganized crowd, shouting at each other. No price was worth dying over. Their unity fragmented, the various gangs tried to decide whether to continue or retreat. As Seventeen and his friends drew in a few deep breaths, the second wave of killers charged onto the scene.

The newcomers, fresh and filled with energy, flowed through and around the disorganized and disgruntled first bunch, sweeping them forward in their rush towards envisioned riches and glory. Odds jumped from formidable to overwhelming. Propelled by a lust to kill, they formed a wall of unyielding human flesh. Madness engulfed the night.

A red haze descended across Seventeen's eyes. The club was gone, but his fists served equally well. He fought without thinking, striking out with mechanical precision, crushing bones with every blow. Knives, bayonets, axes slashed out at him, but he could not be stopped. His wounds healed almost as quickly as they were inflicted. Feet planted firmly in place, he refused to be dragged under. A lion surrounded by jackals, he refused to go down.

Sam Haine, the Changing Man, had vanished; melting into the berserk crowd, his features changed constantly, a chameleon of death dealing deadly stabs from his blade. A thrashing sea of arms and legs, punctuated by continual screams of mortal agony, was the only indication that Madeleine Giovanni still fought. Seventeen had no idea what had happened to Shadow of the Dawn.

Albert, his features grim, was backed up against a huge pile of asbestos. Claudia Johnson and one other mage stood beside him. The other two had perished under the relentless assault. Sparks of pure energy surrounded the trio, scorching anyone who came too close. Howling with fury, the mob pressed closer, using their dead comrades as shields. There was no escape.

A huge man broke from the pack surrounding Seventeen and charged. In his hands, the killer held a massive scythe. The blade swung in a decapitating arc. Ducking beneath the steel, Seventeen grabbed the weapon by the staff. For an instant, bioengineered man and mortal held the ironwood shaft. Then, power surging through his genetically-enhanced muscles, Seventeen wrenched the scythe out of the other man's grip, then returned it to him with interest.

For a moment, time seemed to stop for Seventeen. Like the one belonging to the Reaper, this scythe was well made. Still, it was not his. But in a battle to the death, it would serve. Magickal power poured from him, binding his body and the scythe into one.

With an incredible roar that crashed like thunder through the toxic waste dump, Seventeen raised the scythe over his head. Its curved steel blade flashed with brilliant white light. And with frightful intensity, Seventeen began to kill.

He became the Reaper. His hairless, slab-like face seemed to become shadowy, nebulous, as if cowled like the Dark Angel's own. With each swing, heads flew, blood sprayed, limbs leaped from torsos like husks beneath a blade. In seconds, ten were dead. In a minute, ten more. Back and forth, the scythe swung; with each pass, Death cackled. The crowd around Seventeen backed away, terrified of the unholy monster they now faced.

In the killer's hands, the scythe *sang*.

With each death, the song grew louder. And louder. Soon, the wild death-wail of the scythe drowned out every other noise. The sound filled the night air. Panic grew as Seventeen slashed a path through the ranks of attackers. One ran, tripping over the dead bodies to escape. Another turned in panic, then several more. A few became many. In moments, a savage attack became a rout. Killers disappeared in seconds, like snow in the desert. Except for the dead and dying, the waste dump was cleared.

Gone were the maniacs who minutes before had threatened Albert and Claudia Johnson. Madeleine Giovanni stood revealed, her eyes wild, features placid, drenched red, and close by an acid pit. Sam Haine, a bemused expression on his face, rested by her side. And at the center of a circle of bodies stood a weary, battered Shadow of the Dawn. Swords pointed to the earth, her arms rested wearily against her sides.

Fifty feet away, Seventeen had no chance other

than to shout a word of warning when two figures, broad-shouldered and ghost-like, rose from the piles of the dead behind Shadow of the Dawn. The pair moved with unnatural speed. One wrapped his massive arms in a bear hug around her from behind, pinning her limbs to her body. The other, hands outstretched like claws, grabbed for her face.

A shotgun roared twice. The grasping man flew backward, knocked a dozen feet away. Seizing the sudden reversal, Shadow of the Dawn twisted the short sword in her left hand and thrust up and back, catching the man holding her full in the groin with her blade. Gasping in shock, the man collapsed to his knees, the bear hug broken. As Shadow spun, her long sword whirling in a finishing move, the man's right hand clawed desperately at her face. Nails raked across the warrior maid's cheek, drawing blood. A second later, steel separated his head from his body.

In a display of inhuman stamina, the other attacker, two gaping wounds in his chest, slowly rose to his feet. Calmly, Madeleine Giovanni stepped up to him and tore the man to pieces.

Shadow of the Dawn, her face pale and bloody, was speaking to a young blonde woman dressed in white bike shorts and a black halter top, with an x-shaped cross above her breasts.

"Too damned close for comfort," said Seventeen, as he came up beside the warrior maid.

"They were clev…" began Shadow of the Dawn. Eyes widening in sudden pain, she dropped to the ground.

Sam Haine rushed over and grabbed one of her wrists. Using Verbena magick, the Changing Man could detect dangerous wounds in instants. All color drained from Sam's face.

"Lycosis," he whispered. He looked to Albert. "Anything you can do?"

The giant shook his head. "The poison attacks the blood. There is no cure that I know of."

Sam Haine turned to Seventeen. The old man's face was wet with tears. "Better hold your lady, son," he stammered, his voice cracking with emotion. "She's dying. Poison is rushing through her bloodstream. Only got a few minutes more. And there's nothing we can do to save her."

Epilogue

In the farthest regions of the vast expanse known as the Deep Umbra, there exists a pocket universe, a small Realm known to its inhabitants as Harmony. At the center of this hidden kingdom stands a tower that gleams like solid gold. In this tower, seven people sit around a table. Six women and a being with angelic features that suggest both man and woman. It is the artificial creation known as the pattern-clone; the mysterious figure that calls itself Heylel Teomim, the Abomination. The clone and its six most trusted lieutenants plan their next move in the game of worlds known as the Ascension War.

In the middle of a sentence, Heylel suddenly stops speaking. Its face grows thoughtful, distant, as if witnessing events far from normal sight.

"He understands," whispered Heylel. "Now he understands the power."

RoBeRt WeInBeRg

Robert Weinberg has authored twelve novels, five nonfiction books, and numerous short stories. His work has been translated into French, German, Spanish, Italian, Japanese, Russian, and Bulgarian.

He has co-authored White Wolf Publishing's *Vampire Diary: The Embrace* (included in *The Essential World of Darkness*), the *Masquerade of the Red Death* trilogy (*Blood War*, *Unholy Allies*, and *The Unbeholden*), and *The Road to Hell* (Volume I of the *Horizon War* trilogy). At present, he teaches creative writing at Columbia College in Chicago and is working on the last book of *Horizon War*, *The War in Heaven*.

THE HORIZON WAR TRILOGY

WILL
CONCLUDE IN

ThE
WaR iN
hEaVeN

BY ROBERT WEINBERG

FORTHCOMING FROM WHITE WOLF IN
JUNE 1998

(left margin fragments)
bing
doubt
'onna
Gate
king
of the
wife,
r Ar-
three
d no
4PM.

em-
gold
grees
late
dis-
son.
have
cher
e of
vice
other
liza-
t be
ore.
of the
briel
ael.
sent
ities.

Fitz-Empress

Porthos Fitz-Empress, Hermes *bani* Flambeau, Drua'shi Master, Magister Mundi and Deacon Primus died this week in the destruction of Chantry Doissetep. The well-known magus of the Order of Hermes was a veteran of the earliest battles against the Cabal of Pure Thought, Order of Reason and Technocracy. Porthos contributed to the founding of the Council of Nine Traditions, participated in the creation of the Horizon artificial Realm, and assisted in the vast magickal engineering feat that moved Doissetep' central castle complex and surrounding landscape to the Mars/Forces overlap Realm called Cal Ladiem. Despite his advanced age, he remained active in Council politics; sponsored the genesis of the Ambassador Program; supported greater rights and training opportunities for Orphans, Hollow Ones, and Craft mages; and wrote and edited numerous seminal volumes on Traditional and mystickal history. His last published opus, **The Book of Worlds**, is considered the definitive cross-disciplinary resource for travellers.

He is survived by his daughter, Dindaine Fitz-Empress and an apprentice, Mahmet Kemal, Hermes *bani* Flambeau. Memorial services will be held in the Commoner's Chapel beneath the Hall of LaSalle on Horizon. In lieu of flowers, the family requests friends and colleagues purchase copies of **The Fragile Path**, the deceased's history of the First Cabal. Mourners should send $10 and their address to White Wolf, Attn: Fragile Path Memorial Offer, 735 Park North Blvd., Suite 128, Clarkston GA 30021. Shipping and handling will be donated by the publisher.

Grossman

Albert Marmaduke Grossman *Bani* Sons of Ether died Tuesday in a lab accident. The young physicist had made

(right margin fragments)
Sm
D
for
taki
of v
loc
sto
cat
foll
teri
Par
viv
dau
thre
fam
flo
be
Mo
vice

So
R
fou
pre
nig
bod
and
to
con
Hou
Hel
kno
tria